HOT LIMIT

Hostile Operations Team® - Strike Team 2

LYNN RAYE HARRIS

The Hostile Operations Team® and Lynn Raye Harris® are
trademarks of H.O.T. Publishing, LLC.

Printed in the United States of America

First Printing, 2023

For rights inquires, visit www.LynnRayeHarris.com

ISBN: 978-1-941002-79-7

Chapter One

RYDER HANSON HAD NO DESIRE TO DIVE INTO A frigid lake on a cold, windy, gray-ass day, but he was gonna do it anyway. The woman floating face down, arms spread out, body bobbing in the choppy water, made the choice for him.

Ry peeled his sweatshirt over his head, kicked off his hiking boots, and swore a blue streak as he got a running start down the dock. He had no idea how long she'd been there. He'd noticed her from the kitchen window a split second ago. He'd been reading the morning paper, and he'd gotten up to get a cup of coffee when he'd noticed her. Like a piece of drift-wood. He'd thought he was seeing things at first, but fuck all if she wasn't real.

Ry dove into the water, arms out in front of him, body arcing the way he'd been taught during all the brutal hours of combat swim training. The lake wasn't deep, no more than four feet at his dock, but he knew how to dive into much shallower water if need be.

The water was cold enough to shrivel his balls and make him scream like a little girl if he let it. He wasn't about to let it. He'd bobbed in colder water than this waiting for a pickup after a mission, and he'd trained in colder water too.

He just hadn't expected to go in today.

Ry powered through the water until he reached her. He flipped her over so her face was no longer submerged. There were cuts and bruises on her skin. She was deathly pale and her lips were blue, but there was a pulse. Shallow and thready.

Fuck. She wasn't even wearing a coat. Probably lucky since that would have weighed her down.

Ry turned her head to the side so water could drain from her nose and mouth and then put his mouth over hers and performed rescue breathing. He did it four times and waited. Her chest moved, thank fuck.

He put everything he had into swimming for the dock again, one arm wrapped around her and the other stroking for all he was worth. He'd been so damned happy and proud when he'd put an offer on this place just last month. He'd been saving, looking for the right property, and he'd found it near the town of Mystic Cove where one of his teammates lived.

One of the pluses about it was how remote it was for being within fifty miles of DC.

Where the fuck had this woman come from then?

Ry reached the dock, managed to push the woman onto the weathered wood, and followed her up. Her chest was still moving and her pulse was stronger. He turned her to the side again. When she started to cough, he breathed a little easier. Not that she was entirely out of the woods yet, but it was better than a few moments ago.

He needed to get her warm, and he needed to get her to a hospital. He had medical training, so he wasn't entirely clueless about what to do, but he didn't want responsibility for her any longer than he had to have it.

He scooped her into his arms and carried her inside, kicking the door closed and heading straight for his bathroom. He laid her on the floor and started the water running in the big bathtub. He hadn't even used the tub yet. Funny this would be the first time.

Once the water was the right temperature, he put her in the tub and let it keep filling. She lay back against the rim, her eyes still closed, her chest moving. She started to whimper as he peeled his wet clothes off. He grabbed a towel and scrubbed himself dry, then hooked it around his hips. He couldn't leave her to get more clothes, and he couldn't shower yet either. Not until he had her warmed up and out of the water.

He wouldn't take a chance of her slipping beneath the surface while his back was turned. He took the time he had now to study her. She looked to be in her twenties, with dark brown hair slicked against her skull. It fell to just below her shoulders.

There was a cut on her left cheekbone, some scrapes on her chin and cheek, and a bruise beneath her left eye. She had finger marks on her collar bone and at the base of her throat. Her fingernails were torn and ragged, and one had ripped partially off. It was starting to bleed again now that the water was warming her.

"Jesus, sweetheart, what happened to you?"

She wore what looked like leggings and a sweatshirt with Princess Leia on it. She had no shoes or socks, and nowhere to stash any ID. He wouldn't know who she was until she woke. He could do a search for missing persons, maybe that'd turn something up. He could also snap a pic and send it to Sky "Hacker" Kelley, see if maybe Hack could find something.

But that seemed to be a bit too intrusive just now. If she didn't wake after he got her warm and dry, maybe he'd do it then. Except he'd be taking her to the hospital by then, so maybe he'd just wash his hands of the whole thing. Let them figure it out.

She was still whimpering, only now he could understand words. Words that tore his heart in two.

"No, please, no…"

He hunkered down beside the tub and frowned. "It's okay, you're safe. I've got you. No one's going to hurt you."

She shuddered, her head moving back and forth as if denying what he was saying. He thought she might be convulsing, and he reached for her to stop her from sinking under the water.

Her eyes snapped open. The terror he saw there stunned him at first. Then it angered him.

"It's okay," he said again. "You're okay."

She opened her mouth. And then she screamed.

———

ALL SHE COULD REMEMBER WAS the feeling of suffocating. Of hands wrapped around her throat, choking her. There was a bag too, or maybe it'd been a blanket. Then there'd been nothing, except ice. She'd been colder than she'd ever been, and now she wasn't.

The pain in her body was like needles stabbing her over and over. Like she was a piece of fabric being flattened beneath a cosmic sewing machine. Everything hurt.

Then there was the man. He was big... and naked. *Mostly* naked, she amended. He had a towel around his waist and he was too close. Had he grabbed her? Was he the one who'd choked her?

Who'd brought her here and submerged her in a warm bath?

A warm bath? Alaina struggled to draw breath, to get control of her shivering, shaking, terrified body. Why was she in a warm bath? And why did she have all her clothes on?

"Hey, hey," the man said, holding out both hands. He knelt, not too close, but close enough he could shove her under if he got annoyed. "It's okay. Nobody's going to hurt you. I promise. Tell me who you are, and I'll get you home again."

Alaina sobbed. She couldn't seem to stop herself, no matter that she wanted to find her voice and tell him—beg him—not to hurt her. He said he wouldn't, but she knew better. She'd been around men like him before. Big, strong, handsome. Sweet words could hide dark thoughts. She'd lived it as a child. Seen it too often since.

"I found you," he said, his voice soft and soothing. "In the water. Near my dock. You were unresponsive, so I brought you inside and put you in the warm bath to help regulate your body temperature. I'm sorry you're scared, but I mean you no harm."

Her throat was raw from screaming, and her eyes stung with tears. Worse, they would swell soon, and then it'd be hard to see. She fought to stop crying so that didn't happen, to find her voice, but everything hurt and fear rode her hard.

An image popped into her head and made her

tears choke off like someone had turned a tap. A little boy. He had blonde hair and blue eyes, and he was the sweetest thing. "Everett," she gasped. Memories flooded her then. She'd dropped him off at school this morning—

Alaina tried to claw herself to her feet as the fear closed in on her again. Fear for her little boy this time, not for herself. Alarm crossed the man's features as she struggled. He held his hands out again.

"Hey, hey. Calm down. Who is Everett? Did he do this to you?"

"N-no," she managed, her teeth chattering. "I h-have to go. Get him."

"You almost drowned, honey. You can't go charging out of here looking for this Everett. Tell me where to find him. I'll get him for you."

Her heart was a hammering lump in her mouth. Dizziness closed in on the edges of her vision. "No, please," she whispered as nausea clogged her throat.

The man took a couple of steps away, then picked up a pair of sodden pants and fished out a wallet. He dropped the pants and return to her, opening the two sides of the wallet to reveal a driver's license and a military ID card that said his rank was sergeant. The photos on both were the man in front of her.

"My name is Ryder Hanson. I'm in the Army. I just moved here, and this is my house. I found you in the water, and I gave you CPR and brought you here to warm your body temperature. I'm going to take you to the hospital, but I needed to stabilize you first. You're safe, and I won't hurt you."

Alaina was still shivering, still finding it hard to say the words she wanted to say. She could find the thoughts, and then they floated away like wispy clouds on a breeze. She tried to gather them back, but they would not come.

"Alaina," she managed. "My name is Alaina."

Alaina what? She was drawing a blank, though she knew it was there. Just beyond the tip of her tongue. She knew who she was, knew she had a six-year-old son named Everett, but grabbing the information from her brain and saying it aloud was more taxing than it should have been.

The pain in her skin was easing as her body warmed, but there were other pains. Her hand stung from where one of her nails had ripped below the quick. And there were deep pains, like someone had kicked and punched her. Her cheek stung and her throat hurt. Her side. Ribs?

"I want to help you, Alaina. I'm going to get you to a hospital, and I'll find Everett for you, too. Is there anything else you can tell me? Do you know who did this to you?"

Alaina's eyes filled with tears. All she had was that impression of suffocating and darkness. She shook her head, then wished she hadn't when the pain split her skull in two. "Hurts. Everything."

"I know, Alaina. I'm sorry."

She closed her eyes against the pain and tried to concentrate on his voice as he started to speak to someone on the phone. She didn't know him, had never seen him before, but there was something trustworthy in that voice. She believed him when he said he wanted to help. Then again, she'd believed people's promises before and been wrong.

She didn't want to live that way, mistrusting everyone, but maybe she had to. Maybe there was no such thing as a good life for her. No such thing as a good man. For Everett's sake, she hoped that wasn't true. But how could she ever know?

She felt the prick in her arm too late. Her eyes snapped open, meeting Ryder Hanson's. He was frowning at her as he held a needle in one hand. She hadn't heard him approach. Stupid for closing her eyes. Stupid, stupid, stupid.

That's how you end up dead, girlfriend.

"I gave you a shot of painkiller. It should help. I need to get you out of that tub, Alaina, and it's going to hurt."

She stared up at him until his face began to grow fuzzy. Her head lolled onto the rim of the tub and the ceiling blurred. She drifted, though a part of her was fighting inside. She needed to stay alive. What would Everett do without her? Who would take him if she died? Who would love him?

There was no one but her.

Water drained from the tub, leaving her cold

where it no longer touched. She felt the brush of Ryder's hands against her shoulders, beneath her knees. She tried to struggle, but she couldn't seem to control her muscles.

"It's okay," he said softly, lifting her up and carrying her somewhere. He set her down again, and then she was wrapped in a blanket like a baby. "I need to throw on some clothes, then I'm taking you to the hospital."

Alaina drifted. She didn't know for how long, but then he was back, lifting her again. Her body protested, but all she could manage was a whimper. She had the feeling it didn't hurt as much as it could have. She could feel her wet clothes, but the blanket seemed thick and warm.

Ryder put her down again, talking to her as he settled her. She forced her eyes open and took in the interior of a vehicle. Panic flared again, and she began to struggle. Or did she? Because Ryder didn't blink at her efforts. He belted her in place then went around to the driver's side of the car. She fumbled at her side, trying to undo the buckle so she could escape, but nothing happened. Her limbs weren't obeying any of her commands.

She tried to stay alert, but it was impossible with the drug flowing through her system. She had an impression of moving, of stops and turns and speed, and she wanted to scream. He'd said he was taking her to the hospital, but what if it was a lie? What if he was the one who'd attacked her? What if he was sadistic and this was simply part of his torture? Making her think he was helping, then finishing what he'd started.

Alaina squeezed her eyes shut. If this was it, if this was her end, she prayed Everett would end up with a family who loved him. She could almost accept death if she knew he'd be loved.

Almost.

Chapter Two

Mystic Cove was too small to have a hospital, so Ryder drove Alaina to the next big town over. He'd called Easy and Jenna to ask where they thought he should take her, and that was the answer he'd gotten. He was still too new in town to know where everything was, but he'd known where to get the answer.

He'd also gotten an outpouring of support and questions about what he needed them to do. He'd said he didn't need anything right now, but thanks. The team had just returned from a grueling mission to the jungle, and everyone was busy decompressing with their families. Except him. He'd been busy closing and moving in to his new house.

He hadn't accepted help with that because he hadn't had much to move. He'd bought new furniture, but it hadn't been delivered yet. He was sleeping on a mattress on the floor while he waited for the bed to come in. Mal's fiancée, Scarlett, had helped him choose some items. Scar was a serious bargain shopper and she'd saved him some coin. Which he'd needed because he'd used nearly everything he had for the down payment.

Today was only his fifth morning waking up with his water view and the quiet peace it usually brought. Until today, when he'd felt like he was being forced to relive one of the worst memories of his life.

He took Alaina to the emergency room, but once he'd gotten her there and filled out paperwork with what little he knew about her and what he'd given her for pain, he couldn't just leave. Not to mention the staff was looking at him with some suspicion for the bruises and scrapes on Alaina's face and throat.

He understood, and he did his best to answer their questions. He wasn't worried, though. He had faith that Alaina would recover, and then the police would know everything they needed to find her assailant. They could suspect him, but they wouldn't find any evidence he'd done that to her. Because he hadn't.

"Sergeant Hanson," someone said.

Ry looked up from his phone and stood. "That's me."

A doctor came over to him. She gave him a warm smile and held out a hand. "Doctor Innes. I wanted to speak to you about Alaina. She's been kicked and beaten fairly savagely, but there doesn't seem to be any internal damage. She's also been strangled, but it doesn't appear to have lasted long enough to break any blood vessels. There are no signs of a stroke, and her brain function is good despite a blow to the head. I think she was also suffocated. It's a miracle she's alive, quite honestly. She's lucky you found her when you did, or she might not be."

Ry swallowed the anger he felt deep inside. Who would do that to a woman and then dump her like she was trash? He noticed the doctor didn't say anything about sexual assault, but that kind of information was a lot more personal and she might not be willing to share it.

"I was home today because I just moved to a new place and I'm on leave. If I hadn't gone to the kitchen when I did…" He shook his head. "Jesus, she almost drowned. And now you tell me someone strangled, suffocated, kicked, and punched her? I mean I knew she'd been in a scrape, but I wasn't sure."

"Someone definitely did. What do you know about her?"

He shook his head. "Nothing. I've never seen her until today. She was in the water off my dock, floating face down. I didn't even know if she was alive when I went in."

"I see. Good thinking getting her in the bathtub. You saved her life, Sergeant, and not just with CPR."

"I'm in Spec Ops, ma'am," he said. "We have some medical training for field duty. No ERs where we go, so it's up to us."

Doctor Innes nodded. "We're keeping her sedated for now, and we'll file a police report. If we're lucky, we'll know who she is in a few hours. You don't need to stay. We have your contact information if we need anything else."

Ry thought he should feel some relief, but instead he felt a sense of responsibility. Someone had nearly killed Alaina, and the only name she'd spoken besides her own was Everett. Who was she, and who was Everett? A boyfriend? She'd said he hadn't been the one to attack her, but he was clearly important to her since his was the first name she'd spoken. Ryder felt like he had a duty to help.

"I'll stay for a while if that's okay."

Doctor Innes smiled a little sadly. "It's fine. You can see her in ICU if you wish. Ordinarily we'd limit it to family, but since we don't know who that is, maybe seeing you will help when she wakes up. If you want to follow me, I'll take you to her."

Ry didn't know what else to do, so he went with the doc. Alaina looked small and bruised in her hospital bed. She had tubes in her arms and monitors hooked up to leads on her chest. She also had an oxygen tube. Her eyes were closed. Her hair was dry now, and it wasn't as dark as it'd appeared when wet. He'd describe the color as a combination of browns and reds, except the reds looked as if they'd been added. Red streaks, but subtle enough to blend until the light caught it just right.

Her skin was pale, and there were bruises beneath her eyes. He remembered those eyes snapping open to stare at him before she'd screamed. They were green like his, but not the same. Darker, with flecks of gold in the irises. Not quite hazel, but close.

"There's a call button if you need anything," Doctor Innes said quietly at his shoulder, pointing to the control hanging near Alaina's head.

"Thanks."

The doc left, and Ry dropped into a chair at the end of the bed. He didn't want to get too close, in case she woke and he spooked her, but he didn't want to leave either. Not yet. He would when she woke, when she knew she was safe. Then he could walk away with a clear conscience.

Or could he? Ry rubbed his palms along the fabric of his jeans, telling himself this was nothing like that summer when he'd pulled his sister from the swimming pool in their backyard. She'd been sixteen and she'd tied concrete blocks around her ankles before shoving them into the deep end and going in with them. He'd been thirteen, a shy chubby kid with low self-esteem and few friends. After that horrific day, he'd gone deeper into himself, gotten chubbier, and thought about tying blocks around his ankles and doing the same.

Ry pressed his palms to his eyelids. Fucking childhood memories gutted you like nothing else ever could. Sheri hadn't lived, and he hadn't died. He'd wanted to, but never quite badly enough. His parents, who'd always been more focused on their jobs, focused even harder on them than before. Ry had spent a lot of time with his grandparents because his mom and dad were gone so often. That's probably what had saved him, quite honestly. He'd been lonely, but he'd had them.

Gram and Papa were loving, sweet people who'd made up for a lot of neglect in his life. Because of them, he'd gotten his shit together. Eventually, despite the fact they owned a bakery and taught him how to bake sugary treats, he'd dropped the baby fat, joined the military, and became a lethal fighting machine who relied on strength and brains to get the job done.

He often wondered if Sheri would be proud of what he'd become. He hoped so. His parents were disappointed, but he'd expected that since he hadn't gone to college or followed them into journalism. His grandparents would have been proud no matter what he'd done. They'd wanted him to take over the bakery, but when he told them it wasn't what he wanted, they were fine with it. They sold the business and moved to Florida where they were enjoying the retired life, and he talked to them often.

Ry looked at the small woman in the hospital bed. She'd brought emotions to the surface he hadn't had to deal with in a long time. It was odd, because his job required him to save people in all kinds of circumstances. He'd done water rescues countless times.

Somehow, though, Alaina was different. Saving her was different, too. He *did* feel responsible for her, even if it wasn't logical.

He took his phone out and did a search online for Alaina and Everett. Just those two names. Since he didn't know how she spelled her name, he went with Elena. He narrowed it to Mystic Cove, since that was the town closest to his place, but nothing came up. He tried Elana and Elayna, then Alana and Alayna. Still nothing. A quick search of variations on that name gave him one he hadn't tried. Alaina.

He plugged that in next with Everett. That time he got a hit. Alaina Montgomery lived in Mystic Cove. He pulled up the address and texted it to Hacker with the name and asked for help. It didn't take long to get a reply.

Alaina Montgomery, twenty-five, single, one son named Everett, six, goes to Mystic Cove Elementary. Alaina works as a cleaner at Hopeful Future in Mystic Cove. It's a shelter and crisis services center for women who've been victims of violent assault, including rape and domestic violence.

"Jesus," Ryder whispered, glancing at Alaina. Had someone seen her there and targeted her? Or maybe there was a violent man in her past. Anything was possible, and he wasn't going to have answers anytime soon.

He texted his thanks, then called Easy and asked if he and Jenna could check into Everett Montgomery's whereabouts. If he was in school, then they'd need to find out who was designated to pick him up when Alaina couldn't. And if he wasn't there, it was time for the police to get involved.

Maybe that was the answer anyway. Maybe Everett's father was a piece of shit who'd come after Alaina and taken his son. Ryder shoved his hands through his hair when the call ended and swore. So many fucking questions and not a lot of answers yet.

He watched the woman in the bed, wanting to know who'd done something so evil to her. Wanting to know her secrets. Wanting to protect her, because that's what he did. Might be none of his business in the end, but he'd pulled her from the water near his dock and that made her his business for now.

He'd stay until he had more answers.

———

ALAINA STRUGGLED to open her eyes. She felt like she was in a sticky dream world where nothing obeyed as she expected it to. Her eyes didn't want to open. Her limbs didn't want to move. But her will said they had to. She *had* to wake up. Everett needed her.

When she finally managed to get her eyes to obey, she was in a dark room. There were beeping sounds and blinking lights. She lay in the stillness, trying to make sense of her surroundings. And then it finally came to her.

She was in a hospital bed.

Panic started to claw at her. Where was Everett?

"He's safe," a voice said, and that was when she knew she'd said the words aloud.

The owner of the voice came into view then. The man who'd put her into a bathtub and then brought her here. Relief rolled through her. He wasn't a serial killer, and he'd done what he'd said he would do.

She let herself look at him. He was tall with a broad chest, big arms, and dark hair cut short. His eyes were green, set into a handsome face with a couple days' growth of beard that would have made her swoon back in the old days. Before she had a child to take care of and no space in her life for anything else.

"Your friend Stacie picked him up from school," he continued. "When it was time for her shift at the center, my friends Noah and Jenna took him home with them. They have a little girl named Alice who's three. Stacie said there was no one else and no father to contact. She knows Jenna from the diner when Jenna was a waitress there. Stacie said to tell you she approved of the arrangement with Everett, and she hopes you're okay with that. She also sends her love."

Alaina squeezed her eyes shut for a moment. If Stacie knew and trusted Jenna, then she knew she could too.

"Thank you," she said when she looked at him again. It came out as a hoarse whisper. Her throat was dry, and talking felt unnatural. He seemed to realize it because he reached for a big cup with a handle and a straw.

"Hey, you thirsty? The nurse said you might be."

"Yes." She tried to take it, but her hands were too weak to close around the handle. Her finger throbbed where the nail had been partially ripped off.

"I got you," he said, holding the straw to her mouth so she could drink.

The water felt cold and good going down. She hated being so damned helpless, but it wouldn't last forever. She had to take help where she could get it, and she had to get strong for Everett. He was all that mattered.

"Thank you. For everything," she said when she could talk again.

"You're welcome. I'm Ryder, in case you forgot. Or Ry. Whichever works for you."

Ryder. Ry.

She liked that name. "Ryder. I-I need to go home."

He tugged a chair over and sat down so he was almost on a level with her. His green eyes seemed a bit concerned. "I know, but it's gonna be a day or two before the doc clears you. Somebody beat you up pretty badly, Alaina. Do you know who it was?"

Fear rose like acid in her throat. She tried to remember, but all she could recall was pain and darkness. She didn't even know if she'd been raped. The lack of certainty made her shiver uncontrollably.

Knowing you'd been attacked and hurt was one thing. Not knowing if you'd been violated in that way was another.

"N-no. I took E-Everett to school and d-dropped him off. I th-think I went home after, but I d-don't remember."

Ryder stood, frowning, as her teeth continued to chatter. "I'll get the nurse."

She wanted to tell him not to leave her, but he was gone before she could get the words out. A few moments later, a nurse came in alone. "What's wrong, hon?" she asked sympathetically.

Alaina blinked up at her. "I don't k-know wh-what happened. Was I r-raped?"

The nurse squeezed her shoulder lightly. "No, honey. Nobody did that to you."

Maybe it was weird to be relieved about that when she'd been beat up and nearly killed, but she was. Alaina closed her eyes and nodded.

She heard the nurse fiddle with her IV and then type some stuff in the computer terminal nearby. "I'll tell your boyfriend he can come back in. You're gonna be okay, honey."

Alaina didn't get a chance to say Ryder wasn't her boyfriend before the nurse was gone and he was there.

"You okay?"

She nodded. "I-I needed to know. Rape."

He looked angry, but she knew it wasn't directed at her. "I'm so sorry, Alaina."

She reached for his hand with her good one and squeezed. He didn't pull away. It was a bold move for her, but she felt like she needed to do it. "It didn't happen."

He looked as relieved as she felt. "That's good."

She let go of his hand and blinked back tears. Her heartbeat was slowing again, and the fear was ebbing by degrees. Her teeth were no longer chattering, though a shiver rolled through her body from time to time. It wouldn't go away completely, not yet, but it wasn't going to overwhelm her either. She tried to focus on what she could remember about the day, push the fear away.

She had an impression of returning to the tiny trailer she'd rented. It was an old RV that her land-lord had parked on a wooded plot of land behind his house. It wasn't ideal for raising a child, but it was the best she could do right now. She'd thought they were safe there. Mr. Herbert didn't bother her so long as she paid her rent. His grandson was often there and acted like he was interested in her, but he'd never asked her out. The property wasn't in a bad area. It was the country, for heaven's sake. The trailer might not be big, but there were woods and fields for Everett to play in. It was what she could afford.

"I'm s-sure I went home after. But I don't remember what happened then. I can't recall going inside or anything."

"Your car's parked there. A couple of sheriff's

deputies have been out to your place. It wasn't broken into and they didn't find anything unusual, but your landlord appears to be gone."

"Hunting t-trip with his grandson," Alaina said. "They left last night. Or maybe early this morning, before sunrise. I'm not really sure, but I don't think they were there when I took Everett to school. H-how long have I been here?"

"I found you this morning, 'bout eight or so. It's almost eleven at night. The hospital let me stay in case you woke up so I could reassure you about Everett."

She was glad. "Thank you. D-does he know?"

He nodded. "Jenna told him you'd had an accident, but you were going to be okay. She said it wasn't good to lie to a kid about something so important. He wanted to see you, but she said you were resting and he could talk to you tomorrow."

Alaina nodded. "She's right. I wouldn't want him to know I'd been attacked. I want to see him, but I'd rather it not be here."

She had bad memories of going to the hospital with her mother when she was a kid. She didn't want Everett to feel the same way. She'd sat in waiting rooms with her poor, bleeding mother and then listened to her tell the doctor she'd fallen, or run into a cabinet door, or how the dog had tripped her when they didn't even have a dog.

Alaina wasn't doing that to Everett. A current of despair rolled through her. How was she going to take care of him now, when everything hurt and she was afraid to close her eyes?

"You okay? Do I need to get the nurse again?"

She focused on the big man at her bedside again. "I'm okay. Do you have my phone?"

"I'm sorry, but I didn't find one on you when I pulled you from the water. The deputies didn't mention finding it either, but I'll see what I can learn. It might be in your car or your home."

She closed her eyes again. "Thank you." She prayed it was. Replacing a phone was an expense she didn't need, plus there were photos of Everett she didn't want to lose.

"Look, I know this is going to be hard for you, and I want to help."

Alaina looked at him. He had kind eyes in a stunningly attractive face.

He continued, "I just moved to Mystic Cove, but I've got a small cottage on my property. I think it was a mother-in-law suite. There's a bed, a couch, a single bathroom, and a small kitchen. I was going to rent it out at some point, but if you want to stay there with Everett while you recover, it's yours. Free of charge."

Her eyes filled with moisture. She blinked it away. "I can't take advantage of your kindness. I have the trailer, and my rent is paid through the end of the month."

"I hear you, Alaina, but until you know what happened, do you really want to stay in your RV?

You'll be alone when Everett's in school. If someone attacked you there, they might come back. They won't know where to find you at my place. And I'll be there for the next couple of weeks before I have to go back to work. It'll give you enough time to figure out what's next."

She *was* afraid to return to the RV. Since she didn't know what'd happened out there, she'd always be terrified it could happen again. If she stayed at Ryder's, she'd have time to find something closer to town. Something with neighbors. Or maybe he'd rent his cottage to her cheaply enough she could afford it. She doubted that, but a girl could hope.

Sometimes hope was all you had left. Hope that life would get better, that you'd be a good mother for your child and give him everything he needed, and that he wouldn't grow up fucked up because of the choices you'd made.

Every instinct she had told her to accept his offer. He was a decent man, and he'd been nothing but kind. He could have left her at the hospital and gone back to his life, but he'd stayed. And he'd made sure Everett was cared for.

"Okay, I accept. But only until I feel well enough to go back to the trailer." Maybe by then the police would have found her attacker and she could feel safe again.

"Good. You'll be secure at my place. I promise."

She believed him.

Chapter Three

Ry waited until Alaina was asleep again before he left. It'd been a long day at her bedside and he needed to get some sleep and fresh clothing before he went back again. He didn't like leaving her when he didn't know who'd attacked her or why.

He'd gone through a list of scenarios in his head when he'd been sitting in her room.

The likelihood she was being targeted by an assassin was pretty low. A professional would have completed the job, not left her half-alive for someone to find. Not to mention she seemed to be what she was, which was a single mom with a young child. She worked in a crisis center, which could increase her exposure to violence.

It was possible she hadn't told him the truth about what she remembered. Maybe she knew who did it but she was scared. Maybe she had a boyfriend or a stalker and that person had attacked her. Whoever'd beaten her and dumped her in the water had been angry, not calculating. It hadn't been a sexual assault, but it'd still been a brutal attack.

Ry really wanted to find the culprit because he'd like to see the fucker charged with attempted murder. Strike that. What he'd really like to do is repay the asshole in kind, but that wouldn't make the HOT hierarchy happy. Didn't need to piss off Mendez or Ghost. He'd just closed escrow on his dream house by the lake, and he didn't need that kind of trouble.

He had a life plan, and it didn't involve fucking up his career. It was about making a home for himself in a place that made him happy, about being open to the future and maybe finding someone to spend it with the way so many of his teammates had. He couldn't deny how happy they were. Hell, Dean "Wolf" Garner and his wife had just had a baby girl, and Ry had never seen Wolf happier, despite the lack of quality sleep since little Paisley had come along.

Not that Ry was looking for a woman to settle down with right this instant. It would happen when it happened. He was drawn to Alaina, but that had everything to do with the circumstances in which he'd found her. He felt responsible. That's all it was.

And that was fine. He could help, and he would. He'd give her a place to stay, help her get back on her feet, and feel good about it. Wasn't anything more than that.

———

RY WENT HOME to grab a few hours sleep, then returned to the hospital early the next morning. Alaina was sitting up when he walked in. There was a breakfast tray in front of her, and she seemed to have eaten most of it. The bruise beneath her left eye had darkened and the scrape on her cheek was scabbed over, but her eyes were brighter today. When she looked at him, he felt a hitch in his chest so strong he wanted to rub it. What the fuck was that about?

"Hey," he said.

"You're back."

"I am. You seem surprised."

She glanced down at her lap, then back up, her green eyes warm as she looked at him. "I am, kinda. You don't have to be here."

He dragged a chair over and sat. "I said you could stay in my mother-in-law cottage, right?"

She nodded, her eyes a little wide as she watched him. Wide, but not scared. That was good.

"Do you know where it is?"

"No," she breathed.

"Exactly. How would you get there if I didn't come back?"

He liked that she smiled. "Okay, maybe I expected you to return. But not so early."

"I'm an early riser," he said with a shrug. Not always, depending on how fucked his body clock got

29

because of missions in different time zones, but mostly. He liked being up early, before the sun, making coffee and waiting for the first rays to peek over the horizon. "I got a friend who's good with computers to do a trace on your phone. The last place it pinged a tower was near your home, but it's dead now."

"Thank you for trying." She seemed resigned. "Your friend Jenna called my room a few minutes ago. I spoke to Everett before she took him to school, and I gave her permission to use his key to go over and see if my phone and purse are at home."

"That's good. How did it go talking to your boy?"

She picked at a half piece of toast left on her plate. Her fingers were slender, her wrists tiny. When she'd been weighted down with water, she'd still been lighter than he'd expected. Made him wonder if she was on an extreme diet or something.

"He's six. He doesn't quite understand why I'm not there. Or why he's not with me." She tossed the piece of toast down. "I need to get out of here. I can't leave him with strangers, no matter how kind. Do you think they'll let me go today?"

"I think they'll let you go when it's time."

She looked a little frantic then. "I can't afford to stay in the hospital. I-I only have basic insurance. I'm a cleaner at the women's shelter, and I clean a few houses in town too. I have to work so I can take care of my son."

"I think you aren't going to be working for a few days," he said gently.

Her eyes welled with tears. She put the heels of her hands over them and pressed. "Sorry. I shouldn't be crying like this, and I shouldn't be telling you my problems. You've already done more than I can ever repay you for."

"I didn't ask for repayment, Alaina."

She sniffled. "I know, but you've spent too much time with me, and you're giving up the cottage you wanted to rent. It's a lot to do for a stranger."

"We aren't strangers anymore, are we? You saw me with a towel wrapped around my waist and you sat in my bathtub. Think that makes us friends or something."

She didn't say anything for a long moment. Her lip quivered a little, but the tears she'd pressed away didn't dare to fall. He got the impression that when Alaina made up her mind about something, her body didn't disobey.

"You're very understanding. And kind."

He didn't deserve the praise, but there was no way to refuse it without either sounding like a dick or scaring her into reconsidering staying at his place. He didn't know why it was important to him that she be there, other than he'd driven by that tiny little RV she called home and shuddered at the state of it.

The siding was filthy with mildew and water spots, and the tires had rotted away at least a quarter century ago. The little porch was neat and tidy, though, and there were a few empty flower pots waiting for spring. There was a wind chime hanging from an L-bracket attached to a nearby tree, and the yard around the RV was well-kept. He imagined it was neat inside as well, but it was small and old and he couldn't imagine a young woman and a six-year old boy living in that thing for weeks or months at a time.

Didn't make sense.

He had a place for them, and he wasn't using it, so why not? Maybe they could work out something about rent if she wanted to stay after she'd recovered. He wasn't rolling in dough, but he got hazardous duty pay and he'd saved a lot to make his dream of owning a water property possible.

He didn't ever want to go back to Buffalo, and Maryland was as good as anywhere. His friends were here. His life. He could visit his grandparents in Florida, and his parents could stop in for a visit if they were in town. Not that they would.

"You've been through a lot. I have a place and I'm not using it," he said, echoing his own thoughts.

"But you wanted to."

"Eventually. I just bought the property, and everything needs some work. The cottage is clean and safe, but dated. There's paneling on the walls and orange bathroom tile. I was planning to change it before I rented it, but that will take time. So it's available, and you aren't inconveniencing me at all. Hell, I might be inconveniencing you once you get a look at that tile."

He winked, and she bit back a grin, dropping her gaze again. "Okay, fine, maybe you aren't that nice after all. Orange tile is an abomination."

"But cheerful. You'll want orange juice every morning, guaranteed."

There was motion at the door. Ry was looking at Alaina and saw the moment her eyes widened. Then her gaze darted away. Ry turned as a couple of sheriff's deputies came in the room, hats in hand.

One of the men gave him a once-over. The other glanced his way and nodded. Ry stood, shoving his hands in his jeans pockets and waiting for what they'd say.

"Miss Montgomery, I'm Deputy Turner and this is Deputy Foss. How are you doing today, ma'am?"

Alaina lifted her chin. "I've been better, officer. And you already know me from the center."

The deputy frowned. "Wasn't sure if you'd remember us."

"I do. I know you both."

"That's good. Can you tell us what happened, ma'am?" Turner asked. Foss stood quietly with a pen and a notebook.

"That's what I don't really know." She turned, her gaze meeting Ry's. "Ryder pulled me from the water and revived me. Without him, I don't think I'd be here right now."

"You don't know how you got in the water?" Foss interjected. He sounded a touch angry.

She didn't meet the deputy's gaze. "No. I took my son to school. I think I went home after, but I don't remember. I don't remember anything until I woke up in Ryder's bathtub."

Foss turned narrow eyes on him. Ry automatically didn't like the way the man stared. Wasn't gonna react though.

"Why was she in your bathtub, Mister…"

"*Sergeant* Hanson," he said coolly. "U.S. Army. She was in my tub because she was submerged in icy water and I needed to raise her body temperature."

Foss grunted as Turner nodded. "Makes sense. Can you tell us where you live, Sergeant?"

He'd given all this info to the hospital yesterday so they could file a police report, but he did it again because these men wanted to assert dominance and he didn't give a shit. Pissing contests didn't faze him in the least. His masculinity didn't hang on the results. When it counted, he'd wipe the floor with anyone who pushed him too far.

"How long you lived there?" Foss asked.

"About five days."

"New in town, huh?"

"In this town, yes. But I've lived in Maryland for four years, and one of my teammates lives in town."

"Teammates?"

"Special Ops."

Foss stared. Ry stared back.

"See any combat?" Foss asked.

"A bit," Ry said. Understatement, but he wasn't giving details to this dick.

"Is there anything else you remember, Miss Montgomery?" Turner asked. "Anything at all?"

She frowned. Then she shook her head. "I really don't. I just have impressions. Darkness, pain. Then water. I didn't see anyone."

"Any idea why someone would do those things to you?"

She hesitated. "Not really. You know we see all kinds of women in the center. Sometimes there are angry boyfriends or husbands in the picture."

Ry didn't like the sound of that. Why would a cleaner be the target of an angry boyfriend or husband? Then again, why not? Abusers weren't rational people.

"And have there been any of those lately?" Foss asked.

"There was a guy a couple of weeks ago, but I never spoke to him. Lidia did, but not me. He was angry that his wife left him. Bridget called the sheriff's office and you came over, Deputy Foss."

He nodded. "I remember that one. You haven't seen him since?"

"No. I never even spoke to him."

Foss was busy writing something down. "Doesn't mean he didn't watch the center and choose a target. Living where you do, you'd be an easy mark."

Alaina stiffened. It took everything Ry had not to take a warning step toward the deputy. Of course he'd know where she lived as a law officer. But something about that made Alaina uncomfortable, and that caused Ry's protective instincts to flare even if there was nothing he could say at the moment.

"I live where I can afford to," she said primly. "It's not great, but Mr. Herbert is nice and takes care of things when asked."

"Old man Herbert's nice enough, but that rundown RV he calls a trailer isn't fit for dogs, much less a pretty young woman such as you. Still," Foss said, clicking his tongue, "no offense meant. Just pointing out the property is accessible and far enough from town someone could do what was done to you unseen."

Alaina clasped her hands in her lap. Her knuckles were white. Ry had an urge to wrap his fingers around Foss's neck and march him out of there, but he could chalk that one onto the column of things that would not go well with his command. Like hell the man hadn't meant to be offensive. There was more going on here than met the eye, but whatever it was made Alaina uneasy. And Ry didn't like it. That responsibility thing again.

"Anything else you guys need?" Ry asked. "Alaina needs to rest."

Foss's eyebrows twitched down for a sec, but it was Turner who responded. "No, we're good for now. We'll let you know if we find any leads. And you let us know if you remember anything, Miss Montgomery. Anything at all, no matter how small."

"I will," she whispered.

"Good. I'm sorry this happened to you, ma'am. We're going to do our best to find this person."

"Thank you."

Turner gave Foss a look and the two of them left, their boots echoing down the hallway. Alaina kept studying her hands. Finally, she met Ry's gaze. He didn't know what was in those eyes of hers, but it pierced something in his soul. Made him want to save her the way he hadn't been able to save Sheri.

"You all right?" he asked.

She nodded. "I'm fine."

He sat down again. "Do you often have trouble at the center?"

"Not often. It's a crisis center for women who've been victims of rape or domestic violence, or for those contemplating suicide, and it's locked down. We sometimes get angry men yelling outside who blame us for their wife or girlfriend leaving. All we do is counsel and help people by being there and holding their hands when they have to go for a rape exam or talk to the police about what happened. We also help place them in shelters if they need it."

"We?"

"I get paid to clean the center five days a week, but I volunteer too. I'm not a social worker, but I've trained to be a crisis counselor. The program is run by the center, and I've completed it. I sit with people, like I said, and help when they need a shoulder to lean on. I don't do anything except listen and reassure. I've worked the suicide hotline, too, but that's harder in my opinion."

"Could someone target you?"

"I don't know why they would, but yes, I suppose someone could. Like Deputy Foss said, I could have been the random target they chose. I doubt it'd be specific. I haven't been working as a counselor for long. I finished the training a month ago, and I've had a few shifts since. But cleaning is what pays, and I have to be home for Everett in the evenings, though Stacie takes him sometimes if she's off. We watch each other's kids if one of us works an evening shift."

He had so many questions. He wanted to know where Everett's father was. Was he someone who could attack her if they were fighting over Everett? It was something he intended to find out, but not today. She had enough to deal with right now, and she seemed tired after the visit from the deputies.

Doctor Innes came to see her a little while later and delivered the news that if she kept improving, they'd let her go home tomorrow. She would be in pain, and she would need help, but Ry had that figured out. She'd stay in one of the bedrooms in his house for a few days. Everett could share it with her because there were two twin beds Ry had bought from the previous owner. When Alaina was stronger, she and her son could move over to the guest house and have their privacy.

When Alaina fell asleep again, Ry left her to go make arrangements. He asked himself the entire time he drove around town shopping for groceries, then returning home to make sure the spare room was good enough, what the hell he was doing. He'd pulled her out of the water yesterday. Tomorrow, he was moving her into his house.

He didn't know anything about her other than she had a six-year-old son named Everett and what she did for a living. He didn't know how long she'd been in town or what her background was. And he damned sure didn't know what to do with a six-year-old.

But he couldn't abandon her. Something about her got to him in a way he couldn't explain. Not just the fact he'd saved her life. He'd have done that for anyone. There was something in her eyes, some depth of emotion that intrigued him. She had secrets, but who didn't?

Including him. He'd never told anyone in his life since he'd left home about Sheri. Or about finding her. The only people who knew were people back in Buffalo. He didn't know why he didn't talk about it, but anytime he thought about sharing it, his throat closed up.

Alaina's secrets didn't worry him. He could tell a lot about her by what he knew already. She was a woman who worked an unskilled labor job to take care of her son, and she lived in a broken-down RV outside town. But her yard was neat and he knew there would be flowers in those pots in spring. She also cared enough about helping other people to do volunteer work when a second job would've netted her more income.

Alaina Montgomery seemed like someone who'd endured her share of pain and loss. So had he. Maybe that was what drew him, or maybe it was just that she seemed like she needed someone strong in her corner. Not just a friend, because she seemed to have at least one in Stacie, but a protector. Someone who could look out for her and keep her safe.

Someone who could find out who'd tried to kill her and make sure they didn't get away with it. That was his mission now.

Protect Alaina and her son. Find the bastard who'd hurt her.

End them.

Figuratively, of course.

Chapter Four

ALAINA HOBBLED TO THE KITCHEN AND POURED A CUP of coffee before making her way to the dining room table and easing into a chair. Every day was better, but she still hurt. It was worse when she woke in the mornings. She'd learned to ease into the day, though it frustrated her as well. She needed to work, and she still couldn't do much of anything without aching all over. So frustrating.

It'd been a week since Ryder had picked her up from the hospital and brought her to his beautiful white clapboard house on Mystic Lake. He'd helped her from his truck like she was made of glass and then carried her to the bedroom she now shared with Everett.

The house had been sparsely furnished when she'd first arrived, though he'd had some furniture deliveries in the days since. There was a dining table now, but no chairs other than the fold-out kind you got at Walmart. He'd gotten a couch and recliner yesterday, and bedroom furniture for the master the day before that. The guest room she and Everett were in had twin beds and a dresser, but those had been there when they'd arrived.

Ryder had a television and internet, which meant he could stream shows. Something she'd never been able to do for two reasons. One was price. Two was how bad the internet was at Mr. Herbert's.

In the evenings, Ryder let Everett stream shows on Disney+. It made her tear up because her kid was so happy. And because Ryder gave up his television for her kid like it was no big deal. Ryder didn't stay with them, though. He went to the small cottage that sat about thirty feet diagonal of the main house and worked on getting it ready for when she could move over there.

Alaina sighed as she sipped coffee and contemplated the view. The deep blue of Mystic Lake, which was fed by one of the bleeder creeks that came off the Chesapeake, was visible across the entire back of Ryder's house. Anywhere you went in the living room, dining room, or kitchen, you got a water view. There was a dock that jutted a good distance over the lake, and bare trees stood on the bank.

It was lovely, but also stark because she could feel the chill in her bones as she looked at the water. A shiver vibrated through her.

She'd been out there. Floating with the current. Dead for all intents and purposes. Until Ryder saw her.

Alaina shuddered every time she thought about it, and then she thanked God for putting her in the water where Ryder could see her. If not for him, Everett would probably be in a children's home right now, waiting for placement with a foster family. She couldn't bear to think of it.

Her aunt and uncle wouldn't take him, and the man who'd fathered him had never admitted it to anyone, least of all himself. She'd been so young and dumb back then. At nineteen, she'd thought Clint would marry her when she'd told him she was pregnant. He'd always promised they would get married someday, and that'd seemed the perfect time for it.

But when she'd told him about the baby, he'd called her a slut and said it wasn't his kid. Even though they'd been dating for a year and he knew she'd been a virgin when they got together. Not his kid.

And not his wife, either. He'd never meant to marry her. He'd only said it to get into her panties.

That wasn't the first time she'd learned the world was cruel, nor would it be the last. Her aunt and uncle had grudgingly raised her when her mother died, but no way would they help her out with a kid. She was old enough to take care of herself, according to them, and they'd discharged their duty the day she'd turned eighteen.

That a man she'd only met when he'd saved her from drowning had opened up his home to her and her child was nothing short of remarkable. Even better, Everett liked Ryder. He was a shy kid, didn't say a lot around other adults, but he'd started to tentatively talk to Ryder.

Ryder didn't brush him off when he did it. It made her happy to see her son get attention from a male he could look up to, though she was still cautious, still waiting for the moment Ryder would prove his patience had a limit.

If it happened, she'd be back to her RV and to hell with the difficulty of moving around. Everett was her first priority. Always.

She was still at the table when Ryder walked in the door. He'd just dropped Everett at school for her, same as he'd done all week. Her car was in the driveway, but driving was too difficult right now.

As much as it pained her, she'd had to accept help from strangers. Once she'd met Ryder's friends— Noah, Jenna, and their little girl, Alice—she'd known her son would be okay with any of them. Maybe it was because of the way she'd been raised by her aunt and uncle, but she hated to be a burden to anyone. Though Ryder and his friends insisted she wasn't, she still felt that way deep inside.

Jenna had found Alaina's purse and phone in

one of the empty flowerpots on her porch, so at least she had her phone back. It had died because it was old and didn't hold a charge well. The only thing missing had been her last fifty dollars. Maybe not much to anyone else, but it was a lot to her when it was the last bit of cash she had until payday.

Fortunately for her, Ryder hadn't let her pay for any groceries since they'd moved in, though she felt guilty about that too. She took a moment to appreciate him as he strode into the dining room. He was tall and muscled, and so handsome it made her heart squeeze every time she saw him. More than once since she'd started to feel better, she'd imagined pressing her mouth to his, feeling the firm pressure of his lips, and her insides turned upside down same as always.

"How're you feeling?" he asked.

"Still a bit sore, but better than ever," she replied with a smile. And she was. By afternoon, she'd feel good enough to go with him when it was time to get Everett from school.

Ryder poured himself a cup of coffee, then held up the blueberry muffins she'd noticed this morning and pointed. She shouldn't, but she nodded. He snagged two and brought them over, sliding one to her on a plate.

"Grandma's recipe," he said as she bit into it.

Alaina wanted to moan. It was a very good blueberry muffin. "I thought I smelled something baking last night. But I figured you'd whipped up a box mix."

He gave her a look of mock horror. "No way. Gram would spin in her grave if she were dead, which she is not."

Alaina grinned as she took another bite. "Glad to hear it. And glad she gave you her recipe."

She couldn't cook to save her life. If it couldn't be boiled or dumped into a saucepan and heated, maybe toasted, she was out.

"Everett chattered all the way to school. Thought you might like to know that."

Alaina blinked in surprise. Everett was warming up to Ryder, but wow. "What about?"

"Fishing." He polished off the muffin. "I think I may have oversold the prospect of catching fish from the dock when the weather is warmer."

Alaina's heart beat a little harder at the idea of this man showing her son how to fish. "I'm sure he'll have fun whether he catches anything or not."

Ryder nodded. "Probably. But man, it's gonna seem like forever before he gets the chance. I told him it'll be a couple of months at least."

Disappointment flared. A couple of months. They'd be back in the RV by then. Not a thought she relished. She liked not having to move things around to create space for a bed every night, and she liked not having to think about the limited supply of hot water in the tiny tank that supplied the RV. She typically saved that for Everett's shower and she showered at the center. On days she didn't work, she took a very fast shower and used dry shampoo so she didn't have to spend time washing her hair. Staying with Ryder was heaven compared to that, even if she did feel increasingly burdensome to him.

"I think maybe Everett and I could move to the guest house now. Give you back your television and your evenings."

If she thought he'd disagree, she was disappointed. He took a sip of coffee and nodded. "Sure, we can do that. It's ready for you now. Scarlett's bringing some side tables and a chair later today."

She'd heard him talk about his friends Mal and Scarlett, but she hadn't met them yet. Scarlett was a bargain shopper and thrifter. Alaina was a thrifter too, but more for necessity than fun. She didn't have an eye for stuff. She just got what she could use. It was amazing what people got rid of when they wanted something new.

"I look forward to meeting her."

"She wants to meet you, too. Word of warning though. Mal will probably be with her. He's, uh, extra."

Alaina was intrigued. "What's that mean?"

"Means he's goofy, and you never know what's coming out of his mouth. He's fun, though."

"Mmm." She swirled her coffee, working up the nerve to ask a question. One that was beginning to make more sense now that she'd eaten a blueberry muffin he'd baked from his grandmother's recipe. "Hey, um, why does Noah call you Muffin?"

He let out a long-suffering sigh. Then he pointed at her half-eaten blueberry muffin as if to demonstrate. "My grandparents owned a bakery in Buffalo, where I'm from. I learned how to bake a lot more than muffins, but blueberry is my favorite. And I was, shall we say, a bit of a chubby kid. With a muffin top."

Alaina blinked. Her jaw must have slipped open a little because he nodded.

"It's true. Hard to believe, I know, but there's pictorial evidence. Which is how I got stuck with the name. That and I made the mistake of baking homemade muffins for the guys one time. Call signs aren't always flattering. I've got a teammate named Wolf—now that's fricking cool, right? We have Saint, Wolf, Hacker—self-explanatory—Mal, the fucker. Easy, Gem, Zany, and me. I'm the one stuck with Muffin."

Alaina couldn't help but giggle. A muffin top? On him? She didn't remember his naked torso from the day he'd rescued her, more's the pity, but he'd carried her against his hard body and there was no way he had an ounce of fat on him.

"Yeah, I know," he said, waving a hand. "Laugh away. I'm used to it."

She bit the inside of her lip, thinking he was feeling a little self-conscious, but then he shot her a grin and she didn't try to hold it back anymore.

Damn he was gorgeous.

It'd been years since she'd been with a man. In truth, she'd only ever been with Clint. Once Everett was born, she'd vowed not to be distracted with men or dating. Her little boy deserved all her time and attention, and she'd worked hard to give it to him, moving the two of them to Maryland a year ago.

She'd needed a change from South Carolina. Nothing was ever getting better there. Too many people knew her in the small town of Aurora, and she was tired of seeing Clint's wife and kids around town, knowing that he refused to acknowledge his oldest. She'd stayed far too long hoping he might one day want to see Everett, for her son's sake, but she'd finally acknowledged it wasn't ever going to happen. She'd gone to see him once in his office, because Everett was sick and needed medicine she couldn't afford, and he'd thrown her out and told her not to ever come back or he'd have her arrested for harassment.

She'd gotten the money from the kindness of a friend, but she'd known she needed to get Everett out of that environment where he wasn't ever going to be good enough for the man who'd fathered him.

It'd been challenging to leave everything she knew, but also good. She was happy in Mystic Cove, which she'd found six months ago after bouncing around the DC area for a while. Mystic Cove was more affordable, and Mr. Herbert's RV, no matter how shabby, was a godsend after sharing apartments with roommates she didn't fully trust.

A feeling of despair threatened to overwhelm her, but she pushed it back. She'd lost several days' work, which meant things would be extra tight for a while, but for now she had Ryder and his friends to help her out. She felt guilty relying on him to take Everett to school and pick him up, to prepare meals and let her kid use his television for kid shows, but she didn't have the ability right now to do it herself. She'd offered to pay him, but he'd refused to accept.

"So you bake more than muffins?" she asked, tearing off another piece and popping it in her mouth.

"Yep. Cakes, pies, scones, bread, croissants. If it's full of carbs and quite possibly bad for you, I can do it. I used to stay with them a lot because my parents often worked late or took assignments out of town. Gram taught me how to bake because I was apparently too rambunctious otherwise. If she kept me busy with measuring and mixing and baking, I didn't annoy her."

Alaina pictured a little boy standing on a stool to reach the counter, mixing ingredients in a bowl. "What did your parents do?"

"They're newspaper journalists. They put in long hours and traveled a lot for stories when I was a kid, but not so much now. Hell, they're lucky they still have jobs the way everything's going online and consolidating."

"Oh. I'm sorry. It sounds like a fascinating job, though."

"It was. I guess it still is, but it's less certain than it used to be. People don't want to believe facts anymore, or that real reporters still exist and do their best to report facts only. You've got the entertainment networks masquerading as news now. They don't care about truth at all, just whip up their viewers with whatever extreme thing they think will get them the most eyeballs. Makes staying in business harder than ever, which affects journalists everywhere. It's tempting to say to hell with the facts and let's just write about whatever gets eyeballs. Luckily, they're at the end of their careers, not the beginning."

"You didn't want to be a journalist too?"

"Nope. I don't like anything that involves that much writing. I'm more of an action kind of guy."

"So you joined the military."

"I did. My parents wanted me to go to college, but I didn't want them to have the burden of paying for it. Plus I wasn't ready. I knew I wasn't. I just wanted to get the hell out of Buffalo and see the world."

Alaina understood wanting to get away from a place, but her reasons were less about the place than some of the people and the way she'd felt continuing to raise her son there. "What's wrong with Buffalo?"

"Nothing. It's a great city. Great food, great

people. Too much snow, though. If I never shovel another driveway, I'll be happy."

"It snows here, you know," she said with a grin. They'd had snow at Christmas, and more in January.

"Yeah, true. But even when you shovel snow here, it's nothing like back home. It's so easy it almost doesn't count."

Alaina laughed. "I'm from South Carolina. Any snow is too much snow."

He looked intrigued. "What made you move to Maryland?"

Of course he would ask. She'd asked him, after all. "I wanted somewhere new. There's nothing for me back there."

"Everett's father?"

Alaina had known it would come up eventually. "He's not involved in Everett's life. Never has been. Never wanted to be. We weren't married, and he was starting his freshman year at Clemson when I got pregnant. It was a lot easier to deny he was Everett's father than to take responsibility for a baby."

"Ouch. Sorry."

Alaina shrugged and took another bite of her muffin, which she had apparently torn to bits on her plate. "It's okay. It bothered me seven years ago, of course, because I was nineteen and scared. Now I'm glad he's all mine. Clint graduated a few years ago and married a doctor's daughter. He's perfectly happy without Everett in his life."

"So he's not someone who'd come up here to confront you about something and lose his temper?"

She understood why he might think that, but she snorted. "No way. He's got a cushy life with his new wife and no reason to screw it up. I haven't heard from him in years. I used to run into him in town, but he never acknowledged me. I'm sure he's ecstatic that we're gone."

Ryder's brow knit tight. "Everett's a great kid, Alaina. Any man who doesn't want his own kid isn't worth your time or Everett's. But I know it had to have been hard for you raising him without help, and I'm sorry."

She could feel the tears just below the surface. "It hasn't always been easy, but it's worth it. He's worth it."

Ryder nodded. "Of course he is."

God, this man. There was so much she wanted to say to him, but she didn't know him well enough. Even though she was in his house, eating with him every night, talking to him, sleeping in a room down the hall from his. She trusted him enough to know he wouldn't hurt her or her child, but that didn't mean she needed to let herself feel more than she should. He had his life together. He could do better than a single mom living hand to mouth and a six-year-old that wasn't his.

"I really can't thank you enough for all you've done for us. If I could cook, I'd fix you a great meal in thanks. You've got me beat on the cooking thing, though. All I can do is tell you how grateful I am, and pay you back when I'm working again."

Even though doing so would come at a cost since she was already behind on everything else.

"You don't have to pay me, Alaina. I told you that."

"I know. But this is your home, and you've only recently moved in. We're imposing."

"You aren't. I'm used to being alone, unless I'm hanging out with my team or traveling with them, but it's been nice having people at the table with me."

Alaina ducked her head, her cheeks heating for no reason whatsoever other than the intensity of his green gaze. That and the way she was thinking about his lips on hers again. "I appreciate that, but you need your space back. And I don't want Everett getting too used to your cooking or your television. It'll be hard enough for him when we have to go back to our place as it is."

Ryder's gaze didn't waver. "So don't go. Stay in the guest house. Rent it from me. It's not that much farther to Mystic Cove from here than it is from where you live now."

Alaina's throat was tight. "Thank you, but I can't. I can't pay any more than I'm paying now, and your place is a lot bigger. It's worth more, and you shouldn't take less just to help me."

He blew out a breath. "Pay me whatever you're

paying Mr. Herbert. I'm fine with that. I'd rather know I had someone who needs the place and will treat it right than go searching for tenants who may or may not throw wild parties when I'm out of town."

Alaina sniffed a little. "How do you know I won't throw parties? They might be wild parties for six-year-olds, but they could get kinda crazy. You never know with kids."

He laughed. "You don't have to decide right now. Let's get you moved over there, and you can let me know how you like the place, okay? But it's yours and Everett's if you want it. You'd be saving me the trouble of finding someone, and that's a plus."

Alaina's heart throbbed. "Okay, we can do that. If Everett likes it and it makes sense, we'll let you know."

"Good. Tell me when you're ready and I'll help you take your things over there."

"Thank you. I will."

He nodded. "I'll be working on some things in the garage. Come get me any time."

Chapter Five

Ry stood beside Alaina in the much smaller guest cottage, aka mother-in-law suite, as she took it all in. It had questionable seventies decor that he'd done his best to clean up. She still walked slowly, but she was definitely on the mend. The bruising on her face was mostly covered with the makeup she'd applied, and she didn't wince with pain every time she moved. That was a good thing.

There'd been no progress on finding her attacker. It'd only been a little over a week, but the sheriff's department had nothing. The only thing Alaina had reported missing was fifty dollars, and that didn't seem like much of a reason to go to the trouble to beat someone senseless and move their body five miles to the water to dump it.

Though crazier things had happened. Could have been someone high on meth or prescriptions drugs seeking whatever cash they could find. Alaina's phone was too old to be worth much, and she didn't have credit cards. Maybe another person had moved Alaina after the attack. An accomplice or someone cleaning up after their loved one.

The attack could have also been motivated by revenge for something she'd done, but Alaina didn't seem to have any enemies. She'd gotten calls from her friends at the center, and she hadn't seemed upset or especially quiet after any of them.

He wanted to ask Hacker to look into some stuff for him, but his teammate was currently on vacation with his wife. It'd have to wait until he was back home again. For now, Ry would keep her safe and make sure nobody got to her.

He watched her study the cottage, her sage green eyes giving nothing away. The walls were dark paneled, the kitchen was a small galley style against one wall, with a sink, a counter, a stove, and a refrigerator. There was one row of overhead cabinets, and a built-in banquette with a table near the window. The living room wasn't big, but there was a couch and a cabinet for a television, though both had seen better days. The previous owners had left all the furniture in the cottage because it was old.

The floors were vinyl, stained in some places, but not too terrible. She walked into the bedroom, the only bedroom, and took that in, too. There was a queen-sized bed he'd have to get a new mattress for soon, and a bedside table. There was also room for a fold-out twin cot where she could put Everett. Or she could put him in the living room on the cot. Ry had one of those coming because Mal and Scarlett were bringing it over. And the bathroom did indeed have orange tile, but it was more of a sherbet color than a true orange.

"Very 1970s," she said as she turned back to him. He stood in the doorway, watching her.

"Yeah, I'd planned to gut it and retile everything. Put down some new ceramic tile flooring—the kind that looks like wood—paint the paneling, maybe paint the kitchen cabinets too. It's not a bad place, just needs some TLC. Now do you get why it'd be criminal to charge you anything more than what you're already paying? If you wanted to stay, that is. It's yours for free while you recover."

She clasped her hands in front of her body. He wondered if she realized how it pushed her breasts together and made them seem plumper. Made his heart speed up in a way that surprised him. He wasn't an eighteen-year-old virgin anymore, and he didn't get hot and bothered over a little bit of cleavage.

Until now.

"It's a little dated, but it's a nice place, Ryder. Nicer than living in one-hundred and fifty square feet of space." She turned to gesture toward the window. "And there's a view of the water, plus the trees and grass will be beautiful in spring and summer. And fall, when the leaves turn."

"So you like it then." It wasn't a question.

She nodded. "I like it. But I'm not saying yes to renting it yet. I need you to be certain about that."

Ry moved toward her. She didn't back away, but her eyes widened a bit as he approached. He made himself stop. The last thing he wanted was to scare her. But he also wanted to touch her. Damnedest thing, this compulsion.

"I told you, Alaina, you'd be doing me a favor. Besides, I saw those flower pots and the wind chimes at the other place. You like to make your space pretty. You'll do that here, and you'll be helping me because I know shit-all about plants."

Her grin was sudden and almost blinding because it transformed her from small and frightened into beautiful and confident. Alaina Montgomery had a killer smile. He wanted more of them. He knew that with a clarity that shocked him.

"I'm pretty good with plants. I can't cook to save my life, but I can clean and I can work in the yard. If you let me clean your house in addition to the rent, then we may have a deal I can feel good about."

He didn't want her to feel like she had to do more than pay rent, but he also recognized that she needed to feel like she was paying her way. He could do that, even if he'd rather she just take his offer as it was.

He held out his hand. "Then let's shake on it—but

the cleaning can wait until you're back up to speed, okay?"

She put her hand in his. Little sizzles of electricity raced up his arm. She lifted her gaze to meet his, and he had the craziest urge to cradle her in his arms and kiss her senseless.

"It's a deal," she said, her voice breathy and soft. "So long as Everett likes it, and I'm sure he will."

"Deal," he repeated before he let her hand go, because he couldn't find any other words to say. He hoped Everett liked it. He couldn't imagine the kid wouldn't, but he still knew nothing about kids. He liked Everett, though. The kid was quiet until he knew you, and then he didn't stop. Ry had been a little panicked at all the chatter this morning, but then he'd realized he didn't have to say much in response. It was true he'd mentioned fishing, but at the time Everett hadn't said much about it. Not so this morning.

A million questions, a million additional thoughts, and Ry had dropped the kid at school and welcomed the silence for the ride home. Was that what it was like to be a parent? Bursts of chatter that made you kinda crazy but you enjoyed them anyway?

Maybe so. He'd thought he was doing Alaina a favor taking Everett to school, and he was, but he hadn't realized how monumental it could be to Everett. Ry was the male figure in his life by default at the moment, and that was a serious responsibility. He had to be careful with it, not just randomly promise the kid they'd do things together.

He *wanted* to fish off the dock with Everett when the time was right, but he realized maybe he shouldn't have planted the idea in the boy's mind so soon.

"I'll get your things, if you like," he said.

Alaina turned. "Oh, I can help."

The sound of a car door got his attention. His phone pinged with a text a second later. "It's Mal and Scarlett. You ready to meet crazy Mal and his far more sensible other half? We can get your stuff later."

Alaina clasped her hands in front of her body again and nodded. "I think I'm ready. He's not too crazy, is he?"

Ry laughed. "Crazier than a fox in a henhouse, as my grandma used to say."

She gave him a wry look. "I'm not sure I know what that means, though my granny said something similar. I believe it was crazier than a shithouse rat, though."

He laughed again. "Either way, I think it's pretty crazy." He went over and opened the door, hollering to Mal and Scarlett. They strode toward the cottage, a table tucked under each of Mal's arms.

"Chair's in the back of the truck with the cot, and I found these beauties at the thrift shop just this morning," Scarlett said as they approached. "Better than the ones I was going to bring. I picked up some pictures, too, in case you want to hang anything."

"Any dogs playing poker?" Ry asked.

Scarlett rolled her eyes good-naturedly. "No, 'fraid not."

"Dang, I was hoping." He turned to see Alaina behind him, not too close, twisting her hands together as she waited. He felt a tug of sympathy for her as he moved to let Scarlett and Mal in. "This is Alaina Montgomery. Alaina, Scarlett and Mal."

Alaina smiled as she held out a hand. "Hello. Pleased to meet you both."

Ordinarily Mal would do something goofy like push her hand aside and hug her anyway, telling her that's how they did it in Texas. But he knew enough of what she'd been through to keep that part of his personality reined in. Ry appreciated the caution. He thought Alaina was strong, but even the strongest could break when least expected.

Everyone shook hands, and then Mal went back to retrieve the chair. Ry grabbed the tables and led the way inside. Scarlett directed them where to place everything. "What do you think?" she asked Alaina.

Alaina seemed surprised to be asked. "I think that's great. I should admit I'm not a decorator though."

"Neither am I," Scarlett said with a smile. "I just know what I like. And I love bargain hunting, so if you want help with any decorating, I'm your girl."

"Please," Mal said, clasping his hands together

and dropping to his knees. "Please go shopping with her and put me out of my misery."

Scarlett laughed and pushed his shoulder. "You like shopping with me, you big idiot. It was practically our first date."

"Told you he was crazy," Ry said.

Mal looked offended. "You said what? I'm shocked. Shocked."

"You really aren't," Ry said mildly. He turned to Alaina. "This guy dumped a bucket of blueberry muffin mix on my head a couple of months ago after I got out of the shower in the locker room. Had to shower again."

"Hey, it wasn't me. It was Hacker," Mal said in mock offense.

"Dude, he set it up. But *you* gave him the idea. Same as if you'd done it to me so far as I'm concerned."

Mal got to his feet, grinning. "I am gifted that way, aren't I?"

'That's one way of looking at it," Ry said.

Mal turned his megawatt grin on Alaina. "Don't you believe what this guy says, Alaina. I'm fun, not crazy. Ain't that right, Scar?"

Scarlett put her arm through his and sidled against him. "You are completely fun, baby. And maybe a little bit nuts."

"Nuts for you," he said, gazing down at her.

"Hey, do that on your own time," Ry said. "Scarlett, before this caveman drags you home again, can you help us out here? What would you do about curtains and all that girly crap women like?"

Scarlett arched an eyebrow. "Girly crap? Crap?" She huffed, then went over and stood by Alaina's side. "Mal, you two go grab the pictures and the cot please. Then y'all get out of here. Go stare at the water and think about fishing or something. I'm going to talk to Alaina about what *she* wants."

"Yes, ma'am," Ry and Mal said at the same time, shooting each other a look as they headed toward the door.

———

ALAINA HADN'T KNOWN what to think at first, but she liked Ryder's friends. She'd been nervous, and then she hadn't. Between one moment and the next, Mal and Scarlett had made her feel comfortable. Especially Scarlett.

They walked around the cottage, looking at it from all angles, Scarlett folding her arms and studying the room with an intensity that Alaina didn't have. At least not when it came to configuring a space. It wasn't that she didn't want it. She loved HGTV as much as any woman, but she didn't understand how to go from crappy room to beautifully decorated space no matter how she tried. Plus she only saw decorating shows at the center these days.

"I really think this is a great space," Scarlett said. "Can't you just see it with white walls? It'll be so bright in here. Put up some soft curtains on rods with clips—we could use patterned sheets for that—and it'll change everything."

"I can't really spend a lot of money," Alaina began, looking at the chair, side tables, and hanging pictures in frames Scarlett had brought with her today. In fact, she could spend *no* money.

Scarlett shook her head. "Not you, girlfriend. Ryder. It's his place, and he needs to make it worth the rent. I'm assuming you're going to stay, right?"

Alaina looked at the gorgeous view from the windows, at the space it took her more than two steps to cross, and back at Scarlett. "Yes, I'm staying. It's already worth the cost to me just the way it is."

Scarlett smiled. "It *is* a nice place. Ryder knew what he wanted and he didn't stop until he found it, even when people told him it would never happen. But it did!" She sighed. "I might get a little carried away with envisioning changes. Still, Ryder should paint it, and he can put up curtains and blinds too. That's not a lot, really. It's the least you'll need with the windows bare like this."

Her mom had used aluminum foil to darken bedroom windows when Alaina was little. It was cheap and effective, but probably not what Ryder would want done. Though she could ask him. Not that she liked the foil option, but it was low cost and the bedroom was all that would need it.

"It's fine as it is. Really," Alaina said, hastening to add, "I love your ideas. I just don't want to ask Ryder to do anything when he's done so much already. When I get more settled, I'd love your help, though."

Scarlett gave her a sweet smile. "You got it, Alaina. Anytime you want to shop or paint or anything, you call me. It's my relaxation. Work and school can be stressful, so I like to do something I find fun."

"What do you do?" Alaina asked.

"I'm a physical therapist assistant, but I'm going back to school to be a physical therapist. It's hard work, but I love it. Plus it's where I met Mal."

They talked a little about what Scarlett did, about how she'd been Mal's therapist for a leg injury. How he'd offered her the apartment over his garage when her roommate decided to sell her house to get married, and how they'd eventually fallen for each other.

Alaina heard the underlying similarities and the way Scarlett seemed to hope things might work out the same for her and Ryder, but what man wanted a relationship that included a little kid in the mix? Not to mention she didn't have the bandwidth for it. Ryder was nice enough and sexy as hell, but Everett's well-being was her priority. End of story.

Scarlett asked questions, but they were easy ones.

Where Alaina worked, then how it worked at the crisis center with counseling and support services, about Everett and the things he liked. Alaina knew that Ryder had probably coached her, but she appreciated it. She didn't want to talk about what had happened or speculate about the kind of person who'd attacked her and dumped her unconscious body into the water. It was ugly and made her anxious because there was so much she still didn't know. May never know if her experience at the center was any indication.

Some women never recalled what happened when they were assaulted. All she knew was she hadn't been raped, and that was something she held onto as tight as she could. She hadn't been violated that way. But why had she been attacked if not for that? It certainly hadn't been for her last fifty dollars. And it wasn't like she'd been in a relationship with anyone, violent or not.

Then again, she didn't have to be. She could have been the unlucky woman in the wrong place at the wrong time. Whatever the case, there was a violent man—she assumed it was a man because it usually was—loose in Mystic Cove.

Alaina shuddered. That was the other reason she wanted to stay in the cottage. She knew Ryder was in the military, and she knew he did some sort of dangerous special operations stuff, like a Navy SEAL or a Delta Force soldier. The down side was that he could be gone for weeks at a time when he was working.

But for now he was her security. She prayed it was enough.

"You think we've made the guys wait long enough?" Scarlett asked with a wink.

Alaina peeked out the window at where they stood on the dock, gesturing at the lake and trees. Mal pretended he was fishing, and Ryder shook his head. Then the two of them were laughing and pushing each other up and down the dock.

"Maybe we better go out there," Alaina said. "Before one of them lands in the lake."

Chapter Six

ALAINA AND SCARLETT REJOINED THE MEN, WHO stopped horsing around the second they appeared. It didn't bother Alaina to walk down the dock. She had no memory of the water, other than Ryder's bathtub.

There was a bigger space at the end where you could fit chairs and a small table if you wanted to sit and stare at the water. She could imagine summer mornings with coffee, or fall evenings watching the sunset and the leaves turning. She imagined sitting there with Ryder while Everett perched on the dock with a fishing pole and a bucket, his legs swinging from the edge.

Careful.

It wasn't her home, and though she'd agreed to stay and rent the cottage, that didn't mean it would work out. She couldn't let herself get complacent about the situation. She had to work and save and eventually find a place that was hers and Everett's alone. A place where they wouldn't have to speak to a landlord or get permission to plant a few flowers.

Not that she'd ever get a house of her own on a cleaner's pay. Maybe she should take on a few more clients, learn to function on less sleep…

"Y'all want to grab lunch?" Mal asked, interrupting her thoughts. "I'm starved."

Scarlett had slipped her arm around his waist, and now she laughed as she gazed up at him. "You ate a big breakfast not more than two hours ago."

"I know, honey, but I gotta keep my strength up." He patted his belly. "You made me go shopping, and that takes energy."

"Oh, Mal. You are so full of crap."

He gave Scarlett a noisy kiss on the forehead. "And yet you love me anyway."

"I definitely do."

Alaina almost thought she should look away, but she didn't. It made her feel lonelier than ever to watch Mal and Scarlett. They had something she'd never had. And never would, at least until Everett was grown and safely launched into the world. It'd probably be too late by then anyway.

"I could eat," Ryder said. "Alaina?"

She started. "Um, no, I'm fine." She couldn't afford lunch out. She'd stay here and eat some of the leftovers from dinner last night, though she kind of wished she could go and hang out with them.

"You don't have to eat if you don't want to," Ryder said. "You can join us though. We should call Easy and Jenna," he added to Mal and Scarlett.

"Definitely," Mal said.

"I'll text Jenna," Scarlett said. "We can go to the Early Bird Diner if she doesn't mind. Their pie is so good."

"Come on," Ryder said gently. "Join us. I'm buying."

Her stomach chose that moment to growl. Not the quiet kind of internal growl that let you know you were hungry, but a full-on monster growl everyone could hear. Alaina wanted to disappear, but they'd all heard it.

"I guess I am hungry," she said, because what else could she say? "But I can get my own lunch."

She'd eat a grilled cheese sandwich. Something cheap. She'd been to the diner before, and they had inexpensive items as well as full meat-and-three lunches made to fill up a horse.

"No," Ryder said, shaking his head. "I'm buying because we're celebrating. You can buy the next time."

Her heart thumped. "What are we celebrating?"

"I got a tenant today. Didn't you hear?"

His grin was too much. Too beautiful, too sexy, too inviting. She wished she could slip an arm around him and feel his lips against her forehead, but that was a fantasy. Still, he made it hard to say no.

"Hey, that's pretty terrific," she said, playing along. "I guess I can't say no when you put it like that."

"Nope, you can't. We'll grab something to bring home for dinner tonight, too."

"Sounds like a plan." She didn't know if he was just being nice, or if he felt sorry for her because he knew she didn't have much. Either way, there was nothing she could say in front of his friends.

"Jenna says they're in," Scarlett said. "They'll meet us over there in half an hour. Jenna's aunt is visiting, so we'll have Aunt Maggie and Alice too."

"I love Aunt Maggie," Mal said with a sigh. "She gets me."

"She feeds you pancakes."

"And she feeds me pancakes."

"Come on, doofus. Y'all want to ride together?" Scarlett asked.

Ryder shook his head. "Nah, you shouldn't have to bring us back when it's not on the way. I'll drive Alaina over."

"See you there," Scarlett said as she and Mal started toward their truck.

"I have to get my keys and wallet," Ryder said to Alaina. "Need anything?"

She started to say she could get it herself, but she told him she needed her purse and jacket. It was warmer today than it had been recently, but she thought she might get cold in the diner even with the sweatshirt she wore with her jeans.

Ryder went inside, and Alaina made her way to his truck. Scarlett waved as Mal turned around in the drive, and Alaina waved back. She liked these people. She liked Ryder. They made her feel like she belonged.

But she knew she didn't. She couldn't get used to any of this because it could all be over tomorrow. She was an outcast, same as always. She'd learned that lesson early in life, and nothing had changed. Alaina Montgomery was on her own, and she had no business equating friendliness with belonging.

Worse, she had no business bringing people into Everett's life if they were just going to leave. Not that she could keep everyone out. People came and went, after all. He would get used to the natural fluctuations of life. It was the sudden shifts she wanted to protect him from. Getting attached to someone and then having them leave you without a backward glance or an ounce of remorse.

Like Clint.

Ryder returned with her purse and jacket, then opened the truck door for her. She got inside and clipped the seatbelt while he went around to the other side. He started the truck and backed it up, turning around and heading for the road. His hands flexed on the wheel and she knew he was thinking about something.

"I hope I didn't push you too hard to come with us," he finally said. "I know Mal can be intense all by himself, but add in all of us, including a toddler and Jenna's aunt, and it might be overwhelming for someone trying to take it easy."

Alaina's throat tightened at his thoughtfulness. "It's okay. I'm an introvert by nature, but I like your friends. They're kind, and they've been nothing but helpful to me and Everett. I wouldn't want them to think I didn't want to be around them."

"They'd understand if it was too much."

She loved that he was concerned about her feelings. "It's not. I'm feeling a lot better. Besides, it's time I got out again. If I can do this, maybe I can start back to work soon."

"Maybe so. But don't push it too far too fast." He shot her a look just as her mouth opened to tell him she had no choice. "I know what you're going to say, but I'm telling you as someone who pushes his body to the limits of endurance on a regular basis, you have to let the body heal when it needs it, or you'll flame out and need even more time to recover. That won't help you or Everett."

She didn't argue with him. What he didn't understand was she didn't have the luxury of waiting to work. She'd take it easy. Everyone at the center would understand. She might lose her private clients, but she could get more. Many people wanted a housecleaner because they worked long hours and needed help.

One way or the other, she was clawing her way back up the ladder and replacing every dime she'd lost in the last week.

She was used to surviving. Used to relying on herself because relying on other people had never worked out. You could only get kicked in the teeth so many times before you stopped trusting anyone to be there for you when you needed it.

"You don't have to bring home anything for dinner," she said softly, changing the subject. "I don't want you thinking you have to provide everything for me and Everett. We'll be fine."

"I don't think that," he said. "But we'll be at the diner, and it'd be easy to grab one of their ready-made casseroles to bring back. Look, I know it's tight for you right now. You aren't working, and that bothers you. You don't really know me all that well, and you're worried you're going to be indebted to me if I keep getting you food and letting you live rent-free until you're back to work. Maybe you think I'm the kind of guy that's been adding everything up so I can ask for payment when you least expect it."

Her silence must have spoken volumes because he huffed a breath.

"I won't, Alaina. My family's Catholic, and though I'm more than a bit lapsed, I still believe in doing good works. I was raised by the kind of people who'd give you the shirt off their backs. My grandparents took me to volunteer at a homeless shelter every Thanksgiving for as long as I can remember, and we worked at a soup kitchen in the evenings when the bakery was closed. Most of those people just needed a hand up. They were working, but they couldn't get ahead. There's no shame in that."

Alaina bit the inside of her lip and told herself she wasn't going to cry. What he'd said was nice, not terrible, but she couldn't help how it made her feel.

She was a project to him. A person down on her luck who needed help. That wasn't a bad thing, but it hurt too.

They reached the diner, and Ryder pulled into the parking lot. Before he could shut off the engine, she spoke, trying not to let her voice waver.

"I've provided for Everett since he was born. I appreciate any breaks I get, but I'll still be providing for him next month and next year and five years from now. I'm not ashamed of the work I do. My boy doesn't go without the important stuff, and never has. I won't eat if it means he gets less than he needs, and I won't sleep if it means I can work harder to provide more than necessities. I thank you for all your kindness, really, but I don't want to be a feel-good project for anyone."

Before he could say a word, she opened her door and hopped out, wincing as pain radiated through her body. He was at her side faster than she'd expected, and he put a hand under her elbow to support her.

She tried to jerk it away, but he held on firmly. "I'm sorry, Alaina."

She stopped and turned to face him. "Do you even know what for? Or are you just saying that to placate me?"

Inside, a little voice was telling her to stop. Telling her she had it good at his place, getting his cottage for the same rent as she'd been paying for an old, outdated, dilapidated RV. But she still had some pride, even if it wasn't much, and she didn't have to let him make her feel poor and needy, even if she was both those things.

Jesus, Alaina! Why are you being so pissy to him? You do need a hand up, and you can't get ahead to save your life.

"I'm not trying to placate you," he said, his green eyes shadowed. "But I can tell you don't eat enough. You go without so Everett doesn't have to. All I'm telling you is that you don't have to, either. And not because you're a feel-good project. I pulled you from the water. I saved your life. And yeah, I feel a connection to you now. I feel responsible for your safety, and I want to find out who did that to you. I don't want to see the fear in your eyes when you get asked about that day, and I don't want to watch you go back to that shitty RV and struggle to make ends meet. I like having you and Everett around. I said that before, and I meant it. Let me feed you today, let me feed you both tonight, and when spring comes, you can do whatever you want to my property that makes you feel like it's an even trade. I'm trying to help you. When I need it, you'll help me. That's what friends do, right?"

She blinked back those stupid tears again. "I don't have many friends."

Because she was cautious, and she'd learned there were different levels of friendship. Not everyone who claimed to be a friend would actually put themselves out for you. She had Stacie at the center, and there was Bridget and Lidia too, though they weren't on the same level as Stacie.

"You've got me, you've got Easy and Jenna, and now you've got two more with Mal and Scarlett. Sound good?"

He was looking at her expectantly. She wanted to hold onto her hurt and anger, let it keep her from getting too close and wanting too much, but it whooshed out of her in that moment. Maybe it was a bad idea to let it go, but she was tired of holding onto it. She held too much in her heart, and it was heavy.

"Yes, okay. Sounds good."

His smile was everything. She told herself not to crave it so much, but it was like standing in the sun and feeling its warmth after a long winter.

"Great. Let's go eat a big lunch and have some fun. You ready?"

She nodded, and he turned her and hooked her arm over his before leading her slowly to the diner's glass doors. Before they got there, one burst open and a man walked out. For just a second, Alaina felt herself go cold.

Deputy Patrick Foss strode toward them with a couple of takeout containers in a bag. He didn't smile, but then again he almost never did. Alaina didn't like him. He'd been dating Bridget for a couple of years, apparently, but that hadn't stopped him from flirting with her. He'd go to the center to see Bridget, or on a call, and he'd always find a way to say something suggestive to her. She didn't tell Bridget because that was the last thing she wanted to do, but she kept hoping the other woman would see he was a jerk and break up with him. Hadn't happened yet, though.

"Miss Montgomery," he said as he approached. "It's good to see you out of the hospital. How are you doing?"

"Fine," she chirped, unwilling to admit she was still in pain. "Getting better every day."

His gaze slid to Ryder and he nodded. Ryder nodded back. She could feel the slight stiffening of Ryder's body, as if he was preparing for a fight. He didn't say anything, though, and she appreciated that. The sooner Foss went on his way, the better.

"That's good to hear," Foss said. "I better get this food over to the office. Y'all have a nice day."

He started to walk away. Anger flared inside and she called out, "Have you made any progress in finding the person who attacked me?"

He stopped and faced them again, his pale blue

eyes flickering with irritation. "We're investigating every angle. It takes time. I can't comment on our progress when it's still ongoing, but I assure you we're doing everything we can to find whoever did that to you."

His gaze slid to Ryder again and lingered as if he was suggesting something.

Alaina thought she heard a low growl in Ryder's throat. She swallowed, gripping his arm a little tighter. He looked down at her as if to reassure her. There was anger in his gaze, but it wasn't directed at her.

"Be careful out there, Miss Montgomery," Deputy Foss said. "You never know who means you harm. Have a nice day."

Chapter Seven

RY WAITED UNTIL AFTER LUNCH WAS OVER AND THEY'D said their goodbyes to everyone before he asked Alaina the question that'd been on his mind. She blinked at him as they sat in his truck. He'd started it but hadn't shifted into gear.

"No, I don't like him," she finally said. "He's been seeing one of the psychologists at the center for the past couple of years. She thinks he's going to marry her, but he's a jerk. She'd be better off without him."

Ry didn't like the man either, but that had everything to do with the way Foss had bristled the moment he walked into Alaina's hospital room and saw Ry there. He'd as much as implied that Ry was a threat to Alaina when they'd bumped into him earlier, and that had nearly made Ry throat-punch the asshole.

"You must have a reason," Ry prodded.

Her jaw worked. Then she turned to fix him with

her green gaze. "He hits on me at work. He comes to see Bridget, and when her back is turned because she's busy, he says suggestive things to me. I don't like him because of that."

Ry didn't like the sound of that at all. It was slimy as fuck. "Suggestive how?"

She threw her hands out. "How do you think? He wants to rock my world, take me to the stars, show me a good time, loosen me up. He thinks we could have fun together, and maybe I'm the one for him instead of Bridget." Her nostrils flared. "It's all bull-shit. Even if I said yes, he wouldn't stop seeing Bridget for me because I have a kid and that's not something he wants to deal with. He just wants to fuck me."

Ry shouldn't be surprised at the way his gut clenched at the word *fuck* coming from her mouth, but he was. She didn't seem to notice. He was glad. Now was not the time to get mildly turned on because a woman said *fuck*.

"He's one of those guys that'll get married to the good girl and then be a serial cheater," she finished. "I don't like men who can't honor their commitments. I told him the last time to leave me alone or I'd report him to his superiors, but he only laughed."

Ry wanted to go to Foss and tell him if he even looked at Alaina again, Ry would make his life hell. Wanted to, but couldn't. The specter of General Mendez and Ghost making *his* life hell for it was very real. Still, if the man made her uneasy again, Ryder *would* deal with it.

And there was another thing to consider. If Foss had been making moves on Alaina and she wasn't playing, maybe he'd snapped. Maybe he was the one who'd beat the shit out of her and dumped her body. It would explain why there'd been no evidence. If he was investigating himself, he could make it disappear.

If Ry found that out for sure, to hell with Ghost and Mendez coming down on his ass. He'd hurt the motherfucker so bad Foss would be drinking dinner out of a straw for the next year, minimum. *If* he survived.

"I'm sorry, Alaina," Ry said carefully, unwilling to share the direction of his thoughts with her. "It's obvious you're uncomfortable when Foss shows up. I wanted to know why."

"Now you know. I want to tell Bridget, but I don't see any good coming of that. We're friends, but not super close. If I tell her the boyfriend she thinks is Mr. Wonderful is hitting on me when she's not looking, she might think I'm making it up. She *will* think I'm making it up because he'll deny it and she'll believe him. He's a law enforcement officer, and he's lived in Mystic Cove his whole life, same as her. I'm the outsider, the one who's jealous or attention-seeking or whatever." She shook her head. "I've tried to think of how I could tell her, but I can't. All I can do is hope he shows his true colors before it goes on much longer.

He won't stop hitting on other women, so it'll come out eventually."

Ry tapped his fingers on the steering wheel, his brain churning. He couldn't do anything about Foss yet, but he could damned sure keep Alaina away from him.

"When you go back to work, I want you to let me know if he does it again. Not because I'm going to charge over there and beat him up, though believe me I'm tempted. But you need to tell someone. I'm new in town, too, but I've got friends and I'm in the military. That holds weight with people. They may not listen to you, but they'll listen to me. Sucks but it's the truth."

She'd dropped her chin to study her lap. Her hands were so small, her wrist bones prominent. She'd eaten well at lunch though. Meatloaf, mashed potatoes, green beans, and banana pudding. He'd been glad to see it. She hadn't argued about him buying, hadn't tried to order a slice of toast and a glass of water. She'd eaten. Made his heart feel good.

When she sighed and lifted her head, her eyes were shiny. "I feel like I should say that I can take care of myself. That it's nothing you need to get involved in. But honestly, I'm grateful. I have a hard time accepting help for a variety of reasons, but I'm going to take your help with this because I don't know what else to do. So long as you promise you aren't going to go all caveman and get into a fight."

He held up his right hand and separated his fingers in the Spock salute. "On my honor, I will never throw the first punch at Deputy Sleazebag. If he comes for me though, I can't promise not to fight back."

And that was the truth.

She studied him then held up her right hand in the Spock salute, mirroring his. So she *was* a Trekkie. Damn, that made him happy.

"It is agreed. Live long and prosper," she intoned.

He laughed. "Live long and prosper."

She grinned and they dropped the salute. He liked to see her smile. Alaina was pretty in that wholesome girl-next-door-who-you'd-never-noticed-before kind of way. Once you did, you couldn't unsee her.

She reached for her seatbelt and buckled it as he put the truck in gear. "Just so you know, I don't think for a second that you're the one who attacked me. I mean, I did when I first woke up because I didn't know what was going on, but when you were at the hospital, when you stayed by my side and made sure Everett was taken care of? I knew it wasn't you. Foss wants me to think it could be because he doesn't like you, but I know better."

He'd kind of hoped she hadn't realized what Foss was insinuating about him, but he should have known she would. Made him dislike Foss that much more.

"Thanks. I appreciate that." He sighed, and then he told her the truth. "My job involves violence,

Alaina. I won't lie about that. But it's always to help people or to prevent mass violence against civilians."

"Have you ever been violent with a woman?"

He didn't like the sudden tension in her voice, but he wouldn't lie about that either.

"There are nuances to that question. Have I ever been violent with a woman I was dating, or even a random woman who pissed me off for some reason, like cutting me off in traffic? No. But sometimes enemy combatants are female, and I'll take them down if it means my team gets to live. I can't apologize for that. It's not violence against a woman at that point. It's war."

"You're right," she said softly. "I didn't think about that. I'm not accustomed to the military."

"You'll learn. We have a whole language you haven't encountered yet. Just wait until the acronyms start flying. You'll think you've entered a foreign country and can't understand a thing."

He wanted to make her laugh again, wanted to steer her off the idea of combat and back to safer topics.

"Really? Like what?"

"TDY. CONUS. EER. SITREP. MOS. AAFES. OPSEC. BAH. FOB—I could go on, or is that confusing enough?"

She laughed. "Wow. What did you say?"

"I didn't say anything. I just told you some of the more common acronyms. TDY is temporary duty.

CONUS is the continental United States." He ticked off on his fingers as he kept defining them. "Enlisted evaluation report. Situation report. Military occupational skill. Army and Air Force Exchange Services—that's basically a department store—operational security. Basic allowance for housing. Forward operating base. The military lives and breathes their own language, and it gets even more nuanced between the services. You hang around with us, you'll pick it up in no time."

She was still smiling as she watched him. He wanted to keep looking at her, but he had to drive. Alaina was strong and proud and convinced she had to do it all herself, but he liked when she let him help. When she smiled, like now.

"Thanks for lunch today," she said. "Not just buying it, but convincing me to go. I had fun."

"You're welcome. I'm glad you were there."

Her smile widened. She bit her lip and looked away, and he wondered what she was telling herself. He didn't ask because he knew she wouldn't share. He'd already pushed her enough for now.

One day, she'd tell him her secrets before she told anyone else. He didn't know why he thought that, but he did. Was as certain of it as he was of his own name. He'd made the mistake of implying she was a project, but she was more than that.

He wanted to make her safe, and then he wanted to unravel the knots around Alaina Montgomery's heart and set her free. And maybe, just maybe, he'd fill the empty spaces in his own if he did.

————

"WE GET TO STAY?" Everett asked, his little blue eyes wide, his cheeks red from playing outside before dinner.

He'd been running in the yard. At one point, Ryder had gone outside to play catch with him, and the two of them came back inside when Alaina called to tell them dinner was ready. It was a chicken enchilada casserole that Ryder had picked up at the Early Bird Diner today, and all they'd had to do was pop it in the oven and set a timer. Alaina had made a salad, because she could cut up vegetables, and now they were seated at the table in the cottage and Ryder was dishing a helping of the casserole onto Everett's plate.

Alaina nodded as she met Ryder's gaze. His lips quirked and an eyebrow lifted. She told herself not to read any meaning into the look he gave her. There was nothing to it other than a conspirator's look. He was *not* looking at her like he wanted to take her in his arms and kiss her senseless.

"Yes, we are staying right here," Alaina said. "Unless you want to go back to Mr. Herbert's?"

"No!" Everett yelled before Alaina reminded him to use his inside voice. "No," he said a touch quieter.

"I like it here. I like Mr. Ryder's dock, and I like that my bed doesn't move at night."

He was talking about the way the cushions in the RV shifted sometimes. She'd done everything she could to secure them, but Everett was a wild little sleeper and he often kicked at least one free.

"Then it's settled, bud," Ryder said. "You and your mom will stay here, and you can visit me anytime."

"Can I come watch your TV every night?"

"Everett, Mr. Ryder has his own shows to watch. Our TV will get hooked up soon as I can go get it."

"Okay," Everett said with that little kid hangdog look that said he'd just been denied the greatest adventure of his life. "Our TV's so little, though. And we don't got Disney+."

"Don't *have* Disney+," Alaina said.

"Don't have Disney+," Everett repeated.

"You can watch my TV, buddy," Ryder said, reaching for Alaina's plate. "But not every night, okay? You let your mom know when you want to come watch, and she can ask me if I'm available. Sound good?"

Alaina had cringed at first when Ryder started to speak, but now she was grateful. He hadn't told her kid it was okay to come over whenever he wanted like she'd thought he was about to do. Ryder had put the ball firmly in her court, and he'd let Everett know he wouldn't always be available for television nights.

"Yes, sir," Everett said as he dug his fork into the food and took a bite. One thing she'd never had to worry about was Everett's palate. He probably wouldn't eat sushi, and he definitely didn't like carrots, but he wasn't super picky about most food. Thank God since she wasn't a cook and couldn't afford fancy stuff.

"Tell me when, Alaina," Ryder said as he lifted a scoop onto her plate.

"A little more, please." He smiled at her as he complied. She accepted the plate from him and took a bite. The casserole was cheesy and good, and though she didn't usually eat so much in one day, it wasn't because she was picky or anything. She either didn't have the time, or she couldn't stomach one more hot dog for dinner.

Alaina liked food. She'd just never really learned how to cook it. Her mother had died when she was eight, and her aunt viewed her as more of a burden than anything. She and her husband were childless and they hadn't appreciated gaining an eight-year-old to take care of. Her aunt was a typical Southern cook, fixing everything by feel and taste and years of prac-tice, but she hadn't shared any of that with Alaina.

"Taste all right?" Ryder asked.

Alaina started as she realized she'd been drifting. "Yes, delicious. Sorry, I was thinking about something. Nothing important."

"Mama, do you know that starfish don't pee?"

"Really? What do they do?"

"Ammonia is removed through tubes on their feet."

"Wow, how cool is that? Did you learn that in science class today?"

He nodded. "We're learning about the ocean. It's fun."

"Sounds very fun. First grade is so interesting. Do you have reading homework to do after dinner?"

"Yes, ma'am. We're reading a book about a bear and I'm supposed to read a page to you so you know if I'm doing it right."

"Then we'll do that."

"Can you stay and listen too, Mr. Ryder?"

Ryder seemed a little shocked, but he recovered quickly. "Sure, bud. If it's okay with your mom, I can stay."

She couldn't tell if he wanted to or not. "It's okay with me. But if you have other things you need to do, we understand, don't we, Everett?"

"Yes, ma'am," her son said dutifully.

"I can stay for a bit."

"Awesome sauce!"

Alaina smothered a grin at the way her kid said those two words. They were probably not cool anymore, but they had been when she was a kid. Or so she'd thought. Ryder gave her a look across the table that she didn't quite understand, but it made her heart thump. It was a sexy, intense look. Or maybe he was trying to tell her thanks for giving him an out. Could go either way, she supposed.

Everett continued to chatter about school, informing them about his best friend Nate and how excited they were for their upcoming class field trip to the Smithsonian Air and Space Museum.

After dinner, Everett and Ryder took care of the dishes and put the leftover casserole in the refrigerator. Then Ryder sat on the couch beside her and Everett got his book. He read well, only stumbling over a couple of words, and when he was done he hugged them both and said thank you for listening.

"Can we go watch TV now?" he asked, his little face hopeful.

Ryder gave her a subtle nod that said it was okay. Warmth flowed through her like sunshine. "Only for an hour," she said. "Then it's time for a bath and bed."

"Yay!" Everett bounded toward the door, and Ryder held out a hand to help her up.

Her skin zapped where he touched her, the sensation traveling up her arm and ending as a small shiver down her spine. "You don't have to let him watch your television, Ryder. It's okay to say no."

Everett was already out the door and skipping toward Ryder's house.

"I know," he said. "But I like him. He's a good kid, Alaina. He's polite and respectful, and he listens to you."

Pride threatened to swell her head to ridiculous proportions. It hadn't always been easy, but she was determined to raise Everett to be the kind of person who was honest and good.

"Thank you for spending time with him. He likes you a lot."

It worried her a little, but Everett was going to get attached to people. Sometimes, those people wouldn't stay.

"I'm glad." He hesitated. "I haven't spent much time around kids his age, but I want you to know I'm aware I have to be careful what I say. I don't mean swearing, though there's that too, but promises. That kind of thing. I wasn't thinking when I told him we could go fishing. And I do want to teach him to fish, but I know I have to be careful not to get his hopes up, especially about things I haven't cleared with you."

There was a lump in her throat. A giant, emotional lump. He cared about not disappointing her kid. That meant a lot.

"I appreciate that. He hasn't had a man in his life, well, ever, really. He might look up to you a lot, and I'm grateful you know to be careful, especially since we're going to be neighbors. I want him to feel comfortable with you, but I don't want him thinking you're going to be a dad to him. He knows he doesn't have one, and he knows other kids do."

She faltered, but he didn't look angry or annoyed. He nodded, his eyes intense.

"I know, Alaina. I understand. I had absentee parents. I had grandparents, but I know what it's like to want a mom and a dad present. To crave that attention. I swear to you I'm aware how cautious I need to be with him."

"Thank you," she said, her throat tight.

He grinned. "You know, when we get your TV hooked up, I'll give you my login. That way he can watch anytime and you don't have to always come to my house."

"That's very sweet of you, and I may take you up on it, but I kind of like that it's not so accessible for him. I'll think about it."

"Good. I think there are parental controls available if you want to try that. No pressure. Go on in, Everett," Ryder called out when her son stopped at the back door and turned to look at them. "It's open, and you know how to operate the remote."

Alaina stopped on the path and faced Ryder. He was so much taller than she was. Broad and muscled. She imagined he was pretty scary when he was suited up in his military gear with his weapons and body armor. He didn't scare her, though.

"I know you said I don't have to pay you back," she began. "And I'm working really hard on not looking at this like I owe you, but everything you've done for us—" Her throat tightened again. "I'd be dead if you hadn't found me. Everett would be lost in the system. I just want you to know, when I say I can never repay you, it's about more than renting me a house or letting my son watch your TV or buying us dinner."

He smiled softly. When his hand came up and brushed a strand of her hair off her cheek, she didn't pull away. His fingers were gentle as he skimmed them over her skin. He didn't linger, though she found herself wishing he would.

"I know, Alaina. If it makes you happy to keep thanking me, you can. But you don't have to. It's my job to do the hard things, to go where none dare. I walk into burning buildings, jump out of perfectly good airplanes, and face down enemy fire to do what I do. Saving you was something I'm wired to do. But the part where I invite you to live in my rental cottage and spend time with me while your son watches television? That's all you. Because I want to be near you." He ran his fingers over her cheek again, down her throat, skimming her throbbing pulse as a grin formed on his perfect face. "You feel that charge when I touch you?"

She nodded, because she couldn't speak.

"I feel it too. I crave it, if I'm honest." He dropped his hand and took a step back. "But it's too soon to explore it further. One day, though, I intend to kiss you. We'll see what kind of spark flares then. You game?"

Was she game? Her panties were currently on fire. Need flooded her system, threatening to make her incoherent. Or worse, to say something stupid. But it'd been so damned long. Years. Not since she was eighteen and flush with hormonal urges that she'd gratified in the backseat of Clint's Ford F-150.

"Yes," she managed to squeak out before he thought she'd lost the ability to speak. Which she damn near had.

"That's good news, Alaina." He held out a hand. "Let's go watch some kid stuff with Everett."

She put her hand in his and let him lead her inside.

Chapter Eight

IT TOOK SIXTEEN DAYS OF REST AND HEALING BEFORE Alaina managed to go back to work. She was still a bit slow, a bit achy, but she was starting to suffer from cabin fever and she desperately *wanted* to work. The doctor said it was fine so long as she didn't overdo it.

The first day she drove herself to the center, she was filled with apprehension. Ryder had offered to take her and pick her up, but she'd refused. She had to get back into the habit of doing things for herself. Of taking care of herself and her son, because Ryder had a life and a job and wouldn't always be there to watch over her.

Deputy Turner had come over a few days ago to inform her about the state of the investigation. They had no leads, no suspects. It terrified her and made her angry at the same time. How could someone attack her, put her in a vehicle, and dump her into the lake—and *no one* saw anything?

He'd been apologetic. He'd said they were still checking into it, but she might have to accept they wouldn't ever find the culprit. Especially if it'd been a random attack motivated by a desire for drug money.

She'd trembled with anger and fear when he'd said that. Ryder had looked furious, standing nearby with legs spread, his impressive—and tattooed—forearms folded over his chest, and a scowl on his face. He'd made her feel safe with his presence. Like she could face anything. Like he was in her corner and always would be. Maybe he would. She hoped so, though it was far too early to think about such things.

It had only been nine days since she'd moved from Ryder's house to the cottage with Everett, but she was physically a world better than she had been when Ryder had first taken her back to his place. She was fully mobile again, and she could look after her boy.

Everett loved their new home. He was happy with the yard and the lake, though she'd threatened him under pain of death to *never* get in the water without permission or when no one was around. He was also not to go onto the dock without telling her. Maybe she was being a little paranoid, but what if he fell in and nobody knew?

He took it all in stride. He played happily in the yard after school if it wasn't too cold, then went to Ryder's to watch TV on some nights after Alaina made sure it was acceptable. She went too, and she and Ryder talked while Everett watched a kid show. Sometimes she watched with him when he asked her to, but most of the time she and Ryder chatted.

She learned more about his teammates. She'd only met Noah and Mal so far, but Ryder promised she'd meet the rest of them when they got together for one of their potluck cookouts. She thought it was wonderful they liked each other well enough to hang out when they weren't working. Ryder said it was more than that and they were a family. They relied on each other too much not to be. Their lives were at stake, and they had complete trust in each other.

Alaina liked the women she worked with at the center, but they weren't a family. Not really. She was closest to Stacie, probably because they had kids the same age. None of them got together outside work, though. Stacie had three kids, Bridget was wrapped up in her relationship with Deputy Foss, and Lidia was a newlywed. There were others, but Alaina was closest to those three.

They were waiting for her when she walked inside the center.

"Oh my God," Bridget said, rushing over to hug her.

Alaina hugged her back, wincing just a little at the strength of Bridget's squeeze. Bridget was nearly six-foot tall and willowy, but she went to the gym regularly and didn't seem to know how strong her hugs were. "It's okay, Bridge. I'm okay."

Bridget pushed her back to arm's length and looked her up and down while Stacie and Lidia stood nearby, also studying her. A few of the other women came out to welcome her back as well. It was nice, and she felt as if she'd been missed. But it wasn't a family.

"I came by to see you, but you weren't home," Bridget said. "Then Stacie told me you were staying with the guy who pulled you from the water."

Alaina felt herself coloring just a little. "I'm sorry I didn't text everyone sooner. I wasn't thinking straight."

"Of course you weren't, honey," Lidia said. "You nearly drowned! Nobody here blames you for not giving us the minute details about what was happening or where you were staying. You had more important stuff to worry about."

"Who is the guy?" Bridget asked. "Stacie said he just moved to town, but he has friends here. Jenna, who used to work at the diner, and her husband."

Alaina nodded. "Yes. His name is Ryder and he's in the military, like Jenna's husband. They work on the same team."

"Like a Navy SEAL or something?" Bridget said.

"Something like that. I've met a couple of them, but there are more. Anyway, Ryder just bought property on Mystic Lake, and he has a small cottage he offered to rent me. So I took it."

"I'm so glad you left old man Herbert's," Stacie said. "That trailer of his is on its last legs."

"And then there's Keith," Lidia said with an eye roll. "Always lurking."

"Keith never bothered me," Alaina replied. Mr. Herbert's grandson was there a lot, and he seemed like he might be interested in her the way he hung around and asked if he could help with things, but he'd never crossed a line. He also seemed to really love his grandfather. They did things together all the time. Hunting trips, fishing, hanging out. Keith cooked on the grill in the evenings, and Mr. Herbert was happy for the company.

"He's harmless," Bridget said. "Not real social, but he was always that way in school. Didn't talk much to anybody."

"I know," Lidia said. "He's just always been kinda creepy to me. Always hanging around, never saying much. Plus he's got those intense eyes."

Alaina knew what she meant. Keith had a dark stare that was a little unnerving at times. It was almost like he didn't know he shouldn't stare at people, but then he'd look away and you'd wonder if you were making too much of it.

"He's not weird," Stacie said. "He's just shy, and that makes him awkward."

"Anyway," Bridget said, raising her voice and

emphasizing *any*, "we are so happy you're back. It hasn't been the same around here without you."

"I've missed being here. I wanted to come back sooner, but the doctor said I needed to rest. I'm ready now, though."

"We did the best we could without you," Lidia said apologetically. "I hope we didn't leave too big a mess."

Alaina shrugged out of her coat and went to hang it on a hook. "I'm sure y'all did a good job. And I really want to get back to volunteering, too. Just let me know when you need me to take a shift."

The three women exchanged a look that had Alaina's stomach bottoming out. Bridget was the one who spoke.

"Honey, we think you need to take a bit more time with that. You know it's not easy being in the room with someone and trying to help them get through a tough event. We just all think, since you've been through something of your own recently, that you need to heal a bit more before we ask you to sit in a hospital room or at the police station with someone who's been assaulted. You have your own things to work through, and it's not fair to you or the person who needs you to be present for them in that moment."

Alaina's throat was tight. She wanted to be on call, wanted to be there when she was needed. But Bridget was right. There was every chance it would call up bad feelings for her, and she might choke. That wasn't going to help anyone, especially someone who needed support for a traumatic event.

"Okay," she forced out. "If you think it's best."

Bridget put an arm around her. "We do, Alaina. Give it time. You'll be back to volunteering before you know it, and we'll be happy to have you. And if you need to talk about anything, I'm here for you. Or I can refer you to another therapist if you like."

"I'm fine," Alaina said with a sniff, trying not to let her disappointment show. "I don't remember much, so I'm fine."

Bridget hugged her a little harder. "If you do, don't keep it inside, okay? Talk to me."

Alaina nodded. "I know. I will."

"Good."

"I better get my cleaning supplies," she said brightly.

"Don't overdo it," Stacie admonished, giving her a quick hug.

"I won't. Not with all you mother hens to stop me."

"Damn right," Lidia said, also giving her another quick hug.

The women went back to work, and Alaina busied herself with getting her cleaning cart together, trying not to let disappointment get her down. It was the right decision not to be on call. She knew it, but it still hurt. She'd worked hard to complete the crisis training that allowed her to volunteer, and now she wasn't able to do it. Every time she felt like she took a step forward, she ended up sliding backward farther than she'd come.

Patience. She needed patience because it wasn't forever. This was a small setback. It wasn't permanent. Get strong again, get her head on straight, and go back to doing what made her feel useful to others. She knew they were concerned for her, and maybe if she knew precisely what had happened to her she'd be in worse mental shape, but whoever had attacked her had done it swiftly. She hadn't seen a face. At least she was pretty sure she hadn't. She didn't even remember reaching her trailer that morning, much less how she got into the water.

But considering the closest access to the lake was a good five miles from Mr. Herbert's, someone had put her in a car and taken her there. And nobody had seen a thing.

It was *frightening.* She woke up in a cold sweat sometimes, her heart pounding like crazy. She didn't like having her back to a door, and she didn't want to be alone for more than a few minutes.

When Everett had been in school and she'd been in the cottage alone, she was fine so long as she knew Ryder was close by. He was good about checking on her during the day, but his leave was ending and he was going back to work soon.

It worried her to be alone, but she would have to learn to deal with her fear. What choice did she have?

None. Alaina Montgomery was a survivor. That's what life had done to her. She didn't expect it to change now.

———

ALAINA CLEANED ALL MORNING, emptying trash cans, scrubbing toilets, sweeping and mopping and polishing, then stopped for lunch with the ladies. They ordered food from the Early Bird. Alaina hadn't planned on ordering anything, but Bridget insisted it was on her so Alaina got a small turkey sandwich and fries.

The women gathered in the conference room, chatting about everything that'd been going on lately. Nobody asked questions about the attack. She hadn't expected they would.

This wasn't the kind of place where curiosity got the best of people. These women were accustomed to counseling other women in all kinds of situations. One thing you didn't do was push someone to talk about things they didn't want to talk about. Maybe a therapist might, not that Alaina knew for sure, but that wasn't the job of the crisis counselor. Their job was to help someone navigate the aftermath of an assault.

These women would be watching Alaina to see if

she needed any support, but they wouldn't push. Bridget might, but only if Alaina gave her an opening.

And she wouldn't.

She would be just fine. She had Ryder in her corner. He'd been there for her when she woke up in the hospital, and he'd remained since, taking her into his home, helping her take care of her child, surrounding her with his friends. Not what she'd expected, but she couldn't imagine it any other way. He was her rock, at least for now.

She liked him. Maybe more than she should, but it was too late to stop. He'd said he was going to kiss her one day soon, but that was days ago and he hadn't so much as given her a peck on the cheek. Probably for the best since she couldn't afford the distraction in her life. She'd told him Everett was her priority. Maybe he was respecting that, or maybe he'd decided he didn't need to get involved with a single mother after all.

Everett was a good kid, but he was also a handful at times, and Ryder had admitted he didn't know much about children. She hadn't either until she'd been thrown into raising one. Wasn't easy, that's for sure, even when the kid was a good one like her son.

Once lunch was done, Alaina went back to cleaning. She usually cleaned in the mornings, then moved on to her private clients, but today was the first day back and there were extra things to do. Supplies to be inventoried and ordered, extra scrubbing, laundry.

She threw a load of towels into the dryer, then went into the supply closet to count rolls of paper towels and toilet paper and bottles of water. She'd been there for about five minutes when she heard a male voice. Her heart thudded as she stopped and listened.

"Baby, you know I didn't mean anything when I flirted with Stacie," Deputy Foss said. "I love *you*."

"I know you do," Bridget said. "I love you, too. But I don't like it when you flirt with other women. You're mine."

Alaina's stomach twisted. He *did* mean it when he flirted. That was the disgusting part. And Bridget couldn't see it.

"Aw, I'm just being nice, honey," Foss said. "Helps people feel safe and comfortable talking to me. You don't want the women in here not to talk to me, right? I'm here to help. If I make Stacie comfortable, then imagine how some poor girl who's just been raped will feel when she has to talk to me about the assault."

"I know," Bridget said, groaning. "I just get jealous. I'm sorry."

"You know you're my girl," Foss said. There the wet sound of kissing, and then a moan from Bridget. Alaina shuddered at the thought of Patrick Foss touching her the way he was very likely touching Bridget. Foss wasn't a bad looking man, but he was too pervy and he didn't respect boundaries. Bridget didn't see it that way, of course. To each her own.

"I have to get back to my office," Bridget said. "I have a call with the regional director in a couple of minutes."

"Okay. I'll see you tonight, honey. And then I'm gonna rock your world hardcore."

"Counting on it, baby," Bridget said. There was another noisy kiss, and then Bridget's heels clipped down the hall.

Alaina waited a few more moments before she dared to peek her head out of the closet. Foss was standing there, leaning against the wall, arms crossed over his chest. His eyes lasered into her, and Alaina swallowed.

"H-hi, Deputy Foss. I didn't know you were there."

"But I knew you were behind that door," he said. "Were you enjoying what you heard? Did it make you hot?"

He was a barrel-chested man, heavily muscled, and his brown uniform shirt stretched tight over his chest. His name plate was gold, and he had a sheriff's star pinned beneath it. His hat was on, and he looked menacing and unpleasant to her. Probably because she was comparing him to Ryder.

"Uh, I didn't hear anything. My first day back," Alaina said brightly. "I'm feeling much better."

"Are you now?" Foss pushed away from the wall

and closed the distance between them. Alaina wanted to shrink away, but she stood her ground. She thought of Ryder telling her to let him know if Foss harassed her, imagined Ryder knocking Foss's lights out, and it made her feel better. Even if she didn't want him actually getting into a fight with Foss, the mental picture of Foss on his ass was a good one.

"Yes, thank you. If you will excuse me, I have to get back to work. It's been piling up while I was away." She started to shoulder past him, but he wrapped fingers around her upper arm, stopping her. A shiver rolled down her spine, dread pooling in her stomach.

"You need to be careful, Alaina," he said, his fingers biting into her. "You don't know that military guy at all. He's being nice to you, but he only wants you to spread your legs for him. He doesn't care about you."

Alaina glared back. "And you do?"

"I could." He trailed his fingers down her arm. "I could care a lot if you let me."

He was disgusting. Her skin crawled where he touched her.

"You belong to Bridget, Deputy Foss. I just heard you tell her that you love her, and I know she loves you, though God knows why. I'm not the kind of girl who hurts my friends by sleeping with their boyfriends."

His expression turned mean a split second before

he was in her face. "You know what I think, Alaina? I think you better watch yourself with that soldier. He's violent and unpredictable, and you might not survive the next time."

Her heart hammered. "Ryder didn't beat me up and put me in the water. Someone else did. You need to be finding out *who*, not accusing him without any evidence."

He straightened, looking angry. "And you need to leave the investigations to the professionals, you dumb bitch."

He turned and strode away, his boots echoing on the tile. Alaina's pulse throbbed, and she leaned against the wall to catch her breath. She'd made Foss angry, and that wasn't a good thing since he was a cop. She thought about calling Ryder, but what could he do? Go find Foss and punch him? Where would that leave him if he did? He might be a badass soldier, but Foss had a badge and a jail he could put Ryder in for a few nights.

She definitely didn't want that. Alaina sucked in a few calming breaths and grabbed her cart so she could finish cleaning and go home where she felt safe. She thought about marching into Bridget's office and telling her what'd just happened.

She wouldn't do it, though. She'd been at the center for a little less than six months. Bridget had lived in Mystic Cove her whole life, and so had Deputy Foss. Alaina was the outsider here. If she got between them, if she caused trouble, she'd be the one to suffer for it.

Best to keep her mouth shut and do her job. Before she lost it and had to move away to find another.

Chapter Nine

R<small>Y WAS IN THE KITCHEN WHEN</small> A<small>LAINA PULLED INTO</small> the driveway around three. Today was the first day he hadn't been there when she'd picked Everett up from school, and it felt strange. He'd gotten used to taking her to the school, waiting in the pickup line, then listening to Everett's chatter all the way home again. But today was Alaina's first day back at the center, and she'd insisted she could get Everett on the way home from work. He hadn't wanted her to tire herself out, but he also knew she needed to get back to normal in her life.

That was a good thing because he was headed into work next Monday. After nearly three weeks off, the whole team was. He didn't know when they'd be sent on a mission again, but it was inevitable. Alaina needed to be comfortable taking care of herself and her boy again, so he hadn't pushed her to let him get Everett for her.

Everett emerged first, running toward the front door of the cottage. Alaina stepped out of the car, looking a little tired. She moved slowly, and Ry had an urge to go help her carry in the grocery bags she pulled from the back seat. He was about to go outside when Everett returned without his backpack and took a couple of the plastic bags from her hands.

Ry watched Alaina walk a little stiffly from her car to the open door. She was healing, but she'd probably overdone it today. She would have wanted to do a good job, show everyone she was fine. She would never admit she wasn't, either.

She'd started to fill out with regular meals, but she was still thin. Her hair was shiny and healthy, hanging to just below her shoulders, the red streaks picking up the sunlight. He'd asked her about those. She'd told him her friend Stacie had gone to cosmetology school, though she'd had to drop out when she couldn't afford to continue. She sometimes practiced what she'd learned on her friends if they let her, just to keep her skills up.

If anyone could help Alaina through any emotions surrounding what'd happened to her, it would be her friends in the crisis center. He hoped she'd talk to them about it.

Because she hadn't with him. She said she didn't remember, and he believed her, but he also knew trauma had a way of working itself free when you least expected it. He'd watched his parents become distant over his sister's death, and he'd experienced night terrors and panic attacks for years because of it.

He didn't anymore, but he couldn't deny that finding Alaina unresponsive in the water had awakened feelings of helplessness and despair that he'd thought were long gone. Maybe that was why he felt so responsible for her. Didn't explain his attraction to her, though. That was an entirely different set of feelings he was attempting to deal with. But Alaina was still vulnerable, and he was very aware that acting on his attraction could feel like an obligation to her.

He didn't want that. If she was into him, then fine. But how was he going to know? That was why he hadn't kissed her yet. He'd told her he planned to, and she'd said it was okay. Then he'd got to thinking that maybe she'd said that because of everything he'd done for her. Which was why he hadn't pursued it.

Alaina disappeared into the cottage and shut the door, and Ry went back to priming the cabinets so he could paint them. Fifteen minutes later, his phone buzzed with a text. It was Alaina.

What are you doing for dinner?

Ry wiped his hands on a towel and picked up the phone. *Don't know. You?*

Alaina: Everett wants you to come over for dinner if you have time. I should warn you it's nothing fancy. In fact, we're having hot dogs with mac and cheese. From a box. You can say no if you want.

He thought about saying no. Maybe it was best since he would only wind up wanting to kiss her again and arguing with himself about whether or not she felt obligated to let him.

But he wanted to go. He wanted to know how her day at work had been. Hell, he just wanted to see her, even if he didn't act on his attraction to her.

Sounds good to me, he typed. *Can I bring anything?*

Alaina: Nope, just yourself. Also, do you think you could find time this weekend to help me get my things from the RV? I'd do it, but I think I'd like someone with me.

He knew that asking was a big deal for her. *Sure. When do you want to go?*

Alaina: Saturday around noon? Everett's going to Chuck E. Cheese with Stacie's kids, so he'll be with them for a good four hours or better.

Ry: Can do. What time you want me there tonight?

Alaina: Five? Everett has homework first.

Ry: See you then.

He put the phone down and went back to the cabinets because they weren't going to magically paint themselves. By the time he finished coating the cabinets with primer and taking a quick shower, it was a couple minutes to five. He snagged his phone off the counter, tucked it into the back pocket of his jeans, then headed out the door and over to Alaina's place.

He liked the light flickering behind the windows,

liked the sound of chatter coming from inside. For a man who'd moved to the country for solitude, he was doing a damn fine job of surrounding himself with people. He liked it, though. He wasn't a hermit. Far from it. He'd just wanted the peace and quiet of the water and his own property where he didn't have to listen to traffic whizzing by or deal with people knocking on his door selling everything imaginable. If they weren't selling shit, they were trying to get him to go to their church. He didn't want any of it.

Ry knocked on the door. A second later it flew open and Everett stood there, his cheeks red, his eyes bright. "Mr. Ryder! Yay!" He turned his head and shouted, though Alaina was right there in the kitchen. "Mommy, Mr. Ryder is here!"

"I know, honey," Alaina said, stirring something on the stove. "Ask him to come in and get him something to drink."

Everett whipped around again, this time opening the door wide. "Please come in. Would you like water or tea?"

"Thanks, buddy," Ry said as he entered the cottage. "How about water?"

Everett ran to the kitchen to get a bottle of water from the fridge. Ry closed the door since Everett had forgotten and went over to the table. There were paper plates and plasticware at each setting along with a folded paper towel for a napkin.

The cottage was looking homey these days. Alaina

had cleaned it, so the subtle smell of lemon hung in the air. Scarlett had come by with Mal to hang curtain rods and curtains, which Ry had paid for despite Alaina's protests he didn't have to. There were pictures on the wall, a vase of flowers on the table, and a throw blanket on the old couch.

There was also a folding screen in one corner that Scarlett had brought over a couple of days ago. Ry could just see the bottom edge of the cot peeking out from behind it. Smart way to give Everett his own space away from his mother.

"How was work?" Ry asked Alaina.

She gave him a soft smile as she turned sideways to stir the pot and look at him. "It was fine. I was glad to see everyone."

"That's good."

"The mac and cheese is almost done. The hot dogs are done, and I heated the buns. We have the usual condiments, plus cheese and onion and chili if you like chili dogs. I should probably warn you the chili is from a can."

"Sounds good to me." Everett bounded over with a bottle of water and set it down in front of Ry. "Thanks, little dude. How was school today?"

"We learned about dinosaurs! And me and Carter and Nate played kickball at recess."

"Carter and Nate and I," Alaina said.

"Carter and Nate and I played kickball at recess," Everett said. "I'm going to Carter's party at Chuck

E. Cheese on Saturday. Do you like Chuck E. Cheese?"

Ry nodded, though Chuck E. Cheese was definitely not high on his list of places to frequent. Arcade games, shouting kids, loud noises, a giant mouse, and pizza all in one spot? No, thanks. Though he envisioned attending kid parties there in the future at some point. His teammates were busy starting families, and there were bound to be parties and invitations when the kids were old enough.

"Did you wash your hands yet?" Alaina asked Everett.

"Not yet."

"Then go in the bathroom and wash up. Dinner is almost ready."

"Yes, ma'am!" Everett yelled before bounding away.

"He seems happy," Ry said.

Alaina turned off the burner and brought the pot to the table, setting it on a potholder. "He is. He's always a happy kid, but I think being somewhere he can actually move around inside, plus having you here tonight, has him pretty excited."

Ry grinned. "He sees me practically every night. Not sure why it's exciting, but I'll take it."

Alaina retrieved hot dogs from the oven where she must have put them to stay warm, and a basket with buns. The condiments and a small bowl of chili were already on the table.

"We're both happy you're here," she said as she sat across from him. "So how was your day?"

He was still processing what she'd said about being happy he was there. She wasn't giving him a chance to say anything about it, though. He followed her lead, filing it away for later.

"I primed the kitchen cabinets. Gonna paint them white because that's what Scarlett said I should do. Though I might paint the bottoms gray or green. She said those were options too."

Alaina nodded. "Good choices. Are you replacing the countertops or anything?"

"Yep, getting quartz countertops and tiling the backsplash myself." He laughed. "Honestly, I can't believe I'm doing it, but Scarlett talks a good game. Plus the renovations on hers and Mal's place are pretty great. I'm convinced that having a nice living space is good for you. Makes you happy to be in it."

"That's true," she said. "Which is why I can't thank you enough for letting us stay here. It's like having a home, and that means a lot to us both."

"You're welcome."

Alaina smiled. He thought she might say something else, but then Everett rushed back to the table and threw himself into the banquette. "I did it! All clean."

"Hold them up and let me see." Alaina inspected. "Good job, sweetie. Ryder, would you like to go first?"

she asked as Everett reached for a bun. He drew his hand back politely.

Ry wanted the kid to get his food first, but he understood that Alaina was teaching him manners. He thanked her and took a bun for himself. She offered him a hot dog and he took that too. He started dressing it as Everett got his own.

Ry ate two chili dogs and a big pile of mac and cheese, and they chatted about everything from Everett's teachers to the weather to Alaina's day at work. When they were done eating, Ry and Everett cleaned off the table while Alaina sat and drank her iced tea. She protested she could clean up, but they didn't let her.

"No, Mommy, you cooked," Everett said very seriously.

"Thank you, honey," Alaina replied, her eyes glowing with love for her boy. It made Ry's heart hitch. Had his parents ever looked at him like that after Sheri died? He'd wanted to scream sometimes that he was still alive, still right there, but he'd never found the courage. Instead, he'd retreated into gaming and eating junk food and being a surly teenager.

He didn't think Everett would ever be surly, but then again it kind of went with the territory of being a teenager.

They ended up over at Ry's place after dinner. He'd baked a cheesecake yesterday, so they ate slices with raspberry sauce while Everett proclaimed it the best cake ever.

"You baked a cheesecake," Alaina said when Everett went into the living room to watch television. "Just because."

Her eyes were a little wide, and Ry laughed. "Yeah, just because. My grandma quizzes me whenever we talk, so I have to keep my skills up."

Alaina grinned. "I think that's sweet."

Ry shrugged. "She spent too much time teaching me, so I can't disappoint her."

Alaina took the plates to the sink and started to wash them.

"You don't have to do that," he said.

"Yes, I do. You cleaned my kitchen because I cooked. Now I'm cleaning yours."

"Fair enough," he said.

She stacked the plates in the drainer and nodded at the cabinets. "I like the idea of darker lowers. But white works too. I don't know how you're going to decide."

"I'll probably ask Scarlett. Unless you want to decide it for me."

She shook her head. "Oh no, no way. I like making my space pretty, but that's for me. I'd be afraid you'd hate what I suggested."

Ry folded his arms and leaned back against the counter. "Just for kicks. Tell me what you'd do if it was your kitchen."

She nibbled her lip. He found himself concentrating on that little action far too much. He forced his eyes upward, meeting hers. The corners crinkled as she thought about her answer.

"Honestly? I'd want white uppers and pale blue lowers with gold hardware. To reflect the water. I'd probably go beachy, except this is a lake and you might want to go more manly with greens and grays and stuff. Though the interior is already white-washed, so beachy would work."

He found himself considering. "Pale blue, huh?"

Alaina put her hands on her cheeks and shook her head. "Oh Lord, don't listen to me. I don't know what I'm talking about. But we have magazines at the center, and some of them are about decorating. I look at them when I'm taking a shift and it's slow. There was a kitchen in one with lots of light coming in. The walls were white, and the cabinets were like I said. There was a farm sink, and a butcher block island. It was very pretty. I remember thinking if I could live somewhere nice, that'd be what I'd want. A bright kitchen where I could bake cookies and make meals for me and Everett. Bear in mind I can't bake or cook things that don't come in a box with directions, so that's out. But it was a nice little fantasy."

"I could teach you to bake."

"You could?"

He nodded, though a part of him was wondering what the fuck was he getting himself into. He just kept getting deeper and deeper with this woman. But he *liked* it. Liked her. And yeah, there was a kid involved and that made it a more serious decision. But he was ready for it.

He wanted kids, though it'd always been a someday thing. Everett was not someday. He was right damn now. But that wasn't nearly as scary as Ry would have thought it'd be. Not that he was going to be the kid's dad if they dated, but he had to be willing to be.

"Yeah," he said. "I can cook a few things, too. I'll teach you what I know."

Her cheeks were pink. "Wow. Thank you. I'd like that."

He was busy studying her, the way her skin glowed, the sparkle in her green eyes. There was something else he should offer to teach her as well. Not as fun, but something she needed to know. He'd been thinking about it, but he hadn't wanted to scare her. Maybe now was time to test the waters.

"Sure thing. I can also teach you some self-defense moves." Her eyes widened, but she didn't shut him down or look scared. "Just in case you ever need it. It's good stuff to know."

She huffed a breath. "You're right. I *do* want to learn self-defense. Maybe if I'd known what to do, I wouldn't have been in the water. And maybe the sheriff's department would have caught the person by now. If I could have incapacitated them, I could have called 911." She lowered her voice so it didn't carry to where Everett sat. "It bothers me he's still out there. If I'm honest, it scares me. I went back to work at the center and I wasn't scared, but when I imagined going out to Mr. Herbert's alone, I started to shake. That's why I asked you to go."

"I don't mind going, Alaina."

She nodded. "I don't want to be anywhere alone, but I have to start cleaning for my private clients again. Some of them aren't home when I go. I let myself in, and I clean. It scares me. I want to get over it. I *need* to get over it."

He hadn't known her before the attack, but it was obvious she'd been independent and determined. Now she was afraid, and that was so wrong to him.

"I'll teach you some things you can use to fight back, and we'll make sure you aren't entirely alone, okay? You'll have someone to call if you need them. When I'm done teaching you self-defense, you won't feel helpless ever again."

The tightness in her body ebbed by degrees. "You are really too good to me. I've been nothing but trouble since you found me. I'm still trouble."

"You aren't trouble," he said swiftly. "And I'm not too good to you. I'm just being me, and I like being around you."

She blinked. And then her gaze dropped away and her cheeks grew pink again. "I like being around you, too."

It hit him then, that overwhelming urge to kiss her he'd felt before. Everett was in the living room, watching television, his back to them. Ry closed the distance between him and Alaina, looping an arm around her waist and tilting her chin up with his fingers. She didn't shrink away from him as he studied her.

"I feel like I should ask," he growled.

"You don't have to ask," she whispered back.

Her eyes were closed before he dropped his mouth onto hers. When he did, she melted against him, a soft moan in her throat.

It was all he could do not to press her against the counter and let her feel how much she affected him. It was too soon, though. He knew it, and he wasn't going to scare her by being too aggressive.

When he broke the kiss—sooner than he wanted because Everett could turn around at any moment— she blinked up at him, her soft green eyes hazy, her lips parted and shiny, her fingers clutching his shirt. He could tell the moment she came back to earth because she straightened, blinking as she took a step back.

"You okay?" he asked.

She nodded. "I'm fine."

"I don't want to push you, Alaina. I don't expect anything from you, so don't get it in your head you owe me, okay? If you don't want to kiss me, then tell me. You aren't obligated."

"I know that," she said, her eyes flashing.

"Good." He liked that she got a little angry about it. Meant she still had a backbone where he was concerned.

He thought she might stomp away, but instead she closed the distance again, this time running her palm along his shirt. Smoothing the fabric. Her touch set him ablaze, but he didn't do anything about it.

"Sorry I wrinkled your shirt."

"I'm not."

"Mommy," Everett called out.

Alaina took a quick step back. "Yes, sweetie?"

"Will you come watch with me?"

He'd turned to look at them both. His gaze was expectant. He didn't look like a kid who'd witnessed them kissing, and Ry relaxed a little.

"Of course, baby. Let me help Mr. Ryder dry these dishes, okay?"

"You don't have to," Ry said. "I'll do it."

"And then will you come watch too?" Everett asked.

"Sure thing, bud. Go on," he said more quietly to Alaina. "I got it."

"Okay." She started to walk away, then turned back and squeezed his hand. "I enjoyed that kiss. Very much."

That's what he wanted to hear. Because he couldn't wait to kiss her again.

Chapter Ten

ON SATURDAY, ALAINA TOOK EVERETT TO STACIE'S house and dropped him off. Stacie met them at the door, smiling. She let Everett in to go find Carter, then turned to Alaina.

"You sure you don't want to go with us? Screaming kids, video games, pizza?"

"I can't," Alaina said with a laugh. "Ryder's going to help me pack up my stuff at the RV and haul it over to his place."

Stacie sighed. "I don't blame you. That is one fine man you've got there."

Alaina's skin prickled with goosebumps. She'd enjoyed the last few days with Ryder teaching her self-defense moves in the evenings and then cooking dinner for her and Everett. She'd tried to learn that, too, but she'd been too tired from learning how to stomp insteps and jab her fingers into vulnerable spots to really pay attention like she should have. Not that he'd minded when her attention wandered. He'd told her, *'One thing at a time, Alaina.'*

He'd also asked her, when she was squeamish about the idea of jamming her keys into someone's eyes, that if it was kill or be killed, could she do it? She'd thought of Everett going into foster care and the rage that'd flared inside gave her the answer she needed. For her child, she could do anything.

"He's not my man. He's just a friend."

"Maybe so, but don't think it can't change. But if you don't want him, I wouldn't say no to a ride on his disco stick." She waggled her eyebrows.

Alaina rolled her eyes and laughed. "Really? Lady Gaga? Is that the best you can do?"

Stacie grinned. "It's all I've got on short notice. And yes, so long as he didn't mind my crazy life, I'd hump him like a dog in heat. My crazy life being that I'm single, supporting three kids, and always dealing with their deadbeat dad who never pays child support on time, if at *all.*"

"I'm sorry, Stacie," Alaina said, skipping over the dog-in-heat comment. "I hate that he's doing that to you."

Stacie let out a dramatic sigh. "It's typical, right? We hear it over and over at the center. At least he was never violent. Just useless."

"Same here." She'd told Stacie about Clint, though not his name or where he lived. They had deadbeat exes in common, though at least Stacie's coughed up child support from time to time. "I better get back so we can go to Mr. Herbert's place."

"I'll drop Everett off later. Don't worry about coming back for him. I'll text you first."

"Thank you so much. Love you," Alaina said, waving.

"Love you too! Have fun. Don't do anything I wouldn't do. In fact, do all the things I *would* do. Ride that man, honey. Then tell me all the details so I can be wildly jealous."

Alaina laughed as she got into the Toyota and put it into gear. She thought about the kiss she'd shared with Ryder as she drove back to his place. She'd told herself not to get involved, not to let anything distract her from her primary calling as Everett's mother. But holy hell, Ryder was hot and sexy and made her feel desired. It was hard to say no to that.

Just because she let him kiss her didn't mean it had to go farther. Though she couldn't deny that a part of her wanted it to. What if she let it? What if they had sex, and it was good, and then they had a lot more of it until he was tired of her or decided he didn't have time for a woman who already had a child?

Alaina's bubble of happiness burst. She wanted Everett to have a home and a family besides just her, and though she couldn't ever guarantee she'd be able to give him the latter, she could certainly give him the former. Ryder had given her the opportunity to provide a nice home for her child, and there was no way she wanted to screw it up.

If she had sex with Ryder and they broke up, where would that leave her and Everett when it came to renting the cottage? No way could she go back to Mr. Herbert's broke down RV, and not because it was old and broke down, but because she couldn't bear to be there by herself ever again.

By the time she got back to Ryder's place, her stomach was churning with all her thoughts of doom and gloom. She hated it. But her life had been too filled with adversity not to consider it. Not to think of it first rather than last. She wasn't someone who had the luxury of believing everything would work itself out if only she stayed upbeat and positive. She'd tried that, and it didn't work.

Ryder strolled outside as she parked her car. She thought about telling him they could go separately so there would be more room for her belongings, but he had a truck and he'd see right through that excuse. Not to mention the price of gas. She couldn't afford a bunch of random trips around town, especially when she hadn't worked for two weeks.

She got out of her car and locked it. She always locked it, and her home too. It amazed her that some of the people in Mystic Cove didn't lock their doors, but she'd heard it over and over since moving to town. Some folks had been there their whole lives, and even with a major city just up the road a bit, they felt isolated enough to live the way they always had.

"You ready to go?" Ryder asked as she walked over to his truck.

"I think so."

He opened the door for her and she got inside. She still wasn't used to anyone opening doors for her, but it was nice.

"I grabbed a few empty boxes and put them in the back," he said. "If we need more, I still have some."

"I'm sure what you have is fine." The heat of embarrassment crawled along her spine and tickled her scalp as he shut the door and went around to the other side. "The RV is small, and we don't have a lot of stuff."

He shrugged as he settled in the driver's seat. "That's fine. I don't either, except now I've had to buy furniture instead of just using whatever the apartment I'm renting comes with."

Alaina didn't know if he was trying to make her feel better on purpose, but it was working. She knew this was the first home he'd ever bought. "You rented furnished apartments?"

"Pretty much. Except for the bed. Always got my own mattress. Never saw the point in buying stuff for an apartment I might not be living in next year, so I always found them furnished or took friends' cast offs."

"There's no need to buy furniture for an RV. It's already furnished."

And the bed was lumpy and smelled like mildew for the first month, until she'd sprayed enough Febreze and aired it out often enough. Everett's bed was the couch that converted to a bed at night by pulling a handle and flattening the seat and back. Those cushions weren't mildewed, but they never seemed to stay in place overnight.

"I thought about buying one and getting some land, but this place came available and I couldn't say no."

And thank God he had. If he hadn't been inside the house at the right moment, she probably wouldn't have survived. "So you won't have to move again?"

"It's possible I'll get sent somewhere else, because that's military life, but I think I'm set for a while with this unit." He glanced at her. "We're kinda special-ized. Takes time to build teams, and you don't tend to break those teams up when they're working well."

"But people leave sometimes, right?"

He didn't look at her. "They do. Not always because they want to."

Her heart thumped. Jenna had told her what Ryder and his teammates did was dangerous. Jenna had been trying to make Alaina feel safe, but instead she'd focused on how something could go wrong and she might never see him again. It wasn't a feeling she liked.

"The team's gathering at Easy and Jenna's tomorrow for dinner, by the way. You and Everett are invited."

"Oh. I don't know. I mean…"

What, Alaina? You mean what?

Her thoughts were a jumble. She wanted to go, and yet she was apprehensive too. His whole team. The men and women she hadn't met yet. Just because Noah, Jenna, Mal, and Scarlett were nice to her didn't mean they would all be.

"Come on, say yes," he cajoled. "I want you to come. If you're thinking you and Everett are after-thoughts, you aren't. The plan just came together this morning, babe. Jenna wants you there."

"Okay. We'll go. Do we need to bring anything?"

"Nope. I got chip and dip duty, so I'm swinging by the store to grab those on the way."

She hadn't been to a cookout at someone's house in years. Not since Everett was a baby and one of her coworkers invited her over. She'd had to leave early because Everett wouldn't stop crying, unfortunately.

They reached Mr. Herbert's property, and Ryder turned down the long drive that led to the house and the RV beyond. There were a lot of trees lining the drive and surrounding land. Alaina had liked that when she'd first viewed the RV. She'd thought it was cozy. Not anymore. There were so many places for someone to hide. Someone *had* hidden out there somewhere, and then they'd attacked her.

Alaina's heart began to hammer. She must have made a noise or something because Ryder stopped the truck on the long driveway and turned to her.

"You okay?"

She sucked in a breath. "I-I'm trying. I don't know why I'm getting upset, but I feel like I can't breathe."

It was panic, pure and simple. She knew that, but it was a lot harder to acknowledge when she was the one experiencing it. She'd held other people's hands through panic attacks, patted them and told them it would be okay. She'd never had one of her own, though. It was a frightening experience.

"Hey." Ryder put the truck in park and reached over, his fingers cool on the back of her neck. "Put your head between your knees and breathe. In and out. Slowly."

She did as he said, working to pull in air and cussing herself for being such a wimp. Though she also knew that panic responses weren't a weakness or being wimpy. She wasn't at fault here, and she needed to give herself grace. She knew what to do, and she focused on doing it. On the man soothing her.

"You got this, honey," he said, his fingers skimming her spine in rhythmic little circles. "In. Out. In. Out."

She kept breathing, squeezing her eyes shut as she drew in breath after breath. Her heart still beat hard, but maybe not quite as hard as before.

"We don't have to do this," he told her. "I can take

you back home and return alone, or we can try another day."

Alaina almost took him up on it. But then she got mad. At herself, and at the person who'd made her so scared. At the world for never letting her get up and stand on her own two feet without knocking her down again.

"No," she grated. "I want to get my things today. Then I never want to come back again."

"Okay. Just let me know when you're ready. There's no hurry. Keep breathing. You're safe with me. I have a gun, and I'm trained in Krav Maga. I can disarm a man with a weapon and have him on the ground begging for mercy before he knows what happened to him. I've faced countless people who've meant me harm and dropped them before they could act. I'll do that for you, Alaina. So long as I'm here, no one—and I mean *no fucking one*—is going to hurt you. I'll take them out before they can touch a hair on your head ever again. I promise."

"Thank you," Alaina whispered, staring at the floorboards, her eyes misty with tears. No one had ever promised to keep her safe before. No one. She was twenty-five fucking years old, and no one had ever made her feel the way Ryder did just now.

She forced herself to sit up again, swiped her cheeks angrily, and sucked back her tears. "I'm fine. Let's go get this over with."

Ryder frowned. "You're allowed to be upset,

Alaina. What happened to you was bad, and even if you can't remember the details, your body knows. It remembers what you can't. The fact you're here now and still want to go to the RV? Badass, babe. Total badass."

Alaina shook her head. "You don't have to say that. I don't feel like a badass at all. But you are, and that helps."

"Trust me, we're both badasses, babe. So let's go get your stuff and put this place behind you."

"Ten-four, ghost rider."

She didn't know why she said that or where it came from, but he laughed.

"See," he said. "Total badass."

———

ALAINA WAS a little shaky as she stared at the dilapidated RV.

Ry waited to see what she'd do, if it was too much for her and she'd need to stay in the truck. He'd understand if it was. She reached for the door handle suddenly, as if she'd made a decision, and opened it.

"Let's go."

"You're the boss."

Ry got out and went around to join her. He could just see Mr. Herbert's house through the trees. When they'd driven past it, there'd been two trucks parked out front. Alaina said that one belonged to Herbert's grandson, Keith. He came over regularly to help with things that needed done, and the two of them often went hunting or fishing. They'd been on a trip the day she'd been attacked. That was probably what had allowed someone to make it back here with a car unseen.

Keith had lived in the RV for a while, but he'd moved out and gotten his own place when he went to work at a home improvement warehouse store about fifteen miles away. That's why it'd been available for Alaina to rent. Someone in the crisis center knew about it and told Alaina, and she'd jumped on it because it was cheap.

And no wonder. It'd be a miracle if it survived another year. One good summer storm with high winds would crumple the old trailer like a sheet of paper. He was pissed anyone had thought to charge her money for it. He'd felt guilty enough offering up an out of date cottage at the same price when she'd insisted on paying, but his place was a fucking palace in comparison.

Alaina led the way up the wooden stairs to the front door. She hesitated, then inserted the key in the lock and pulled the door open. Before she could step inside, he put an arm out to stop her.

"I'll go first. Check it out."

He thought she might argue, but she dragged in a deep breath and nodded. "Thank you."

He stepped inside the small space. She stopped on

the threshold, her hands clasped in front of her. Nervous.

It smelled a little musty, probably from being closed up for three weeks, but it was clean. Everything was put away neatly. There were a couple of throw pillows and a blanket on the built-in couch. She'd hung artwork on one wall. A watercolor print of flowers in a frame and another of a bird. There was a small television sitting on the dining room table with a DVD player hooked up. There was also a small stack of children's movies and shows.

"It's not much," Alaina said, looking around. "But it served us well for the past few months."

"You need more room," Ry said, his voice a little rougher than he intended. But he couldn't get over the fact she'd been living in this shit hole with a rambunctious six-year-old and doing her best to make a home for them.

"And now we have it, thanks to you."

"Happy I could help."

"You have. So much."

She drew in a breath and took another step inside to join him. Ry admired that she did it when she was scared. He knew she wouldn't call herself brave, but she was.

"We just have our clothes and shoes, and a few personal items," Alaina said briskly, all business now. "The television and DVD player, and the movies. The dishes were here, but the food is ours. I picked up a couple of items at the dollar store—spatulas and stuff —but I can get those. Everett has some games and toys, too."

"How about I get a couple of boxes and you can start gathering things? When you fill a box, I'll take it to the truck."

"Sounds good."

He hesitated when he reached the door. "You gonna be okay for a sec while I retrieve the boxes?"

She nodded, her chin thrust out in determination. "Yes. Fine."

Ry hit the yard and strode to his truck, opening the tailgate to reach inside for the boxes. The crunch of a twig a few feet away in the trees made him stiffen. He kept getting the boxes and pulling them onto the open tailgate, listening for the sounds of someone moving closer. He wanted them within range before he turned.

"Who are you?" a male voice asked coldly.

Ry turned then. A man stood there with a pistol at his side and a hard look on his face. Ry took him in, cataloging details. About twenty-five, worked out or worked manual labor, dark eyes, shaggy hair, and a Glock 19 with the extended mag in his hand. It wasn't raised, which bought the guy a point or two, but Ry wasn't exactly thrilled about it.

"Name's Ryder. I'm helping Alaina move her things. You are?"

"I live here. Where's Alaina?"

"Inside. Packing."

The man's eyes narrowed. "How do I know you aren't just stealing her stuff?"

"Alaina," Ry called. "Can you tell this guy I'm not stealing your stuff?"

Alaina appeared in the door, looking alarmed. He hated scaring her, but better her coming out and defusing the situation than him having to jump the guy.

When she saw who it was, the alarm left her expression. "Keith, hi. No, Ryder isn't stealing my stuff. I told your grandfather I was moving. This is the first time I could get over here to collect my things."

Ry was watching Keith, so he saw the look on the man's face when Alaina said she was moving. Possessive. Angry.

Keith definitely wasn't happy about her leaving. Made Ry's hackles rise. Could Keith have anything to do with the attack? If he'd felt rejected, he might have gotten angry enough to beat her up and dump her in the lake. The theft of the fifty could have been after the fact to make it look like a robbery. He'd supposedly been hunting with his grandfather when it'd happened, but that didn't mean he'd really been with Mr. Herbert the entire time.

"Where're you going?" Keith asked a touch belligerently. He was still holding the Glock, and Ry was starting to consider relieving him of it.

"I found a new place," Alaina said. "A house. It's bigger, and there's more room for Everett to play."

"I thought you liked it here."

"I, um, did. Do." Her gaze went to the gun as if she'd just realized it was there. "It's just… just…"

"You wanna put the gun away, boss?" Ry interrupted as Keith continued to stare at Alaina.

"My property," Keith said, swinging his gaze to Ryder again. "I'll do what I want. You don't like it, you can leave."

"Please, Keith." Alaina had gone pale. "I don't like guns, and you're making me nervous. It won't take long for us to get out of here and leave you alone."

Keith hesitated, shooting a look at Ry, but then he put the gun in a hidden holster beneath his waistband and untucked his shirt so it covered the grip.

Ry breathed a sigh of relief. Not because he was scared of the guy, but because he hadn't wanted to put Keith on the ground with Alaina watching. Telling her he had a violent job was one thing. Showing her was another. What she saw might make her afraid of him. He didn't want there to be any fear in her eyes when she looked at him.

"Thank you," Alaina said, visibly relieved.

The hunger in Keith's gaze only grew stronger as she smiled at him.

"I hear you're a hunter," Ry said, his gut burning with irritation. "Whatcha hunting?"

Keith turned resentful eyes on him. "Squirrel. Coyote sometimes. Why?"

"Just wondering where you go. I might like to check into doing some hunting myself. I'm new in town, so I don't know all the places."

Keith jerked his chin and sniffed. "Sorry. I hunt on private property. Can't help you."

"Really? Sorry to hear that." Ry scratched his chin. "Is it anywhere near the lake?"

"No. You writing a book or what?"

"Nah, just making conversation. Thanks for the info." He turned to pick up the boxes and headed toward the RV. Alaina was still in the doorway, and he knew without looking that Keith was staring at her again. Ry wanted her inside, packing, and then he wanted her out of there. He thrust a box at her and she took it, her smile wavering only a second as she gave him a puzzled look.

"Gotta get packing, babe. Everett will be home soon."

"You're right. Bye, Keith. Thanks for stopping by."

Ry admired her even more in that moment as she waved at Keith and ducked back inside. She didn't know what was bothering him or why he was rushing her since Everett wasn't due home for hours, but she didn't question him about it. Ry followed her inside and watched out the window as Keith stared at the RV. Then he turned and strode back toward the house. He might return, but Ry doubted it. There was nothing the man could do with Ry around.

Didn't mean he hadn't done something before, though. Keith Herbert could have been waiting when Alaina came home from dropping Everett off. He could have been in the trees, and he could have attacked her when she left her car.

Maybe that look of possessiveness was more about hurting rather than having. Took all kinds of sick fuckers to make the world go round. Ry knew it better than most people ever would.

"Stacie says Keith is harmless," Alaina said as she gathered clothing and stuffed it in a box. "She grew up with him. Says he's just shy. He was bullied for his awkwardness as a kid. That's probably why he carries a gun now."

Ry got busy unhooking her television from the DVD player. "Maybe so, but he didn't seem too shy to me. And he stared at you a little too possessively for comfort."

She sighed. "He does stare, I'll grant you that. Everyone who knows him says he stares. And I know what you're thinking. You're wondering if he attacked me. But he wasn't here. When I was getting my mail the day before the attack, Mr. Herbert was at the mailbox too. He told me that Keith got a couple extra days off and they were going hunting on the Eastern Shore. He was happy about it. He wouldn't go without Keith. He's eighty if he's a day, and he doesn't want to go alone."

Ry didn't point out that she hadn't been able to remember if Herbert and his grandson left the evening before or the morning of the attack. Alaina wasn't in the mental space to consider that Keith could have been the one to hurt her.

Ry understood it, and he wasn't going to push the idea. But he wasn't going to forget it either.

Chapter Eleven

IT TOOK LESS THAN AN HOUR TO GRAB EVERYTHING and pack it in Ryder's truck. Alaina thought she should feel ashamed about that, but for once she didn't. She and Everett didn't have a lot of stuff, but they had what they needed. Yes, she wished she could give him streaming television and a PlayStation, but maybe he was better off not being online all the time anyway.

She knew he played online at Stacie's house, and she let him use her phone for games when they had a good signal, but Everett didn't seem to focus too much on what he didn't have. That would change as he got older and realized how different his life was from other kids. For now, though, he was a sweet little boy who loved to play outside, loved his friends, and still thought his mama was the light of his life. She would take that for as long as she had it.

Ryder carried everything into the cottage and put the boxes where she wanted them. He set her television on the cabinet that stood against the wall and hooked up the DVD player. While she unpacked clothing, he went up to his house for something.

When he returned, he had a small box that he plugged into an outlet. Lights began to flash before going solid one by one.

"What's that?" she asked.

"A Wi-Fi extender. You can use my internet this way."

"You don't have to do that. You've done so much already."

"I'm not home all the time, Alaina. You might as well use it."

"But you're here now."

"It's fine. Besides, I'd feel better if you had access. Sometimes I get called back to work and have to go fast. It's better you have internet now instead of when I'm headed downrange."

She couldn't help but smile a little. "Downrange. Is that more of that military language you were talking about?"

"Yep. Means I'm deploying—traveling—somewhere, and I'll be gone for a while."

Her tummy sank. "Oh. How long is a while?"

He shrugged. "Anywhere from a few days to a few weeks."

She couldn't find an answer to that.

Ryder walked over and put a friendly arm around her shoulders. She found herself wishing it was more than friendly. Wishing she could turn into him and press a kiss to his firm jaw with the day's growth of stubble. So sexy.

"You won't be alone. I'll message you when I can, and you'll have Jenna and Scarlett to call on if you need anything. Plus you've got some wicked self-defense moves now. You know how to shoot?"

All her warm feelings evaporated as a shadow slid over her heart.

"No," she practically whispered. She'd grown up in South Carolina, and though her uncle hunted, she'd been too terrified of guns to even ask him to teach her. Not that he would have.

"We can work on that, too."

Alaina shook her head as old panic swelled. "I can't shoot, Ryder. I-I don't want to." She squeezed her eyes shut, still hearing the way the gun sounded that day when she'd been a child. So loud. So final.

"Hey," he said, turning her to face him. "What's wrong, Alaina?"

She pulled in a breath, trying to calm her emotions. So long ago, and she still got this way when she thought about it. "I, um, I need some water."

"Okay." He let her go and she fled toward the galley kitchen where she grabbed a glass and turned on the tap. Nothing came out. Tears threatened close to the surface, but she swallowed them down and tried again. Nothing.

"Shit," Ryder said. "I don't know what's going on. I'll check my house, see if the water's off there too. Come with me and I'll get you a bottle of water."

She started to say no, she wanted to be alone, but he'd done nothing wrong. After he'd been so good to her these past few weeks, she owed him a little more than an unexplained breakdown. He said she was strong, but damn if she didn't always show her weak side when he was around.

Ryder strode toward his house and she followed. When they got inside, he went over to the fridge and grabbed a bottle of water for her. Then he turned on the sink. Water flowed from the tap unimpeded. Ryder shut it off and frowned.

"Could be a broken pipe going to the cottage. I'll have to trace the lines and see what I can find."

Alaina stood with the bottle against her cheek, cooling her heated skin. She'd already drank half of it.

"Just my luck," she said morosely. "You help me move, and I break your plumbing."

"Alaina."

She looked up at his face, the chiseled jaw, the perfect nose, the lips that she wanted to feel beneath hers again. *Dammit.* "What?" she asked on a whisper.

"You didn't break the plumbing. I told you the

place needed work, and we probably just found one of the places it needs it most. I'm sorry. I thought I was offering you a functioning house to stay in, but maybe I was too optimistic. I'll get it fixed. Promise."

"I know you will. It's okay. We'll just, uh…" She didn't know what they would do. How could you flush a toilet, take a shower, or cook without water?

"You'll stay here with me. You and Everett move back in until it's fixed." She started to open her mouth and he put a finger over her lips. "Not taking no for an answer. No excuses either. You can keep unpacking over there, bring a few things over here, and use my shower and bathroom until I fix yours. Got it?"

She nodded and he dropped his finger away.

"Good." His gaze moved over her face, studying her in a way that she thought should make her feel self-conscious but somehow didn't. It felt good, like sunshine on a cold day. "Are you going to tell me why the idea of learning to shoot bothers you so much?"

Alaina felt her throat closing up again. Only this time she didn't let herself start to crumble. "My, um, father shot my mother when I was eight. She died."

"Jesus."

Some of the color left his face. A second later, he dragged her into his arms and held her tight. Alaina didn't even try to pull away. She wrapped her arms around his waist and buried her nose in the flannel of his shirt.

He felt good. Smelled good. She liked being with him, and if she were honest with herself, she *wanted* to be in this house with him. More time with him. More conversations, and maybe even a few kisses. Wasn't it time she had a little piece of happiness for herself?

It probably wouldn't last because nothing ever did, but she was so tired of being alone all the time. Maybe a little risk was worth it to keep this feeling for a while longer.

"I'm sorry, baby," he said. "So sorry."

His mouth was on her temple, his lips soft against her skin. He stroked her hair, and little tingles of sensation shivered down her spine, raising goose-bumps in their wake. She kept hugging him, not wanting to let go. She couldn't remember the last time another person had hugged her tight and just held her. Everett hugged her, of course, and his little hugs were perfect—but it wasn't the same as having someone bigger than you hold you and give you their strength when you needed it.

"Thank you."

They stood that way for long minutes. Ryder didn't let go, and she didn't either. She just closed her eyes and pretended he was hers, that this was real, that he loved her and Everett and wanted to be a family with them.

Dangerous fantasies.

Nobody wanted her. Not really. Ryder might want

sex with her, but he wasn't going to want more. Wasn't going to want all her mess and dysfunction. She believed he was her friend, but she had a hard time imagining he'd want more than that.

Alaina sucked in a breath and pushed herself away. She might as well tell him all of it now. That way she wouldn't expect things that were never going to happen.

He was watching her with sympathy written on his handsome face, and her heart clenched. He would definitely sympathize when she was done, but he'd also know how fucked up her life was. Then he could stop hugging her and making her want more than she should.

"My father was an abusive piece of shit," she began. "Oh, he was charming and handsome, and he fooled most everyone. Including me. But he'd hit my mother for the craziest things. Getting the wrong toilet paper, forgetting to heat up the syrup for his pancakes, leaving a cleaning rag on the counter. She'd tell me it was her fault, that Daddy worked hard and got angry, and I was too young not to believe her. Because he was sweet to me, called me his daddy's girl, all the bullshit that narcissists to do gaslight their victims."

Ryder's expression was changing, growing angry. She didn't fear his anger, though. It was *for* her, not against her.

"He never hit me, but he hit her. When I got a little older and started to cry if he yelled at my mom, he'd yell at me, too. He didn't touch me, though. Now that I'm an adult, I think she diverted him, made sure to focus his attention on her. He was always going to turn that anger on me one day."

She shrugged, though it hurt so bad to say these things.

"The day he grabbed my arm and shook me so hard my teeth rattled and I thought I'd pass out because I was dizzy, my mom packed a small bag and we left. He'd been drinking, and he'd passed out on the couch. We went to a women's shelter in town, and we stayed there for a couple weeks. I know they helped her file a restraining order, and I know they helped her get a job and find a place to stay. We were doing okay, I think. She was working, and the bruises on her face had faded." Alaina's chin quivered. "Sorry," she said as she swiped her eyes.

"Honey, no. Don't be sorry." His voice sounded strained. "You don't have to tell me if you don't want to."

She shook her head, hugging herself tight. "I want to. I *need* to. I want you to understand."

"I'm listening, baby."

She didn't mind that he called her honey and baby, though it was going to make everything harder when he decided he didn't want her in his life anymore. Still, that was a problem for another day.

"I came home from school one day after we'd been gone for a couple of months, and he was there. He'd been in jail for assault, though I hadn't known it at the time. He'd just gotten out, and he'd found us. I don't know how. Anyway, they were arguing—and he shot her. I didn't see it, but I heard it. The gun was so loud." She forced the words out of her tight throat. "I ran to the neighbor's apartment across the hall. They called the police, but it was too late. My mother was dead, and that monstrous asshole wasn't. He went to prison. I went to live with my mother's sister and her husband. They raised me, but they never stopped letting me know how much of a burden I was to them. When I met Clint, I was lonely and vulnerable, starving for affection. He was the first person to show me any real tenderness since my mother died. He was my first—my only, in fact—and I thought he loved me. When I got pregnant, he denied the baby was his. My aunt and uncle didn't want anything to do with me because they said I was old enough to take care of myself."

Alaina shrugged, though it hurt so badly to think of all the people who'd rejected her. "I've done the best I could for Everett. I probably should have given him up for adoption, but I couldn't do it. I knew life would be hard, but he's the first thing I've ever had that was wholly mine. That probably doesn't make a lot of sense, but it's how I feel."

Ryder reached for her hand and took it gently in

his. He didn't pull her to him again, and she was glad because she felt as fragile as tissue paper. She could feel his strength in that light touch, and it warmed the chill in her bones. Hardened the steel in her spine again.

"It doesn't need to make sense to anyone but you, honey."

"He could have had a better life if I'd given him up." Her throat ached with the words she'd never said aloud to anyone. Tears spilled down her cheeks again. She couldn't wipe them away fast enough this time. "Sorry."

Ryder wrapped his arms around her, cupping her head and pressing it to his chest. She clung to him, sobbing, angry with herself and also relieved that she'd gotten the words out. It was like releasing a knot inside and finally being able to breathe again.

"You love Everett and he loves you. There's nothing bad about providing a child with love, Alaina. And you don't know that his life would have been better. You've only convinced yourself it would've been, but you can't guarantee that."

"You're right. I just—I feel so guilty sometimes when I see what other kids have and what I can't give him."

"Trust me, you give him the most important thing he needs. Love and an involved parent who makes sure he uses the right words, has manners, and knows that when he talks, his mother will listen to him. Doesn't get much better than that."

Warmth flowed into her cold bones. "You say the nicest things," she whispered against his shirt.

"I'm telling you the truth. My parents loved me, but they were busy with their careers and often gone. When I was Everett's age, I had video games, a television in my room, and all the things you'd think a kid would want. But I didn't have their attention. They didn't have the time to nurture me the way you nurture Everett. That's why I learned to bake. Gram and Papa had a business to run, so they kept me busy helping out. Not that I was much help when I was little, but I learned."

"You did. Best blueberry muffins and cheesecake I've ever had."

He laughed softly. "Also the reason I had that muffin top as a kid. I spent a lot of time in the bakery and not as much outside as I should have. Add in those Buffalo winters when it was harder to play outside for very long, and you have the recipe for a kid who knows too much in the kitchen but also wants to sit around and play video games and shit."

"Looks like you figured it out though." Easy to say while standing with her arms wrapped around his hard body. "Nothing soft going on here."

"No, definitely not," he said against her hair, and her face flamed as she thought about what she'd said. Nothing soft. *Nothing.* Oh boy.

Alaina tilted her head up to look at him. She knew she looked like hell with her tear-stained cheeks and red eyes, but there wasn't much she could do to change it. "I've cried on you enough, Ryder. I need to unpack the rest of our things and then get some stuff together so we can stay with you tonight."

"And I need to start looking for the leak." He ran his palms up her arms and over her shoulders. "I'll call a plumber on Monday if I haven't managed to fix it by then. I won't make you stay here with me indefinitely."

Of course he didn't want them to stay any longer than necessary. He wanted his space back. She got that, but she was strangely disappointed anyway. "I know."

His thumb traced her lower lip, and her skin bloomed beneath his touch. "I know you like your own place, Alaina. I enjoy having you and Everett here with me, but I know it's important to you to have that distance. So I'll work to get it for you."

Good lord, she could love this man. He was too kind, too perceptive, too attuned to her thoughts. No one had ever worked to give her what she wanted before. Except she didn't necessarily want that distance from him anymore. Not that she could say so.

"It's okay. We like being here with you."

He grinned down at her. "Good. Don't think I didn't hear what you said about Everett's birth father being your first and only, by the way."

"That was a bit of an overshare, huh?"

He laughed. "Maybe, but it's gonna be in my head from now on. Because I want to be your second, Alaina. Pretty fucking badly, I gotta tell you. But if you don't want it, then I respect that."

Her blood throbbed in her veins as she imagined it. His naked skin against hers, hands and mouths and tongues exploring. Hoo boy, was it hot in here? Then she thought, fuck it. She'd already shared every truth bomb she had. Why not another one?

"I want that too. But it's not an easy thing for me. I have to think of Everett and how things affect him. If he gets attached to you…"

His thumb skated over her lip again, short-circuiting her thoughts. "He's already attached, babe. Surely you realize it."

Alaina blinked. Oh God, he was right. Of course Everett was attached. Mr. Ryder let him watch his television. Mr. Ryder came over for dinner, promised to take him fishing one day, and listened to him read books for practice. She'd already let Ryder get too close and she hadn't realized.

"Hey, don't look so worried. I'm not going to stop caring about the two of you if we have sex. This doesn't end with me throwing you out and refusing to speak to Everett ever again."

Alaina swallowed. "That obvious?"

"Yeah, that obvious. Just because his father was a stupid fucker doesn't mean I am. I know what I'm getting into, Alaina. You come with a six-year-old, and that's nonnegotiable. If I have a relationship with you, then I have one with him too. And that's what we're talking about, babe. Dating, getting to know each other, being in each other's lives. Just so we're clear."

A relationship. She liked the sound of that. And yet it scared her, too. "Relationships don't turn out so good for me. I'm a little like a kid who's touched a hot stove. I know better than to do it again."

"I can respect that. But if you want to come into the kitchen again, I won't let you get burned. Promise."

"I'll think about it."

He leaned down and kissed her forehead. Nothing sensual, and yet it rocked her to her core. Things were achy down there. She could feel the wetness between her thighs. What would it be like to let him touch her, to slide his fingers into her wet heat? Would she explode with very little effort? Or was it more like she was rusty and it would take time to get everything working again?

She really wanted to know, but before she could do something stupid like grab the edges of his flannel shirt and haul him to her, he let her go and started for the door.

"Gotta find that leak, babe. Daylight's running out."

Alaina watched him disappear outside, her knees suddenly weak as she put a hand out to steady herself against the wall.

Whew, that had been one close call. Another minute and she'd have climbed him like a tree.

Chapter Twelve

RY FOUND THE LEAK. IT WAS A BUSTED PIPE NEAR THE cottage. He found it because the ground was saturated and growing wetter in that area. A few shovelfuls of mud revealed the culprit. An old PVC pipe had shattered. It was closer to the surface than it probably should have been, and it was possible the freezing temperatures over the winter had finally done it in. With the water inside freezing, thawing, freezing again, the old pipe was weak and it'd had enough.

Unfortunately, considering how close the pipe was to the surface, he'd have to dig it up all the way to the main and then sink a new one deeper. Which meant it would take time. He'd ask Jenna if she knew of a good plumber tomorrow when they went over for the team get-together. It'd be faster to hire someone, though it'd cost a pretty penny too.

But how could he take his sweet ass time when Alaina was waiting for him to get it fixed?

When he thought of Alaina clinging to him, crying, telling him that maybe Everett would have been better off without her—well, he wanted to go find that asshole sperm donor and kick his nuts into his throat for him. If this Clint guy had manned up, he could have at least helped provide for his child, not pretend he didn't exist and let Alaina struggle to get by.

Sweet Alaina, who'd had a shitty childhood of her own, who had a heart that didn't quit, and who was determined to give her child the life she hadn't had. One filled with love and acceptance, not indifference and violence. No wonder she hadn't wanted Everett to come to the hospital. She knew what he would see, and it was too much to bear when she'd grown up the way she had.

He'd lost his sister when she'd taken her own life, and that'd been hard enough. She'd been three years older, and she'd doted on him. He'd been too young to realize she'd been depressed.

He couldn't imagine his father shooting his mother and killing her. Altering his entire childhood for the worse. Being shuffled into a home where he wasn't wanted. Being kicked out at eighteen and told he was on his own, then being turned away when he had a tiny baby to care for and needed them most.

Shitty people, all of them. Except Alaina's mother,

who'd found the courage to finally leave an abusive situation.

Ry turned off the water to the cottage so it didn't keep leaking, then went to knock on the door. Alaina was inside, putting hers and Everett's things away. She opened the door, and his heart did a little flip thing in his chest. She'd changed from jeans to a pair of leggings and a gray workout jacket that zipped up. Her hair was in a ponytail, and her pretty green eyes were warm and welcoming. She wasn't afraid of him, or wary. Not that she had a reason to be, but he was glad to see the friendliness in her gaze when she looked at him.

Her brows lifted. "You look, uh, muddy."

"Yep. Found it. Unfortunately had to turn the water off, so it won't be back this weekend. Sorry about that."

She didn't look upset or disappointed. "I understand, Ryder. Stuff happens. It's not your fault."

He hooked a thumb over his shoulder. "I'm gonna go shower. You need anything?"

She smiled. "No. I'm just about done here, really."

"Come over anytime then. When's Everett getting back?"

"He's spending the night at Stacie's. She called a few minutes ago and said the boys were having fun and wanted a sleepover."

Aw, hell. Just like that he was imagining having a

sleepover with Alaina. Naked. In his bed. Took everything he had not to let his dick get hard at the thought. Maybe it was his imagination, but he thought her cheeks were a little flushed.

"You don't mind being alone with me overnight?"

She shook her head. "No, I don't."

He arched a brow. "You realize you told me you haven't been with anyone since Clint and that I've been thinking about it pretty much non-stop, right? Just so we're clear."

She laughed. Her cheeks were definitely red now. "I understand."

"I won't cross any lines, Alaina. You don't have to worry about that."

"I know." Her voice was a whisper.

He took a few steps back, still holding her gaze with his. He didn't know what she saw in his eyes, but he knew what he thought was reflected there.

Need. Hot, naked, unadulterated need.

"Gonna take that shower now," he said. "See you in a bit."

"I'll be there."

Ry went inside and turned on the shower. He shut the bedroom door, just in case, and stripped out of his clothes. Then he got under the spray and let the mud wash away.

Jesus, a whole evening alone with Alaina. He'd cook her dinner, then maybe they could watch a movie. He'd have to sit on the opposite side of the couch, though. As far from her as he could get. When it was over, they would go to their separate rooms. He wouldn't even risk giving her a peck on the cheek.

And then, because he was there, he thought about what it'd be like to bend her over in the shower, to grip her hips and slide into her body. He thought about the steam curling around them, about the way she would moan and writhe on his dick as he fucked her thoroughly, about how he would make damned sure she came before he did.

Ry groaned. He was fucking harder than stone.

He palmed his dick, stroked it, pleasure blossoming in his balls as he rolled his soapy hand up and down his length. He wanted Alaina to stroke him, but he acknowledged it might never happen. Didn't stop him from thinking about her as he pumped harder, thrusting into his fist again and again.

His orgasm hit quickly, rushing through him, hot semen spilling over his fist as he groaned his release. He turned the water to cool, then stood in the shower and watched the evidence wash away as if it'd never happened.

––––––––

ALAINA WAS nervous as Ryder parked his truck on the street in front of Noah and Jenna's house. She felt a little like an intruder though he'd insisted she and Everett were invited.

Everett had no such qualms. He was about as excited as a kid on Christmas morning to have yet another event on his social calendar for the weekend. Her shy kid was positively giddy at the idea of a cookout. They'd picked him up on the way, and he'd been full of information about Chuck E. Cheese and all the games he'd played. Then there was the detailed recitation of what he and Carter, and Carter's little brothers, did last night and this morning.

"You ready, babe?" Ryder asked softly.

"Yes." She'd fretted about what to wear but had finally put on a light sweater and some jeans, finishing the outfit with a pair of ankle boots. It was March, so not freezing but not truly warm either. She felt cute, if not stylish. Presentable.

"Still say you look hot in those jeans," he whispered.

"Stop trying to make me blush."

"Okay, fine. Everett," he said more loudly. "Grab those bags of chips, please."

"Yes, sir!"

"Don't get out of the truck until I open your door, okay?"

"Okay!"

Ryder shot her a grin, then got out and opened the door for Everett, who'd been seated behind him. Together they came around and opened her door. Ryder had taken the chips from him, which was a good idea since Everett was bouncing excitedly on the sidewalk.

The front door to the house opened. Jenna and Alice stood there, waving.

"Hey, Everett," Jenna said.

"Everett!" Alice yelled.

Everett took off running. Alice caught him around the neck and hugged him when he reached her.

"See," Ryder said. "The kid knows he's part of the gang. So are you. C'mon."

His fingers closed around hers. She walked beside him across the yard to the house, fighting butterflies that were no longer due to the prospect of meeting his teammates.

They'd had a nice evening together. True to his word, Ryder hadn't crossed any lines. She'd found herself wanting him to, but he didn't. And since she hadn't been brave enough to take action, nothing happened. Not even a kiss.

She was still chiding herself for the missed opportunity.

After a whirlwind of introductions, Alaina was handed a drink and pulled to the kitchen where the women had gathered to chat and take care of any food prep that wasn't meant for the grill. She didn't say much, but she didn't feel left out because someone inevitably asked her a question when she'd been silent for too long.

There was a bit of a commotion when the last

guests arrived about twenty minutes later. Dean—aka Wolf—his wife Haylee, and their baby daughter Paisley. Everyone swarmed the couple to get a look at the baby. There were lots of oohs and aahs, and then Noah went outside to tend the grill. The men drifted that way one by one, though Ryder hung back and introduced Alaina to the newcomers.

"*You're* Alaina," Haylee said. She was a gorgeous woman with dark hair and caramel skin, and she didn't look like she'd had a baby a month ago. "I'm so happy to meet you. I've heard a lot about you."

"I, um, thank you," Alaina said as she accepted Haylee's free hand.

Haylee laughed as she cut a look at Ryder. "All of it good, I swear."

"Of course it's good," Ryder said, looping an arm around Alaina's shoulders like it was something he did every day. Several pairs of eyes followed the gesture, and Alaina felt herself coloring. "Alaina and Everett are pretty awesome."

"C'mon, dude," Dean said to Ryder as he kissed his wife on the forehead and brushed his fingers over the baby's cheek. "Let's go outside and leave the women to talk about us behind our backs."

"As if," Haylee said. "We have lots of things to discuss that don't involve you boys."

Dean laughed. "Sure thing, darlin'."

Ryder squeezed her shoulders, then put his mouth

to her cheek and whispered, "Relax, Alaina. You're with family."

Then he was gone and she was alone with a group of women who studied her like she was the latest trend. But then they smiled and started talking about other things.

"Come here, girlfriend," Scarlett said, patting the stool beside her. "Pull up a chair and get comfortable. We've got lots to discuss with the men outside."

Alaina didn't know what Scarlett meant, but she joined her. After a while, she relaxed in their company. Nobody stared, nobody asked her questions about the assault, and nobody said anything that was aimed at her specifically.

Nobody made her feel like she didn't belong or like they were humoring Ryder for bringing a guest. She hadn't expected it from Jenna or Scarlett, because she knew them already, but the rest of the women were just as accepting of her as those two.

"Your little boy is so polite," Brooke Rodgers said a bit later. She was married to Ryder's team leader Cade, aka Saint.

"Thank you," Alaina replied happily. "He's a good kid."

"He's going to be a heartbreaker," Scarlett piped in. "If he keeps on like that, he'll have the girls swooning in no time. All those yes ma'ams, pleases, and thank yous he sprinkles like glitter will serve him well when he gets older."

Alaina laughed. "I hope so. He's not always good at remembering his manners, but he tries."

"I'd say he does a good job," Jenna said. "I'm working with Alice on those things right now, and I sometimes despair of a please, let me tell you. She says what she wants rather than asks for it with a please, but we're getting there."

"Everett had his moments too. Still does," Alaina laughed. "We're working on not shouting in the house, but that one's a little more difficult. Especially with Ryder. He gets excited when Ryder's around, and his voice gets louder."

Everett liked having male attention, and he especially liked Ryder's. When Ryder had gone outside to join the men around the grill, he'd invited Everett to go with him. Everett had done so with enthusiasm.

A couple of the women exchanged looks. Alaina didn't have to wonder what it was about. Like with Scarlett in the cottage that day, they were pairing her and Ryder up in their heads.

"So Ryder is good with him?" Haylee asked.

"Yes," Alaina said truthfully. And then she told them what was on her mind, because what the hell? Sometimes it was nice to have someone to talk to. Even if she never saw them again, they were the kind of women you could say things around. She wasn't sure how she knew that, but she did. "There's only been Everett and me since he was born. He doesn't know what it's like to have a man in his life, but he knows he likes Ryder because Ryder pays attention to him. He hasn't really had that before."

The women around the kitchen island were looking at her with interest. Alaina swallowed. Maybe she should have kept her mouth shut. But then Brooke Rodgers sniffled and waved her hand.

"Sorry," she said. "I'm just emotional right now. But that's so sweet of Ryder."

"It is," Alaina said softly.

"Girl, are you…?" Haylee asked, reaching for Brooke's hand.

Brooke shook her head. "I don't think so. I'm not testing yet because it's too soon, but I always get emotional around that time of the month." She sniffed again and smiled at Alaina. "We've been trying to get pregnant. Hasn't happened yet, but it will. I know it will."

"It definitely will," Everly said firmly. Alaina had been surprised to learn that Everly's mother was Congresswoman Fairhope. There'd been a minor scandal of some kind, and she wasn't seeking reelection, but Alaina wasn't going to hide in the bathroom and google for information. Wasn't important anyway. What *was* important was how kind Everly was.

Eva Ryan nodded her agreement. She was gorgeous. She wore a long-sleeved top and jeans, but judging by the ink peeking out from her sleeves and the open neck of her shirt, she had a lot of tattoos. All in grayscale, which made them eerily beautiful instead of overwhelming. Alaina had never had a tattoo and didn't intend to start, but they fit Eva.

"Circling back to Ryder," Haylee said, and Alaina blinked. Ryder had told her that Haylee was a journalist. She wasn't surprised now that she'd been around Haylee. The woman could hold ten different conversations and never forget which conversational trail she'd been headed down in the first place. "He's a good guy. It's just him and Zane left single now that Everly's snapped up Gem."

"Haylee," Jenna said, laughing. "Stop trying to sell Alaina on the benefits of Ryder. She's living next door to him for heaven's sake. She can see for herself."

Haylee laughed too. "Fine, fine. Just wanted to point out he's a catch. So is Zane, but Ry knows how to bake. That gives him an edge in my opinion."

"Yeah," Scarlett sighed. "He sent us home with a cake the other day. So good."

Alaina could definitely agree that baking gave Ryder an edge. Plus she didn't feel anything when she looked at Zane Scott. He was handsome, but he didn't make her pulse race or her belly clench when he was near. Ryder did both those and more.

Bliss Bennett-Kelley opened the slider and came inside. She'd gone out a few minutes ago to check on the food's progress since she'd said she was starving after a late night on the computer. Ryder had told Alaina that Bliss and her husband were expert hackers. White hat hackers who worked for the good guys, not the kind who'd steal your logins and drain your bank account. Not that Alaina had a bank account worth stealing from.

"Another twenty minutes." Bliss picked up the drink she'd set down and took a dainty sip from the straw. "Muffin, Zany, Mal, and Saint are playing ball with Everett, by the way. I think he'll sleep hard tonight," she added with a laugh.

Alaina laughed too. She was happy. It was a good day after all. "I'm glad to hear it. He's had a very stimulating couple of days. Chuck E. Cheese and a sleepover yesterday, and now this. I was afraid he'd be up half the night wanting to tell me about everything he did this weekend."

"Nah. He's running around so much he'll probably drop in the car on the way home."

"You're probably right."

When Everett was that tired, he'd sleep all night without waking. She'd have to make sure she woke him and made him pee when he got home, or he might wet the bed during the night. She'd also need to watch how much he drank between now and when they were ready to leave. He didn't wet the bed too much anymore, but there were times.

The conversation moved on to other things. Alaina got up to look outside. Sure enough, Everett had a football and he was dodging between four grown men, his expression serious as he made for a goal only he knew. It was clear the men let him through. When he reached the other side, he spiked the ball and did a little victory dance. Ryder and Mal high-fived him. The other men came over and did the same, and Everett looked so pleased with himself that Alaina couldn't help the happiness swelling inside her. Tears pricked her eyes, and she sniffed them back.

"Hey, you okay?" It was Haylee, who was cradling little Paisley and bouncing her gently.

Alaina swiped her eyes just in case and smiled. "Yes. Definitely." She hesitated. "I think Everett needs male attention more than I thought. Makes me a little sad he hasn't had enough of it. And I'm ridiculously happy he's enjoying himself with the men now."

"Aw, honey," Haylee said, giving her a hand a quick squeeze. "It's okay. You have Ryder now. He seems to enjoy his time with Everett."

"I think so. I hope so."

Ryder had never pushed Everett to talk to him. Once Everett opened up and started talking, Ryder had never ignored him or told him to be quiet. He included Everett in conversations, and she believed he would deliver on his promise to teach Everett to fish. Even if she had sex with Ryder and it went nowhere, he would still keep his promises to Everett. That was a very comforting thing to know.

The men returned inside with the food a few minutes later. They scattered to wash up, and Ryder took Everett with him. When they returned, Everett held up his hands for her inspection even though she hadn't asked.

"They look very clean," she said, giving him a quick hug before they fixed plates and found seats around the island or at the tables Jenna had set up.

Everett was a perfect little guest, waiting his turn, saying please and thank you. He managed to make a mess of his hamburger, but he wiped his face and didn't talk with his mouth full.

By the time the party broke up, Everett had fallen asleep on the floor beside Alice. Alaina went to wake him, but Ryder stopped her. Then he bent and scooped her son into his arms. Everett never stirred as Ryder cradled him against his chest. There was a knot in Alaina's throat as she watched big, handsome, tough guy Ryder carrying her child like it was the most normal thing in the world.

They said their goodbyes to everyone, hugs were given and received, and Jenna told Alaina to call if she needed absolutely anything when Ryder was at work tomorrow. Everett slept all the way back to Ryder's place.

Alaina woke him once Ryder carried him in and got him ready for bed, making him brush his teeth and pee. Then she tucked him in and he immediately passed out again.

Ryder was waiting for her when she emerged. "He okay?"

"Grumpy at being woke up, but yes, he's fine. He'll sleep like a log all night long."

Ryder smiled. She loved that smile, the way it transformed him from sexy to breathtaking in one fell swoop.

"He played hard, Alaina. I think he had fun, though."

"I think he did, too. Thank you for giving him so much attention."

He shrugged. "He's a good kid. Tell the truth, I see something of myself in him. I was kind of self-contained and unsure at that age, too. And eager to please. *So* eager to please."

"He's eager to please you. You're the first man to really be a constant in his life." She shook her head sadly. "Damn, you've only known us for a few weeks, and *you* are the constant in my son's life. I've fucked up so many times, and now I've let you in, and he won't know what to do if you leave. Not that it's your problem. It's *mine*. I shouldn't have—"

Ryder closed the distance and wrapped her in his arms, stopping her from talking with his mouth on hers.

Chapter Thirteen

ALAINA SLID HER PALMS AROUND HIS BACK, UPWARD until she could feel those broad shoulders. He was big and built, and he held her like she was made of glass. That was another thing she loved about him.

His tongue slipped into her mouth. She didn't resist. She didn't want to resist. Kissing Ryder Hanson was the most excitement she'd had in too long to remember. She'd only ever had sex with Clint, but she'd kissed other men. Before Clint. And a couple after, when she'd tried dating in the early days before Everett was old enough to really pay attention.

It never turned out well. There was never a second date, and she'd given up the idea long ago.

But now? Now she was eager to feel everything she'd been missing. Maybe those women had gotten to her, or maybe she'd already decided that Ryder was a risk worth taking.

Even if nothing came of it, she trusted him not to throw her and Everett away. He might fall out with her over one thing or another, but he wouldn't let Everett suffer for it.

A seed of doubt started to prickle inside her head the longer they kissed. To bloom into something bigger. Maybe she shouldn't do this. Maybe it was too big a risk after all. She'd known him a little under a month. Not long enough to know what he would or wouldn't do.

She didn't get a chance to break the kiss though because Ryder did it for her.

He lay his forehead against hers, his hands cupping her head, thumbs caressing her jaw. She could feel his warm breath against her skin. She shivered with need and indecision, her desire warring with her brain.

"I'm not leaving, Alaina," he said softly. "I don't know where this is going, I don't know if we'll burn up in the atmosphere or keep soaring, but the thing is I want to find out. I want the right to touch you, to take you to my bed, to make you scream my name because it feels so fucking good and you can't help yourself. This is how relationships start, honey. Two people decide to try and be together. They get to know each other, sleep together when they're ready, and they either keep going or they don't. If we don't keep going, we'll figure it out then. And we'll do it in a way that protects Everett's heart."

"Why are you so good to me?" Her throat ached. She wasn't used to this, and she didn't know how to handle it. This wasn't her life. Hers was full of hardship and disappointment, with the exception of her son who was the best gift ever.

"Why wouldn't I be? You're a beautiful woman, Alaina. You love your son, and you work hard to provide for him. Besides working all day, you also volunteer your free time to help women who've been hurt, though you could use the time to rest. You're good to others, honey. Why wouldn't people be good to you?"

When he put it that way, she didn't have an answer.

"It's still early. You want to watch something?" he asked after they'd been silent for a few moments.

She thought about saying no, that she should go to bed, but it *was* early. If she went to the room she was sharing with Everett, she'd lie awake for hours. But she didn't want to sit on the couch, perched on the opposite end from Ryder, and pretend interest in television either.

"No. I want you to kiss me again," she said, her heart throbbing like a jackhammer in her chest.

He sucked in a breath and straightened until she could see the heat in his eyes. "I want that too, Alaina. I want more than that, and I'm gonna try to get it. So I want you to tell me, very clearly, if you don't want more when I try to go there. Understood?"

She nodded. And then she wrapped a hand around the back of his neck and tugged him down. He groaned as she pressed her lips to his—and then his mouth opened and their tongues slid together in a ballet. Or maybe it was a duel. Either way, Alaina's core melted, her pussy throbbing with the need to be touched. Filled.

She knew down to her soul that if she didn't pull away right now, there would be no stopping until her hunger was slaked and her body was boneless.

She didn't want to stop, though.

Her fingers dipped to the waistband of his jeans and she tugged his shirt free so she could slide her hands against his skin, trace the ridges of those washboard abs and feel the perfection of honed muscles on a warrior's body.

Ryder tore his mouth from hers, his breathing a little quicker than before. "What are you doing, Alaina?"

"I-I'm being impulsive. I'm giving myself what I want for once without second-guessing or denying myself. I haven't had sex in seven years, Ryder. Right now, I think I miss it so much I'd beg you if you told me no. So please don't tell me no."

He stood wide-eyed, gaping at her. She thought he was going to shut her down. But then he growled as he bent and swept her into his arms. "I'm not telling you no, honey. I'm telling you yes. And then I'm showing you how good it can be. I'm not just gonna be your second lover, I'm gonna be your best."

———

RYDER CARRIED her into his room and shut the door. Then he set her down, making sure she slid down his hard body until she was on her own two feet. Alaina swallowed as she gazed up at him. Was he reconsidering? Because he wasn't doing anything besides staring at her.

"Ryder?"

He reached for the hem of her sweater and slid it upward. "Yeah?"

"I-is everything okay?"

"More than okay, beautiful. Lift your arms, honey."

She did as he said and he removed her sweater, laying it over a nearby chair. Embarrassment picked at the edges of her desire. Her bra was old and plain. The white cotton was still white, but it wasn't fancy. No lace, no peek-a-boo, no pushup cups. Basic and serviceable. Like her.

She crossed her arms self-consciously. Ryder gently uncrossed them. "Why are you hiding from me?"

"I… I don't have fancy underwear."

His chuckle was deep and amused. "I don't care about the underwear, Alaina. I care about what's underneath. That's what most men care about, you know. The boobs and pussy are where it's at, not the fabric hiding them."

"I haven't done this in a long time. I'm scared," she confessed.

He tipped her chin up with a finger. "Babe, I'm gonna make sure this is good for you. Promise. You trust me?"

She nodded. "Yes."

"You worried about Everett waking up?"

"No. He played hard and ate well. He'll be out until morning."

"That's good. Real good." His gaze dropped to her chest again, and this time he brought a hand up to cup one of her breasts.

It was dark outside, but the lamp in his bedroom was on. She thought about asking him to turn it off, but she wanted to see what was happening more than she wanted to hide behind the darkness.

She still had bruises, but they were yellowing now. Ugly, but not painful like they'd once been. Ryder dropped his hand from her breast and traced one of the bruises, frowning hard.

"Does it hurt?"

"Not much, no," she said truthfully.

"I really want to find who did this to you and beat the shit out of them."

She shivered at the violence in his voice. But she loved it, too. Because it was for her. She didn't want him to hurt anyone for her, but knowing he wanted to? Heady stuff.

"I don't want to think about it," she said. "Not tonight."

"Then we won't."

Ryder cupped her breasts again, pushing them together before taking a step closer and dropping his mouth to hers. He made a sound of approval when she opened to him.

Their tongues tangled, their teeth clashing. They didn't know each other yet, but they were learning. She loved the learning. Ryder kissed her hard and deep, then dropped his mouth to her throat before he dragged her bra down her shoulders to expose her breasts. She gasped and clung to his shoulders when his mouth fastened around one nipple and tugged. Spikes of pure pleasure shot into her core, her pussy, throbbed in her clit as he sucked hard.

"Ryder," she gasped as he pinched her other nipple. Not hard, but just enough to multiply the sensation. He rolled one nipple with this tongue and the other with his fingers, and Alaina thought she might explode from that alone.

It'd been so damned long, and she'd only been a kid really. Then she'd had a kid of her own and she hadn't gotten to explore her sexuality for years. She'd known it wasn't dead, but she'd considered it dormant.

Not now. She wanted to shove him onto the bed,

rip his jeans off, and impale herself on his cock. That's how desperately awake her sex drive was. Like it'd been frozen in ice but the ice had melted because the sun shone down.

But doing something like that would hurt like hell since it'd been so long. She ran her hand over his jeans, feeling the huge bulge of his cock, and her stomach bottomed out.

Easy, girl.

If she didn't take this slow, she'd be walking gingerly for a couple of days.

Ryder sucked her other nipple between his teeth, eliciting a sharp moan from her throat. He wasn't gentle, but he wasn't rough either. It was just enough. Hard enough to make her squirm and soft enough to make her crave even more.

Alaina didn't want to wait for the more. She ripped at his jeans, trying to unbutton them and release him. He laughed softly as he pulled away and reached behind his head to drag his shirt off one-handed.

Good God, that was sexy.

Then he helped her unbutton his jeans and let her shove them down his hips while he removed her bra and pushed her jeans and panties down until she could kick out of them. He kicked out of his, then dropped to his knees in front of her. Alaina whimpered as he pressed kisses to the underside of her breasts, her abdomen, his tongue trailing around her belly button and then downward until it skimmed between her folds.

He lifted one of her legs and draped it over his shoulder, his fingers spreading her open so his tongue could slide into her seam. Alaina gasped as she clutched his shoulders. She ought to be embarrassed, or apprehensive, but she was neither. She only wanted more.

Ryder licked around her clit, then sucked it like he'd sucked her nipples. Hard, firm, perfect. Alaina moaned. She was so wet she could feel her juices dripping down the insides of her thighs, but she didn't care. Nothing was as amazing as the way she felt right now.

"Damn, Alaina, you taste so fucking good. I could do this for hours."

"I'm not going to last that long," she groaned.

"You're not? Guess I have to let you come… then I'm gonna do it again." Ryder pushed two fingers inside her while he licked her clit. Alaina shuddered at the sensations rolling through her. She was so close. He'd been licking her for precisely three seconds and already she was ready to blow.

"Ryder," she cried as he pumped those fingers into her, finding her most sensitive spot. He was relentless, fucking her with his fingers and sucking her clit as her climax built to a crescendo.

When it broke, when she came, Alaina nearly

sobbed her relief as pleasure long-denied rolled through her. It was so overdue she saw stars.

She'd masturbated, of course. It was *nothing* like having a man between her legs. *This man.* She wanted more. She wanted it all.

Maybe she'd regret it in the morning, but right now she wanted to feel every ounce of pleasure she'd been denied.

"Fucking hell that was beautiful," he growled as he stood and pushed her back toward the bed. When the backs of her knees hit the mattress, he picked her up and dropped her onto it, spreading her thighs wide and dropping between them, his broad shoulders holding her open as he drove his tongue into her pussy, his thumb rolling her clit.

"Ryder!"

"Come for me, Alaina. Again."

He fucked her with his tongue before replacing it with his fingers—three this time. Alaina moaned, her limbs trembling. It was so good… so fucking *good.* She wanted his cock, but first she wanted his tongue on her clit again.

As if he knew, he dropped his mouth right where she wanted it and took her to the stars a second time.

"Fucking hell, babe," he said when he crawled up her body, sucking her nipples on the way. Then he plunged his tongue between her lips, and Alaina wrapped her legs around him. He tasted like salt and musk. Like her. He kissed her like a man starved, and she responded in ways she wouldn't have dreamed were *her*.

"Ryder," she whispered as he dropped to her neck, her breasts again. "I need you to fuck me."

His eyes were bright and needy as he looked at her. "Say that again."

Her heart hammered, but she knew it was right. "I need you to fuck me. Please."

"Goddamn, girl." He shook his head as if reminding himself to take it easy with her. Then he reached for the beside table and produced a condom. She hadn't thought of that, and she should have. She had an implant because she'd learned you couldn't be too careful after working in the center, but she didn't know how many women he'd been with. And she damned sure wasn't asking right now.

Ryder ripped open the condom and rolled it on, tossing the wrapper to God knew where. He settled between her legs, then stopped before pushing inside her. Their gazes tangled.

"I want this to be good for you, Alaina. You need to tell me if it's too much too fast."

"Ryder." She said his name gently. Reverently. "I want you inside me. I had a baby, I think I can handle you."

His eyes widened a second, and then he laughed. "Yeah, okay. Still, you'll tell me if you don't like something, right?"

She nodded. "I will. Now please, *please*, fuck me. I feel like I've been waiting a lifetime already."

He dropped his mouth to hers, his tongue plunging deep as he lifted a leg and wrapped it around his hip. And then he pushed inside her, stretching her wide. Alaina clung to him, her body opening to his. Yes, she'd had a baby—but it'd been a long damned time and Ryder was big.

When he was seated deep inside her, he stopped and gazed down at her. "Feel us together," he whispered. "Feel how good that is."

"It's good," she replied. "So good."

"And it's about to get better," he told her. Then he moved, and Alaina squeezed her eyes shut as her breath stole from her chest. She wrapped her other leg around him, holding tight as he drove deep again and again. It was almost too much, but it wasn't. There was an edge to their joining. A sharp edge that she'd never felt before with Clint. It was addictive in ways she hadn't imagined. They hadn't finished yet and already she knew she would do anything to feel this way again.

Ryder hooked both her knees with his arms and pushed them wide until they were nearly at her ears. Alaina grabbed his face with both hands and shoved her tongue between his lips. They fucked harder than either of them expected, until the stars burst behind their eyelids, until they pulsed and trembled and came back to earth different than before.

After a long while in which Alaina thought she couldn't move ever again, Ryder untangled himself from her body and went to dispose of the condom. When he returned, she'd managed to climb out of bed and start searching for her clothing.

"What are you doing?" he asked.

"Getting my stuff so I can go to bed."

Ryder took her by the shoulders and turned her toward his bed. "You were in bed. Get back in it so we can sleep, babe."

Alaina shot him a look over her shoulder. "I can't sleep here. Everett wouldn't understand."

"You said he sleeps hard after a day like today, right?"

She nodded.

"Then stay with me for now. We can set an alarm, and you can be back in your room before he wakes."

Alaina hesitated. But she wanted to stay. So she nodded, and Ryder took the clothes she'd gathered from her hands and laid them all on the chair where she could easily get to them. Then they climbed into bed together, his front to her back, his arms wrapped around her as he pulled her in close.

She loved his warmth, the way he held her, the feel of his dick nestled against her ass. He wasn't hard, but he wasn't entirely soft either.

"You okay?" he asked, his voice a rumble in her ear.

"Yes. You?" She was going to be a little sore, but she didn't mind.

He chuckled in her ear, his warm breath sending little shivers down her spine. "Better than okay, Alaina. Fucking fantastic."

"Me too."

His fingers traced one of the faded bruises on her ribs. "I was worried about this. That I might have been too rough."

Alaina yawned. "Nope. It feels better than it looks these days."

He dropped a kiss to her shoulder. "I set the alarm for five. Will that work?"

"Definitely."

"Good night, Alaina. Oh, and for the record, I want to do this again. Lots of times, in case you were wondering."

"Me too," she said happily. "But we have to talk about that."

"I know. Now go to sleep, babe. You need to rest."

Chapter Fourteen

Ry woke Alaina at five with his fingers between her legs. "Time to wake up, babe."

She moaned and clung to him, and he chuckled as he stroked her faster. His dick was harder than stone, but he'd survive if he didn't get to fuck her before she had to go back to her own room.

She came within seconds, gasping into his shoulder. "Want you," she said, licking his pectoral muscle before dipping to flick his nipple with her tongue. She didn't have to tell him twice. He sheathed himself and pushed into her, groaning at how tight and wet she was.

"Damn, babe. Feel so fucking good," he said as he held himself still and enjoyed the trembling of her pussy around his cock.

"You too. Fuck me, Ry. I want to come again."

That was all he needed to hear. He stroked deep and fast, working them both toward a shattering orgasm. She bit his shoulder as she came, and that spurred his own release. He groaned her name into his pillow, his cock jerking inside her as he spilled his seed into the condom.

When it was over, when he rolled away to take care of the condom, her eyes were closed and there was a smile on her face. She opened them to look at him, and he felt a jolt in his gut.

"That was *amazing*," she said. "I can't believe what I've been missing."

He bent to suck a nipple before he stood beside the bed and grinned down at her. "Can't get that anywhere else, honey. Don't even think about it."

"Believe me, I'm not. I'm sorry I bit you."

He grinned. "I'm not. You can bite me anytime if it makes you come like that."

She stretched, her back arching, drawing all his attention to her pretty nipples pointing at the ceiling. Damn, he wanted to go back to bed and fuck her again.

"I'll keep it in mind," she purred. She turned to glance at her phone on the side table, then sat up with a yelp. "Crap, it's nearly five-thirty. I have to get out of here."

She jumped out of bed and grabbed her clothes, dragging them on while hopping around on one foot.

Ry should have headed to the bathroom, but he was enjoying the show too much. Especially the part where her tits bounced while she hopped around.

She got everything on, then stopped to grin at him in a way that made his heart squeeze. She looked less like a woman who worried about how she was going to do everything and more like one who knew she didn't have to go it alone. She looked happy. He'd done that, and it made him feel like a million bucks inside.

"Have a great day at work, Ryder."

He wanted to hold her. "You, too. Call Jenna if you feel like you need help or want someone to know where you are."

"I will. Promise."

———

RY WENT STRAIGHT to Hacker's desk when he got into work. The guys had found a few minutes to talk alone yesterday at Easy's house, and they'd discussed how the cops blamed a random drug addict for what'd happened to Alaina. A drug addict they hadn't found any trace of. A drug addict smart enough, or with an accomplice, who'd managed to take a bleeding, unconscious Alaina to the lake and dump her close enough to Ry's place that he'd found her in time to save her.

It was plausible, but not the only possibility by far. Hacker insisted they start at the top of potential suspects who might have a problem with Alaina and go from there. The dude liked to be thorough. Or maybe he just liked hacking into official records.

"Her father got paroled a year ago," Hacker said, looking up. "For good behavior and community service. Found Jesus, too. But he didn't come to Mystic Cove to get revenge on his daughter. He started a church, and then he got busted for possession of a controlled substance. He's wearing a leg bracelet and hasn't left South Carolina in the past six months at least."

Ry was actually relieved about that. Not that he gave two fucks about her father, but he'd hate to think how it would've affected her if he'd been the one who'd tried to kill her. "What about this Clint guy? Everett's father?"

Another douchebag he hoped was innocent for Alaina's sake.

"Clint Hubbard. He married Anne-Marie Sykes, whose father is a prominent doctor in Aurora where they live, and they have three kids. He has his own business as a general contractor. His wife had kid number three the day you found Alaina. He was at the hospital with her, so it's not him."

Ry blew out a breath. "Okay. You find anything on Keith Herbert?"

"Yep. Bit of a creeper. There've been some complaints at work. He follows female coworkers around the store according to the internal memos I found. He denies it, says they don't like him and want to get him in trouble. No action taken."

Zany, who'd stopped by to listen, whistled. "You broke into their internal systems?"

"On my own time, asswipe. Not on government time or computers. Remarkably easy, by the way."

Wolf was there too. He shook his head. Dude's eyes were a bit bloodshot, but Ry didn't think it was from drinking. Miss Paisley Faith Garner was probably to blame.

"Seriously, these companies should hire you to shore up their firewalls or whatever it is that would keep you out," Wolf said.

Hacker shrugged as if he couldn't be bothered. "Wouldn't help much. I'd probably leave myself a back door."

"Whatever that means," Saint said as he walked over and joined the conversation.

"Okay," Ry said. "So Keith could have attacked Alaina."

And if he had, Ry wasn't going to be kind in his response. He wouldn't kill the dude, because he liked his freedom, but he'd make sure Keith Herbert suffered a bit before the police got him.

"Maybe. Keith's movements on the day aren't definitive. His phone traveled north about thirty miles

—not to the Eastern Shore like he said—and didn't travel back until two days later. Doesn't mean he couldn't've made the drive, though. He could have left the phone and returned, attacked Alaina, then went north again. Can't access his grandfather's statement to see what he says, but I'm betting he places Keith with him the entire time."

"Probably so," Ry said, blowing out a breath. "What about Deputy Patrick Foss?"

He didn't like the weasel, especially now that he knew Foss had harassed Alaina behind his girlfriend's back. Harassed a lot of women, apparently, and got away with it. He could have gotten pissed enough at her continued rejection to want to teach her a lesson. Maybe it'd gone too far, and he'd had to dump her body somewhere. The clumsiness of it could have been on purpose to throw suspicion away from him.

Since he was part of the investigation, he could have tampered with any evidence that might have implicated him as well. Or he was just fucking incompetent. They might never know who'd really attacked Alaina with Foss on the case.

"That's trickier," Hacker said. "His phone records and whereabouts are harder to access. He's a law enforcement officer, Muffin. Hacking their database isn't simple. Takes more than a couple of days to do it right if I don't want to get caught, and I don't."

"Chicken shit," Mal said.

Hacker rolled his eyes. "I *am* chicken, dude.

Because if Viper or Ghost catch me, I could be in big trouble. And don't think Muffin wouldn't be in trouble with me. The commander and his deputy aren't stupid. I like my life the way it is, thanks."

Ry liked his too. Especially now that Alaina was in it. She'd surprised the hell out of him in bed. She was demure right up until the moment she got turned on. Then she was vocal and assertive about what she liked and wanted. She'd told him to fuck her. Then she'd taken him hard and given him back everything he gave to her. The more he pushed, the more she took. They'd fucked each other like they were starved. Like coming was the only thing that'd keep them alive another day.

Shit. He felt the tingling in his balls, the telltale stirring that meant he was about to get hard if he didn't redirect his thoughts. He focused on the dudes around him. Worked like a charm since the only dick he was fond of was his own.

"Could also be a rando," Zany said. "Doesn't have to be Foss or Keith Herbert."

Ry wanted to growl. "Yeah, I know. Fucking hell, this sucks."

"Considering where she works, it's possible some jackass targeted her just for being there," Easy said. "Angry boyfriends or husbands who want to teach uppity women a lesson."

Men like her fucking father.

"She could have been the unlucky one," Mal

added. "If some dude was hanging around watching the place, he might have followed her home and realized she was an easy target out there in the woods."

"Yeah," Ry said. "At this point, anything's possible. Still seems off, though. You'd think an angry man who wanted to teach a woman a lesson would resort to sexual assault, but she wasn't raped. Hell, for that matter, I'd expect Herbert or Foss to have raped her before they beat her up and dumped her."

"So we're back to the random meth head," Saint said. "Somebody like that only wants their next score and it doesn't matter how they get it."

They all knew that people had killed for much less than twenty dollars. Made no damned sense, but it happened all the time.

"You'd think they'd have broken into the RV to look for more shit they could take," Jake "Harley" Ryan said. "Things to sell."

"Maybe she disturbed them before they could. Then they panicked," Gem said.

"Jesus," Ry grated. "Too many fucking variables and not enough answers. I want to fix this for her. Make sure she's safe and doesn't have to constantly watch for trouble."

Saint put a hand on his shoulder. "I know, Muff. We're right there with you. She's important to you, and that makes her important to us."

"I'll get into the sheriff's department," Hacker said. "Just give me some time."

"Appreciate all of you," Ry said, his throat tight.

"Anything for family." Mal wrapped an arm around his shoulder and squeezed. "You know that."

Yeah, he knew it. And he was fucking grateful for it.

Chapter Fifteen

AFTER ALAINA TOOK EVERETT TO SCHOOL, SHE WENT
to the center and spent the morning cleaning. She
daydreamed about Ryder. About the way he'd kissed
her like he owned her, the way he'd gone down on her
and made her lose her mind last night, and the way
he'd fucked her like he knew exactly what she needed.

She'd slept more soundly in his arms than she'd
slept in forever. And no wonder considering how
they'd worn each other out. When he woke her that
morning with his fingers stroking her clit, she'd been
surprised at how desperately she'd wanted him inside
her again.

If sex was always this good, then it was a crime
she'd gone without for so many years. Except she
didn't remember it being quite so satisfying with
Clint. Maybe she'd been too inexperienced to know

what she needed, or maybe Ryder was just that much better.

Her pussy was a little sore after so long unused, but the payoff was worth it. Alaina thought of Ryder pistoning into her this morning, catching her just right, making her come so hard she bit his shoulder to stop herself from crying out. He'd finished with a deep groan into the pillow, hips jerking with his release. She'd apologized for biting him, but he'd laughed it off and told her she could bite him anytime if it made her come like that.

She'd gone to the guest room and gotten into bed, but she'd been lonely in a way she hadn't felt in a long time. That bothered her more than she liked. She'd spent one night in Ryder's bed, and already she craved him. How the hell was she going to broach the subject with Everett? He was old enough to sleep alone, of course, but he wasn't a dumb kid and he'd know that Mommy was sleeping in the same bed with Mr. Ryder. Which made things complicated.

Not because Everett had any idea what was going on in Ryder's bed, but because that was a mighty big step to take with a man she'd known almost a month. Taking Everett from *Mr. Ryder is a friend* to *Mr. Ryder is Mommy's boyfriend* was a giant leap in her mind. And it would be in his, too.

No matter how much she wanted to be with Ryder, she had to think of Everett first. Had to figure out how to protect his innocent heart should things go wrong between her and Ryder. But how to do that?

Alaina was no closer to solving any of it when she finished work, picked up Everett, and drove out to Ryder's place. Her heart beat a little faster at the prospect of going there without Ryder at home to protect them. She couldn't always be scared, though. She wanted to be normal again.

And she would be. She ran through her mental checklist. She knew how to defend herself if someone grabbed her. She had pepper spray and a whistle. She was also good at watching her surroundings. In fact, she noticed a truck following her at a distance for a few miles, but she kept an eye on it. She was making plans to drive past Ryder's house and work her way back toward town when the truck turned. She blew out a slow breath and kept driving.

No such thing as being too cautious. Ryder had assured her it was okay to be a bit paranoid. That feeling would ebb over time.

"When is Mr. Ryder coming home?" Everett asked when they drove up to his house. The lake view struck Alaina anew every time. She loved the view, couldn't believe she got to live here. It was peaceful, despite the fact she'd been floating out there on the water. Since she didn't remember it, the lake didn't upset her.

There were no cars in Ryder's driveway and no sign of anyone. Ryder had called a plumber to fix the pipe, but the man wasn't due out until Wednesday. Funny how she now wished he couldn't make it for a few more days. As much as she'd wanted her own space for her and Everett, she wanted to stay in Ryder's bed every night. Wasn't going to be easy when she was in the cottage and he was in his house. And he wasn't going to be able to spend the night with her, either. Not with Everett on his cot behind the screen and her bedroom right next door.

"He called earlier and said around six." She hadn't expected a call, but the second she saw his name on her phone, she couldn't answer fast enough. His voice alone made her wet. She'd imagined all the things he'd do to her later, then laughed when he'd asked if she was paying attention to anything he said. When she admitted she'd been fantasizing, he'd whispered dirty things that had her thighs clenching. Then he'd had to go, and she'd felt as if the sun had gone behind a cloud.

"Will he eat dinner with us?"

"Of course, pumpkin. He's bringing pizza."

"Yum!"

Everett just had pizza on Saturday, but since pizza was his favorite, she'd known there would be no complaints.

"I like living with Mr. Ryder. His house is big and it smells nice."

Alaina's belly fluttered at the idea of living with

Ryder, but then her common sense told her she needed to address what Everett said.

"I know, sweetie. But you know we don't really live with Mr. Ryder, right? We live next door."

"I know. But we stay with him more than we stay over there. Plus I've got a bedroom at his house."

Her heart ached.

"That's true, we do stay there a bit, but we have a broken water pipe and we can't stay in our own home right now. And Mommy is in the room with you at Mr. Ryder's, right?"

"But we could move your bed to another room. Or you could stay with Mr. Ryder. Nate says men and women like to sleep together in the same bed."

Alaina nearly choked. "Well, yes, that does happen sometimes when people like each other a lot. But we'll go back to our little home soon."

The thought was depressing after one night in Ryder's bed. She wanted to wake up every morning with him, go to sleep in his arms, and feel like a family for the first time in her life. Maybe she wanted it too much.

Probably did, but she was happy for a change. Not so worried about making ends meet, though of course she intended to work as hard as ever to take care of her child. But she knew if she needed help, Ryder was there. His friends were there. Maybe they were her friends now, too. She hoped so. She still had Stacie,

Bridget, and Lidia, but it was nice to have a few more friends to count on.

"Don't you like Mr. Ryder?" Everett asked.

Alaina's face was hot. "Um, yes, I like him."

"Then you should sleep in his bed and I can have my own room."

Oh lord. Alaina turned to look her kid in the eye. "No more talk of Mommy and Mr. Ryder sharing a room, okay? Adults like to make up their own minds about these things, and it takes time."

His little face fell. Then he sighed dramatically. "Okay."

He couldn't have said it more exaggeratedly if he'd tried. *This kid.*

"Now give me a minute to text Miss Jenna and we'll go inside."

Alaina looked at the house and surroundings while she texted Jenna and told her she was home. She'd promised Ryder she would, plus it made her feel a little safer that someone knew where she was. She'd asked why she couldn't just text him, but he'd told her he often couldn't take his phone into parts of the building where he worked and he might not see a text.

Jenna texted back immediately. *Text me when you get inside so I know everything is okay.*

Alaina smiled as a sense of belonging flared to life inside. *I will.*

"Come on, sweetie. Let's go in."

Everett got out of the car and ran to the door.

Alaina made sure she'd gotten all her stuff, then she locked the Toyota and went over to let them inside. The house was quiet. Once more her breath was taken by the view out the windows. It would be even better in mid to late April when everything was bloomed and green. She could picture hydrangeas beneath the shade tree near the water, their fat blooms attracting bees and perfuming the air.

If Ryder would agree to buy some hydrangeas, she'd plant them. There were other flowers she wanted too, but that could wait. She imagined having a table and chairs in the garden, eating meals out there in the evenings, and watching the sunset. It was Ryder's home, not hers, but she could envision it all. Maybe he would love her vision, too.

After they were settled inside and she'd texted Jenna the all clear, Alaina fixed Everett a snack, then sat him down at the table to do homework while she made good on her promise to clean Ryder's house in exchange for a reduced rent. She stripped the beds, did laundry, and scrubbed the bathrooms. She was in the groove, getting things done, when Everett called to her.

"Mommy?"

She picked up the laundry basket with clean sheets and walked into the living room. "Yes, honey?"

Her baby was looking at her with innocent blue eyes. "I saw a man."

"A man? Where?" Her heart beat in her throat,

but she told herself it was possible the plumber had come out early. He hadn't rung the bell, though.

Everett pointed, and Alaina followed his gaze to the cottage.

"Really? What did he look like?" She tried to keep fear from coloring her voice, but she could hear it. She hoped Everett did not.

There's nothing to fear. Could be the plumber. Could be a hiker. You're inside and they're outside. You have pepper spray and a phone.

"He had a jacket and a baseball cap with a bird. And he wore brown pants."

"Could you see his face?"

Everett shook his head. "I looked up because I was thinking. He was standing by our house, looking in the window."

Alaina's heart throbbed. Looking in the window? "Did you see where he went?"

Everett pointed. "That way."

Into the woods. Alaina peered toward the woods, but she couldn't see anything. The trees were leafing out and providing plenty of cover these days. She went to the front of the house, looking to see if someone had parked out there and she just hadn't heard them.

But there were no cars.

She thought about calling Jenna, but what would she say? That Everett saw a man and he went into the woods? She could tell Ryder that when he got home. It was nothing to panic over.

Alaina went to the kitchen to dry the dishes she'd washed so she could keep an eye on the backyard and woods. After she finished, she went back to the laundry room to throw some more clothes into the washer and turn on the dryer. The dryer balls knocked against the drum as she carried a load of clothing to the dining room to fold it on one end of the table.

She'd just yanked one of Everett's shirts from the basket when a knock on the door startled her enough to make her jump. Was the man back? Had he gone around to the front of the house when she wasn't looking?

"Want me to get it, Mommy?"

"No, sweetie. Mommy will see who's there. Remember, we don't answer the door unless we know who it is."

"Yes, ma'am."

The knock came again, harder this time, and Alaina forced herself to move toward the front door. Her feet were leaden, and her heart pounded double time. She should have grabbed something to use as a weapon. The story Ryder had told her about Jenna disabling a mafia enforcer with her car keys came to mind. She picked up her keys, putting one between her third and fourth fingers. If someone tried to get inside, she'd stab them in the eye just like Jenna had.

Alaina trembled as she put her eye to the peep-hole. When she saw the man on the other side, relief and annoyance flooded her in equal measure. She thought about pretending she wasn't home, but her car was in the drive and he would know better.

She slid the chain from the lock and opened the door. "Hi, Deputy Foss. Can I help you?"

Chapter Sixteen

When Ry pulled up to his house, a sheriff's vehicle sat in the drive behind Alaina's car. A deputy stood on the front porch, talking to Alaina. She'd closed the door behind her and her arms were crossed over her chest. Her posture was defensive, and the deputy loomed over her.

Patrick fucking Foss.

Ry didn't bother parking in the garage. He stopped in the driveway and got out, shouldering his backpack and grabbing the pizza boxes, then strode onto the front porch with all the swagger of a man intending to protect what was his. Alaina looked relieved to see him while Foss looked angry. The other man took a step back as if he'd been caught doing something he shouldn't.

The jury was still out over whether or not Foss was

her attacker, which meant Ry wasn't going to obliterate him here and now, but he damned sure didn't like coming home and finding the man bothering her.

"Babe," Ry said, dropping the backpack and setting the pizza boxes on the small table by the door. He held out an arm. Alaina came to him and he tucked her into his side, kissing her on top of the head as he did so.

Mine.

Foss eyed them, brows drawn low, anger etched on his features. His gaze dropped to the patches on Ry's camouflage uniform. Special Operations Command. Expert marksman. Master parachute badge. If Foss knew what they meant, he didn't let it show.

"Deputy," Ry said coolly. "You find out who attacked Alaina?"

She slipped an arm around him and leaned into him with a hand on his belly. Every protective instinct he had flared to life for her. Alaina was his. His to take care of, his to fuck, *his.* It was more than that, but he didn't know what to call it yet.

All he knew was she belonged to him. Everett too. He didn't know the first thing about being a father figure, but he could learn. He loved seeing the kid happy as he played ball with a bunch of grown men and laughed his butt off as he made goals. He loved the sounds Alaina made when she came, the way her eyes sparkled when she looked at her kid, how protective she was of his emotions and his heart. The two of them filled a hole in his life that'd been there since he was a lonely boy trying to make sense of his sister's death and his parents' distance.

And if this fucker thought he was gonna make Alaina uncomfortable by continuing to harass her, he was sorely mistaken.

"We're working on it," Foss said. "I just stopped by to check on Miss Montgomery and her son, make sure they're doing all right out here."

Alaina's fingers curled in his uniform shirt. Like she was warning him not to make a big deal of it. What she didn't know was that he had no plans to do so.

"We're fine, like I said," she told him. "Thanks for your concern."

Ry squeezed her. "Yeah, thanks for checking in. Alaina and her boy are doing well. I've made it my mission to ensure their safety. Anybody tries to get to Alaina, they have to go through me. That's not an easy thing to do, I promise you."

Foss sneered. "You can't stop a bullet, Sergeant."

"Maybe not, but somebody better make damned sure their aim is perfect and they've got some distance between us. Otherwise I'm taking 'em down and feeding their gun to 'em piece by piece."

Foss put on his hat and gave them a nod before stalking down the stairs and over to his car. He got in, reversed, and drove away without a backward glance. Alaina seemed to melt a little as he disappeared. Tension draining away, which pissed him the fuck off.

But first he had to take care of her. He turned her with his hands on her shoulders. She gazed up at him, green eyes piercing his heart in a way he couldn't explain.

"You okay, honey?"

"Now that you're here, yes."

Ry's gut churned. "What did he want, Alaina?"

"The usual. To warn me off you, to tell me how much he cares, to try and talk me into sleeping with him. Secretly, of course, because he needs time to break things off with Bridget. Oh, and he'll protect me from harm while he's at it."

It was a good thing Foss was gone because Ry had an overwhelming urge to show the guy what a trained operator could do to an enemy.

"He been bothering you at work?"

She looked away. "Not really. He said something the first day I was back, but nothing since. That's why I didn't tell you. I thought he'd gotten the message."

Men like Foss didn't get the message. He was the type who went into law enforcement or the military because he liked having power over others. He thought if he pushed hard enough, he'd get what he wanted. That he was owed it somehow.

"Doesn't look like it."

"I know. I'm sorry. I should have told you."

Ry tipped her chin up and dropped his mouth to

hers for a quick kiss. Because he'd been dying to kiss her since he'd left her this morning.

Her mouth opened, and she touched her tongue to his. Just like that, his dick started to respond. He stepped in closer, wrapped her in his arms again. She clung to him, her fingers curling into his shoulders, a sigh coming from her throat.

And then she stiffened and pushed him away. He let her. "Everett's inside," she whispered.

Ry nodded, his dick aching with the need to get inside *her*. "You can tell me if Foss hits on you, Alaina. I want to know if he keeps doing it or if he's getting the message you're with me."

"I will. I promise. I just—after the last time, I thought he was done. I told him I wouldn't hurt Bridget that way. I thought he understood."

"Just a guess, babe, but I don't think he's the kind of guy who understands why he shouldn't be trying to cheat on his girlfriend with one of her friends. He gets a kick out of it."

Alaina frowned. "I think you're right. I just hope he finds someone else to pursue besides me. And that Bridge figures it out before it's too late." She looked troubled. "I wish I could tell her, but I don't think she'd believe me."

"Why not?"

"Because she's crazy for him. She has a giant blind spot where he's concerned. I'm not the only one who's noticed. Stacie said there was a counselor that used to work at the center about a year ago who told Bridget about Foss harassing her. She was fired two weeks later and left town. I'd rather not end up the same way."

"Understood. But don't keep it from me, babe. I promise you I'm not a loose cannon. I'm not going to go after him and get myself arrested. I *will* make sure he gets the message, though. There are ways that have nothing to do with violence. You have to trust me on that."

"I do, Ryder." She dragged in a breath. "There's something else you should know. Everett saw a man looking in the window of the cottage about an hour ago. I didn't see anyone, but I believe him because he doesn't make stuff up. I didn't go outside and look, but there was no car I could see from the windows. I didn't hear one, but then I didn't hear Deputy Foss drive up either because I'd just turned on the dryer and the dryer balls were banging around too loud."

Ry didn't like the sound of that. "You tell Foss about it?"

"I did. He said it was probably somebody looking for a good fishing hole or taking a short cut. I thought it might've been the plumber coming for a quick look, but he wouldn't go to the woods."

"True. Foss could be right though."

He didn't tell her it could also be somebody looking for homes to break into. If she'd been attacked by someone looking for drug money, maybe they'd expanded their range to give them more prospects.

Fuck.

"I'll have a look around after we get the pizza inside."

"Okay. Can I help?"

He slung the backpack over his shoulder and picked up the boxes. "You can open the door for me."

She stood on tiptoe and gave him a quick kiss. "I can do that, sexy man."

Just like that, he was hard. Thankfully, it wasn't going to be obvious when he walked inside. Camo was good for more than hiding in jungles and deserts.

"Damn, girl, I really want the right to kiss you in front of your boy," he growled.

"I want it too. I'm going to work on it, prepare the ground."

He kissed her again, then dragged himself away. "Open the door before the pizza gets cold, babe."

She grinned as she did so.

Everett jumped up from the table when Ry strode into the kitchen. "Mr. Ryder! You brought pizza!"

Alaina laughed behind him. "I told you he was bringing it. Did you forget, silly?"

"I didn't forget. I'm just excited!"

"Me, too," Ry said. "Pizza's my favorite."

Coming from western New York, he'd grown up surrounded by Italians. Pizza was an art form back home. He'd found a place near work that made proper New York-style pizza, and he'd gone there before heading home today.

"Can you set the table?" Alaina asked Everett as she arranged the pizza boxes on the counter.

"Yes, ma'am."

Ry watched Everett get napkins, plates, and utensils from all the right places. He glanced at Alaina. She looked a little uncertain.

"What?" he asked.

"It's your house. I should have asked you where you wanted to eat. And maybe not demonstrated that my kid knows where all your stuff is like we live here or something."

Ry laughed. "He's a smart kid, Alaina. I'm happy he knows where everything is. I like coming home to you two."

Her smile was soft and sweet. He wanted to bend her backward over the sink and kiss the daylights out of her. Not happening, but he wanted it.

"I better go look around outside," he said. "You two eat without me."

Alaina shook her head. "No, we'll wait. Everett," she called so he could hear her, "we need to wait for Mr. Ryder to do something outside before we eat. How about you show me your homework while he does that?"

Everett skipped around the table and grabbed his notebook before he skipped over to Alaina. Ry loved how the kid took things in stride. It was all due to

Alaina. She was a great mother. It bothered him that she'd wondered for even a second if Everett would've had a better life if she'd given him up. The answer was obvious to Ry.

He went into the bedroom to get one of his personal weapons since his service weapons stayed at work. He punched in the code to open the safe and took out a Glock 19, popped in an extended mag, and tucked it in a holster under his shirt.

There were footprints down by the water. Hiking boots, size ten or twelve, probably. The footprints were also in the mud near where the pipe had burst, and mud had been tracked around the cottage. There was no sign of anyone trying to force their way inside, though.

Ry followed the trail to the woods, stepping beneath the canopy to look for signs of the man's passing. He followed a trail of tamped down grass and leaves until it opened into a bigger clearing and the tracks disappeared. There was a discarded candy bar wrapper in the clearing, but that didn't mean the man had dropped it. Judging by the faded graphics, the damn thing could have blown through on a storm.

Ry stood and listened for any other movement, but all he heard was birdsong and the occasional squirrel scratching in the leaves. If someone had been there, they were long gone by now.

He growled in frustration. Too bad Deputy Foss

hadn't stopped bothering Alaina long enough to check it out. He might have caught the guy if he had.

Ry turned and headed back toward the house. He'd made Alaina and Everett wait long enough for dinner. He didn't know who'd been poking around his property, but he didn't like it. He'd have to get some trail cams up as soon as he could. Until then, he was keeping Alaina close.

That was something he didn't mind that at all.

———

EVERETT WENT to bed at eight, but of course he didn't stay there. He emerged twenty minutes later wanting a glass of water. Then he wanted cheese. Then he wanted Ryder to read him a bedtime story. By the time he fell asleep for real, it was after nine and Alaina was convinced it would never happen.

Some days were like that. Some days the kid collapsed and couldn't be dragged from bed by lions. Other days, he didn't want to sleep and kept trying to find creative ways to stay awake with the grown-ups.

Mostly, it was Ryder he wanted to hang out with. They'd had pizza together, then Ryder took Everett outside and threw a football back and forth as the sky turned orange and purple. Alaina finished the laundry and made the beds before they came back inside. Then it was time to get Everett into the bath and ready for bed, and that's when the pushback began.

First he didn't want to bathe, then he didn't want to sleep. Ryder intervened a couple of times, telling Everett that he loved baths and took them as often as he could, and that getting lots of sleep made little boys grow into big strong men. Everett's whining didn't stop entirely, but it slowed after that.

"You think he's staying there?" Ryder asked when Alaina came out of the bedroom for the fifth time that night.

"I think so. He was sleeping for real, not just closing his eyes because I told him to."

"Damn, don't think I realized it could be so hard to get a kid to sleep."

He had that shell-shocked look she recognized from her first time dealing with a child who kept finding excuses not to go to bed. It was old hat now, and she knew the key was to keep insisting, not to relent. Let him stay up past bedtime once and he'd badger her every night from now on.

"You just have to be more determined than they are."

Ryder scratched his head. "I'd have made a deal with him. That would have been a bad move, wouldn't it?"

She laughed. "Oh yeah. Never let them know they have bargaining power. You will live to regret it."

"No deals. Got it." He grinned and held out his hand. She took it and he pulled her down beside him on the couch. "How long do we have to wait?"

She lay her head back against his shoulder and traced his lips with her finger. "An hour should be safe."

Ryder reached down to adjust himself. "I'll live. Barely. Want to be inside you again, Alaina."

He'd changed into jeans and a T-shirt after dinner. She kind of wished he'd kept the uniform on. It was hot. But his massive dick pressing against his jeans was hot too. She wanted to touch him, but that would have to wait. Her pussy clenched with need.

"I can't wait."

When an hour went by and Everett didn't emerge again, Alaina went to peek at him. He was sound asleep, thank God. She walked into the living room with a smile on her face and an ache in her core.

"Still asleep."

Ryder launched himself from the couch and stalked over to her. He loomed over her like an avenging angel, but he didn't scare her. No, he made her feel safe and protected. He dug his hands into her ass and lifted her high as she wrapped her legs around his waist.

"Thank fuck," he groaned before he kissed her the way she'd been dying for all day.

His tongue speared into her mouth. His hard cock nestled against her clit. She wiggled her hips to increase the delicious pressure.

"Bed. Now," he growled, nipping her lips as he started to walk them to the bedroom.

"Door," he said, and she reached down to open it. Then they were inside and he toed it closed. She twisted the lock for good measure. If Everett woke up, he'd call for her. But at least he wouldn't walk in on the middle of anything.

She'd worry about how to explain her presence in Ryder's room if it happened. Then again, Everett already had a reason why they should sleep in the same room so maybe it wouldn't be so hard after all.

Ryder slid her down his body, stripping her shirt on the way. Then he tugged his off with that one-hand-behind-the-back trick she found so sexy. Alaina smoothed her palms over his pecs, down across the ridges of his stomach. She'd never seen a stomach like that on a person before.

And his teammates called him Muffin. Irony at its finest.

They shed their clothes fast, then Ryder pushed her onto the bed and buried his face between her legs like he had last night. Alaina's heart pounded nearly out of her chest as he devoured her, flicking his tongue and then sucking as he thrust two fingers inside her and found that spot that drove her wild. It took her no time at all to fly apart, gasping his name as she worked not to scream.

Ryder kissed the insides of her thighs, giving her time to breathe and find herself again. Then he licked her once more, and she trembled with the effort not to come immediately. Didn't take long before she broke apart beneath him, stuffing her fist against her mouth and biting her own knuckles to keep quiet.

"Been thinking about this all day, babe," Ryder said as he trailed kisses up her abdomen, beneath her breasts, licking each nipple before sucking it hard enough to make her whimper. Not in pain, though. In need. She'd been neglected for so long that her body craved what he did to her.

"Me too," she whispered.

He traced his fingers along her ribs, under her breasts, taking his sweet time giving her his cock. "You're gorgeous, you know that?"

She ran her fingers over his jaw and into his hair. She loved touching him. Having the right to touch him. He made her happier than she'd thought possible. Maybe it was reckless of her, but right now she was going to enjoy the ride. "So are you."

His grin lit her up from the inside. "I'm glad you think so."

She wrapped her other hand around his big cock, and he hissed in a breath. The spark between them flared bright once more as their hands and mouths took over, touching, tasting, teasing.

Ryder grabbed a condom from the nightstand, sheathed himself, and flipped her over until her ass was in the air and her legs spread. Alaina clutched a pillow to her chest as he filled her.

"God, that's good," he said, his hands on her hips, his cock buried to the hilt inside her. "I love being with you, Alaina. Fucking you like this. I had a hard time thinking of anything else all day."

"I love it too. Please, please, *please* start moving. Make me come again."

"Anything you need, honey. You tell me."

He pulled out and slammed deep again, and Alaina moaned into the pillow. It had never been this good before. She hadn't known what she needed with Clint. Now she did. Not that he could have given it to her.

But Ryder could.

"Touch me," she gasped.

He slicked his fingers over her clit, pinching, tugging, rubbing, until she was a quivering mass of nerve endings. He didn't let her come, though. It was like he knew just how much to give her, just how hard to fuck, to prolong the pleasure and anticipation.

When he finally bent his body over hers, his chest to her back, his cock driving deep, his fingers plucking her like an instrument, she exploded, her eyes squeezing shut as white-hot stars burst behind her lids. Alaina trembled and cried out until her legs were jelly.

Ryder didn't let her sag to the mattress when she was spent. He wrapped an arm beneath her, cementing her to him while he fucked her harder and faster, slamming into her until his orgasm ripped through him and he gasped her name against the damp skin of her neck.

Then they collapsed together, his bigger body

pressing hers down into the mattress, his cock twitching inside her as the last of his release vibrated through him. She loved how he dominated her and managed to be gentle too. It was a turn on like none other.

"That was fucking fantastic," he growled, nipping her ear. "I want you again. Just as soon as I fucking recover."

Alaina panted from the exertion. "Same. But I get to be on top next time."

"Babe, you can be anywhere you want to be so long as it's sitting on my face or riding my dick." He rolled her with him until her back was to his front. "Gotta go get rid of the condom."

She sighed. "I have an implant," she whispered. "If you, you know. Wanted to, um… So long as you're safe too."

He laughed softly against her shoulder. "You can tell me to fuck you, but you can't tell me I can go bare inside you? That's cute, babe."

Alaina colored. "That was before. This is now."

He sucked her earlobe. "You mean you were horny before but now you aren't? Like I said, cute. And I'm safe. This body is a temple, honey. I haven't been a priest or anything, but I always wrap it up before going in." He nuzzled her neck, and the spark of desire in her belly grew into a flame. "Until you, Alaina. Because the next time I'm balls deep inside you, there's not gonna be a thing between us but skin."

The mattress dipped as he got up and went into the bathroom. He was only gone a few moments, but by the time he returned, she'd lost the battle with sleep.

Chapter Seventeen

Ry snapped awake early, some sixth sense stirring deep inside. A glance at his phone told him it was four in the morning. Beside him, Alaina slept soundly. He didn't wake her since she had another hour before she needed to head back to the room she shared with Everett. Instead, he eased from the bed and dragged on his jeans. He palmed the Glock and moved silently out of the bedroom and into the kitchen.

Everything was quiet, but that unease sat heavy on his heart. He crossed to the windows along the back of the house to peer outside, but it was too dark to see anything. There were no streetlights out here, no house lights from next door. There were only the exterior lights from his house, and he shut those off when he went to bed because why be a beacon in the night?

He added a couple more motion-sensor lights to his mental list of security components he needed to get. He was still going over it in his head when a light flashed in the woods from the direction he'd gone earlier today.

He watched and waited for a minute, but it didn't come again. He considered going after the person, because he could sneak up on a friggin' mouse when necessary, but the unease in his gut told him not to leave Alaina and Everett. They were safer with him.

Which wasn't going to do a damned bit of good if Strike Team 2 had to bug out for a mission anytime soon. It was a distinct possibility if the All Hands Meeting they'd attended today was any indication. The world was filled with hotspots, some hotter than others, and they were currently down a team.

Strike Team 6 had been exposed to a potential biological weapon and were being monitored in a secure, undisclosed facility. Which meant his team was on deck again.

Fuck.

He watched the woods a bit longer, then decided he wasn't going back to bed tonight. Much as he'd like to wake Alaina for another round, she needed the sleep instead. He went into the kitchen and started the coffee. He didn't turn the lights on in case someone was still in the woods. He wanted to see out, not have them see in.

Maybe they'd venture closer, or maybe it'd just been an illegal hunter spotlighting game and they were already gone.

About twenty minutes later, he heard the door to his bedroom open. Alaina emerged, yawning, her hair twisted up on her head in a loose knot. She'd dragged on his T-shirt, and it swam on her. He loved the way it looked. The way she looked in it.

His woman.

"You're up early," she said. "And why are you in the dark?"

He tugged her to him, slid his hands beneath the shirt to cup her pretty little ass, and dragged her against him for a kiss. "Couldn't sleep. And I like the dark. I can see you just fine."

"I can see you, too. You could have woke me up, though. For you know," she finished, waggling her eyebrows.

He laughed and set her away. He loved how she could be a juxtaposition of shy and bold at the same time. She fascinated him. "Wanted to, believe me. But I thought I might have worn you out last night."

"Puh-leeze. It was only once. I could have done it again."

"You fell asleep before I got back from the bathroom." He'd gone to throw out the condom and when he'd returned, she'd been passed out cold. Just when he'd been looking forward to going bare, too.

"I'd have happily woke up for more you."

He liked the way that made him feel inside. Warm. Happy. That persistent undercurrent of loss that'd dogged his life since Sheri's death didn't seem so huge with Alaina near. He needed to tell her about Sheri, but it was something that required a stiff drink and broad daylight. The shadows were too dark right now, and the unease still sat heavy in his gut.

"Coffee?" he asked, going over to pour a cup.

"Sure."

He fixed it with cream the way she liked, then took her hand and pulled her over to the table. In summer, he looked forward to heading outside to watch the sunrise while sitting on the dock with his coffee. Too chilly for that now.

"Need to talk to you, Alaina."

She cradled her cup in both hands. "Uh-oh," she said light-heartedly, but he could see the apprehension she tried to hide.

"Hey, it's nothing bad. Not about us anyway." He took a breath. Then he told her about the possibility the team could go on a mission sooner than expected and that he wanted her to stay in town with Jenna if it happened.

She frowned, then shook her head. "That's not necessary, Ryder. I'm doing okay. Everett and I will be fine here. And I don't want to be a burden to Jenna. She's been so nice already."

Ryder tipped her chin up and made her look at him. "Babe, it's what we do for each other. We're a family, me and my team. Our women are part of the team, too. You and Everett are part of us now."

Her eyes glittered. She pulled away and shook her

head. "You can't say that, not really. We haven't known each other long enough. We're having sex. We've spent two nights together. That doesn't make us a family."

He was determined not to let that hurt. He knew she was afraid, but he wasn't letting her push him away that easily.

"We've had sex two nights in a row, but we've spent more time together than that. This is more than sex, babe."

"Ryder—"

"Shh, let me explain. I don't have a problem finding women to fuck. I'm not saying that to piss you off, but sex is not something I'm desperate for or grateful for. I can get it in any bar or nightclub anytime I want it. I didn't move you into the cottage, be nice to you, be nice to Everett, just so I could eventually fuck you. If fucking is all it is, I could fuck someone else. You understand me?"

Her eyes were a little wide, but she nodded.

"Good," he said, tucking a stray lock of hair that'd dropped from her bun behind her ear. "I like you, Alaina. I like Everett. Makes me feel good having you both around. You feel like family to me. And since you're family to me, you're family to my team. Got that?"

"Yes." Her pulse thrummed in her throat. He knew this was difficult for her because she was used to being alone and taking care of herself and her kid without help. The people in her life who should have been there for her in the past had abandoned her when she needed them most. Made it hard to trust. He didn't blame her for that, but he wanted to prove he was different.

"I'm not going anywhere, Alaina. I'll go on missions out of the country, but I'm not fucking around with you. I want to see where this goes between us. You feel me?"

Her expression was doubtful. But then she smiled, and he felt like he'd been given a gift. "Yes, Ryder. I feel you."

He threaded his fingers in hers and kissed the back of her hand. She stroked his hair, and he turned into her touch like a cat seeking scratches.

"There's another reason I want you to stay with Jenna if I'm gone," he said. "Someone was out there in the woods tonight. Maybe the same someone Everett saw, maybe not. Could just be someone spotlighting game illegally, but with everything that's happened, I'd feel a lot better if you and Everett went into town if the team deploys."

Alaina swallowed. "Do you think the person who attacked me could do it again?"

"I don't know, babe. If the police are right, it was a random assault with robbery as the motive. Unlikely it'd happen again."

"But if they're wrong, then it's possible."

He skimmed her lips with his thumb. "We've got

no reason to think they're wrong. I'm fucking pissed at their lack of progress on catching the asshole, but that doesn't mean they're mistaken. I want you in town because I don't know who's out there or what they're doing. I plan to get a security system set up, with trail cams, but that's gonna take a little bit of time."

"Okay, Ryder. We'll go stay with Jenna if necessary."

Relief rolled through him. "Thank you, honey. I appreciate that. Better to be on the safe side."

She nibbled her lip. "How much notice will we get if you have to go?"

"Not much. A few hours. Maybe a day."

She seemed to take it in stride. "So do I call Jenna or what?"

"She'll know the team's deploying when you do. She'll probably call you if you don't get to her first."

Alaina frowned as she nodded. "I'm still scared, Ryder. I hate being scared. Not knowing if it could happen again. I do think it was random, but it bothers me they haven't caught the person who did it. What if I'm unlucky enough to be in the wrong place again?"

Ry kissed her forehead. "That's not going to happen, babe. We've got a plan, and you know how to fight back. You're going to be fine. We're gonna get through this, okay?"

"Okay. I trust you, Ryder. That scares me too, but I do."

"I know. But I've got you. You aren't alone."

"You shower yet?" she asked.

"No."

She threaded her fingers in his. "Me neither, and it's still over an hour before Everett wakes up."

Ry was already getting hard. "You want to shower with me?"

"Oh, I definitely do. Start my day right with an orgasm or two."

Ry stood and tugged her up with him. "Sounds like a winning plan to me."

———

THE GO ORDER came two days later. Ry's gut sank like a stone when Ghost walked in and told them a team of paleontologists from the Smithsonian had been taken hostage in Acamar and Strike Team 2 was being tasked with their rescue.

"You're under lockdown, boys," Ghost said. "Inform your families you aren't coming home, and let's get busy planning the extraction."

Ry called Alaina, closing his eyes when her voice came on the line. Fucking hell this was harder than he thought. He understood what the other guys went through now. The reason they seemed so morose in those moments before their training kicked in and they went to work. Leaving behind your heart wasn't easy.

"Hi, honey." His throat was tight. Goddammit.

"Babe," she said happily. "I'm still thinking about that move last night. The way you made me nearly pass out, it felt so good. I can't wait to do it again tonight. Oh, and Everett's having a sleepover with Carter Friday night, so we can be as loud as we want. I really, *really* want to be loud with you."

"Baby, I'm sorry," he began. "I'm not coming home tonight."

"Oh." He could hear the disappointment in her voice. "Is this what we talked about before? Or have you found true love and this is how you're letting me down easy?"

It took him a second to realize she was joking with him. "Told you this is more than sex, Alaina. I'm sorry I won't be there, honey. Believe me, I want nothing more than to come home to you and Everett tonight."

He wanted to say so much more in that moment. Wanted to tell her about Sheri because she was the first person he'd felt like he could tell, and he wanted to tell her how much she meant to him. How, though he'd only known her a short time, he knew she was the one. He wanted to be a dad to Everett, though it scared him because it was a serious responsibility, and he wanted to be the man she knew she could always rely on.

But he didn't want to scare her. It was too much, too soon, and Alaina had already had too many broken promises in her life. If he said those things, he'd overwhelm her, and he wasn't going to be there to prove he meant it.

"I want you to come home, too," she said softly. She sniffled, and his heart nearly broke. "Be safe, Ryder. Please be safe."

"That's the plan, baby. Tell Everett I'm sorry I can't play ball with him tonight, but we'll do it when I get back, okay?"

"I will." She sounded like she was crying, and he hated it.

He gripped the phone, the words he'd never said to any woman on the tip of his tongue. But now wasn't the time to lay them on her. "Go to Jenna's. Stay in town, and I'll see you when I get home, okay?"

"Yes," she whispered. "Do you know how long you'll be gone?"

"I'm sorry, honey. I never know, but hopefully it'll be quick. I gotta go now, Alaina. There's a lot to do before wheels up."

She laughed, but he didn't think her heart was in it. "There you go hitting me with military-speak again."

"You're learning it, babe. You'll be fluent in no time."

"Bye, Ryder. I—We'll miss you."

The knot in his throat was huge. "I'll miss you both too."

He wanted to say more, but he'd already decided

it was too much for her so he ended the call and went back to where the team was preparing their gear.

Mal looped an arm around his shoulders and squeezed. "Wish I could say the first time is the worst, but it's never easy to leave the woman you love."

"What makes you think I love her?"

Mal snorted. "Dude, your eyes are as red as a college student on Spring Break."

Zany laughed nearby. "What the fuck, Mal? You mean a college student's eyes, right? Because they're drinking and partying?"

Mal rolled his eyes. "No, man. A pale-as-milk college coed in a bikini who thinks she's gonna tan but turns into a lobster instead."

"Oh Jesus," Ry said, but it worked to make him laugh. And got them to move on from the subject of him being in love with Alaina. "Only you, Mal. Only you."

"What? It's a brilliant metaphor, you dumb fuckers."

"Think you mean *simile*," Wolf said as he walked by. "A comparison that uses like or as."

Mal groaned. "Dude, you marry a journalist and think you know everything about the English language. I'll give you a pass since you're a new dad, but work on the arrogance, okay?"

"Nothing to work on when I'm right."

Easy sidled up beside Ry as Wolf and Mal continued to throw insults at each other.

"Jenna's expecting Alaina and Everett. She was planning to call her when we got off the phone. They'll be fine until you get back. The women will close ranks like always and have each other's backs."

"Thanks, man," Ry said, picturing Alaina surrounded by his teammates' women and believing she was one of them. Because she was. "I owe you."

"Nope. Were you there when we busted into that warehouse and rescued Jenna, Maggie, and Alice from Owen Fisher?"

"I was."

Easy cocked a finger gun and fired. "Bingo, my friend. No more talk about owing anyone, 'kay?"

"Yeah, got it."

That uneasy feeling was back in his gut, though, but he didn't know if it was because of the mission or because he had to leave Alaina before he'd solved anything. On some level, he felt like he was failing her.

But she wasn't stupid, and she'd take care of herself and Everett. She'd also have the Strike Team 2 women to rely on. He still didn't know who'd been out at his place, who was lurking in the woods, or whether it had a damned thing to do with her.

He also didn't know if Deputy Sleaze would use his absence to harass Alaina again. Or, worse, if he'd been the one to assault her in the first place. Hacker still wasn't into the sheriff's department servers, and he wasn't going to get in now that they had to bug out.

The timing couldn't be worse. And there was nothing Ry could do about it. He couldn't refuse to go on a mission and he couldn't call in sick. Those weren't options when the US government owned your ass.

The only option he had was to get the job done and get home again so he could protect the woman he loved and give her the life she deserved.

Chapter Eighteen

"I want to play with Mr. Ryder!" Everett whined as she broke the news to him over dinner at the Early Bird Diner with Jenna and Alice. "Why can't he come home?"

Alaina sighed and opened her arms for her child. He threw himself into them and lay his head on her lap. Across the table, Jenna looked at her in sympathy.

"Sweetie, Mr. Ryder has a very important job to do, and sometimes it takes him away for a while. He wanted to be here with us, but he can't be. He said he's sorry he can't play ball tonight, but when he gets back, y'all will have fun again, okay?"

Everett nodded even though his lip trembled. "I want to go home, Mommy."

Alaina patted his back. "Remember, we're staying with Miss Jenna and Alice until Mr. Ryder comes home again, sweetie."

He gazed up at her, tears on his lashes. "Why?"

Alaina wasn't quite sure what to say. She didn't want to scare her child by reminding him about the man he'd seen and suggesting the man was bad.

"Well, honey, Mr. Ryder asked us to stay with Miss Jenna because he didn't want us to be alone. He wanted us to have fun while he was gone."

"That's right," Jenna said. "We're going to have fun together. Do you want to sleep in a tent in the living room tonight?"

Everett turned to her with big eyes. "Can I?"

"If you want to. I'll make you an air tent like my dad used to make for me. You can put a sleeping bag in it and everything. Just like camping, but inside. We'll even make some s'mores on the stove for dessert."

"Mommy, will you camp with me?" Everett asked, his tears forgotten.

Alaina wasn't quite sure about this air tent thing, but if it helped her kid adjust to yet another house, she'd do it. "Sure, sweetie."

After Ryder had called earlier, she'd dried her tears, swallowed her despair that he was leaving, and left the break room at the center so she could finish cleaning for the day. She was down two private clients who'd found another cleaner during her recovery, but Bridget had been giving her extra hours. Today, Bridge had told her she'd decided she could use a cleaner for her house if Alaina was interested.

It was a good thing, and yet her stomach had twisted into a knot at the idea of going to Bridget's house alone. It wasn't that she didn't want to clean for her friend. It was that Patrick Foss was often there. They didn't live together, but according to Bridget it was only a matter of time before they were married and setting up house together.

Alaina had been unable to refuse her friend's sweet offer. Bridge wanted to help and Alaina was grateful for it. She only hoped Deputy Foss didn't turn up while she was there.

Alaina paid her portion of the check and then followed Jenna home. She'd already been by Ryder's to grab some things earlier. She'd gone alone, which she knew Ryder probably wouldn't like, but she'd been careful and it'd been fine.

She'd stuffed some clothing and other necessities into a duffel bag. She'd been about to leave when she strode into Ryder's room and grabbed his pillow. She'd pressed her face to it and inhaled him. Then she took it with her so she could sleep on it and feel as if he were near.

She already missed him. Badly. She'd had a crazy urge to tell him she loved him on the phone earlier, but she hadn't done it. And now she was going to spend every waking moment worrying something would happen to him and wondering if she should have just said it anyway.

Was it too soon? Maybe, but there was no doubt

she was crazy about him. Was he crazy for her? She thought so, but what if she was wrong? She'd thought Clint was crazy for her and look how that'd turned out.

Except Ryder wasn't Clint. If she thought about it hard enough, she knew there'd been red flags with Clint. He'd never wanted to take her to the places his friends hung out. If they went on a date and his friends saw them together, he never said she was his girlfriend. He'd say, "This is Alaina." Not that she was important to him or they were dating. Just her name.

She hadn't met his parents, hadn't been to any family events with him, nothing.

Ryder took her to meet his team. Said she was family. Made sure she was safe with that family while he was gone. Her eyes filled with tears. Dammit, she should have said the words when she had a chance.

Later, when they got Alice in bed and Everett fell asleep in the air tent—which was basically a duvet cover anchored with books on four corners and a box fan—Jenna poured them a glass of wine and they sat in the kitchen, talking about the men's deployment.

Jenna explained as best she could what was going on. Ryder and his team were being sent somewhere in the world to do something dangerous. When it was over, which could be anywhere from a few days to a few weeks, they'd return home. Once they were wheels up and on the way home, they'd get a message through somehow. Until then, radio silence.

"How do you do it?" Alaina asked, her heart hurting in ways that were new to her. He'd been gone a matter of hours and she craved him. Not just sex, but his arms around her. His presence in bed beside her. Feeling like he'd do anything to make her feel secure.

Jenna frowned as she studied her wine glass. "You get used to it. It's the job, and they wouldn't be the kind of men they are if they weren't willing to drop their lives at a moment's notice and go where they're needed. Admittedly, it's hard on relationships. No one on our team, but I grew up around the military and I've seen marriages fail because the military person has to deploy a lot. I knew what I was getting into, but it's still hard."

"Poor Haylee," Alaina said, thinking of the pretty woman and her baby. "Has to be even harder for her with a new baby."

"I think so, but she'd never say. That's why we get together a lot when the men are gone. Brooke and Cade live close to Dean and Haylee, so Brooke's going to go over there and help. Plus I think Haylee's mom is coming up for a visit. It was already planned, so it'll be good for Haylee to have her mom there while Dean's gone."

Alaina loved how close the women were. How they operated like a family when the men were gone. Even when the men were around, but especially when they weren't. Ryder had told her it was like that. He'd also said she was part of the family. Right now, she felt like she was. It was a feeling she wasn't used to, but she liked it very much.

Maybe it wasn't her after all. Maybe she wasn't cursed.

Maybe she'd just needed to find the right people.

———

THE FOLLOWING TUESDAY, Alaina pulled up to the brick house at the end of a dead-end road and looked for a patrol car. There wasn't one, thankfully. There were other houses on the road, but they weren't close together. She could probably be heard at the next one if she shouted, but it'd have to be very loud.

Bridget's house wasn't quite in the middle of nowhere, but it wasn't the suburbs either. Alaina texted Jenna to let her know she'd arrived. The other woman texted back immediately and told her to text again when she was inside.

Alaina had told Jenna about Deputy Foss and his harassment. Jenna had scowled and said that Foss used to harass the waitresses in the diner as well. He was known far and wide as a horn-dog. Bridget seemed to be the only person laboring under the delusion he wasn't.

Alaina went around to the trunk to get her cleaning supplies, then closed and locked her car. She climbed up the steps to the front door and inserted the key Bridget had given her. Once inside, she texted Jenna. It was a little embarrassing to text so often, but Jenna had told her if she didn't get those texts, she'd have to pile Alice into the car and go looking for Alaina.

Alaina got the message and dutifully texted.

She stood in the entry, surveying the house. She'd never been to Bridget's house before, though they'd known each other for the past six months. But if Bridget wasn't at work, she was with Patrick Foss. It wasn't like she had time to throw parties or do girls' nights.

The house wasn't a disaster zone or anything. It was neat and tidy, but Bridget had said she needed help with the deep cleaning. Alaina took her bucket to the sink, filled it with warm water, and added some white vinegar. Then she headed upstairs to the master bedroom to start there. The plan was to clean half the house today and half on Friday. Then, when she had everything deep cleaned, she'd go to once a week maintenance.

She made the bed, dusted the side tables and knickknacks—and the photographs of Bridget with Foss, who actually looked a bit handsome when he smiled—then went into the bathroom to scrub everything with cleanser. She was just swirling the toilet brush around the bowl when she heard footsteps on the stairs. Alaina's heart rocketed to her throat as she backed against one wall, nothing but a toilet brush between her and the intruder.

Had she locked the front door? She *had*, right? She'd been thinking about Bridget and Foss when she'd entered the house, and how blind Bridget was to his faults. Then she'd started to think about Ryder and how much she missed him, how she couldn't wait to get naked with him again.

Maybe she'd forgotten to lock the front door after all. But she also hadn't checked the other two doors, thinking they were locked because the front door was. Her mind raced as she tried to recall all the things Ryder had taught her. She stood a chance so long as she didn't panic. She had to stay cool, look for opportunities.

Unless whoever was out there had a gun. Then she was toast.

A man came into view, silhouetted in the doorway to the master bath. Alaina's insides churned and then melted with dismay.

"Hi, Alaina," Deputy Foss said. "Didn't expect to find you here."

Alaina's heart thumped. Her pulse raced. Fear squeezed tight inside her. Her phone was in her back pocket, but how was she supposed to call anyone without Foss taking the phone away? He was tall and imposing, his sheriff's star gleaming in the sunlight when he stepped inside the big bathroom. He had a radio clipped at his shoulder, and a pistol in a holster on his belt. There were other things too, but she didn't know what all the pouches held.

She yanked her gaze to his face again. "Uh, yeah. Bridget hired me to clean for her. Didn't she tell you?"

He hooked his fingers into his belt and gave her a thorough once-over that made her skin crawl. "Can't recall that she did. I saw a car I didn't recognize, so I thought I'd better check and see if someone had broken in."

The hell he didn't recognize her car. But she wasn't going to say that. Not to mention he'd come down that dead-end road on purpose because there was no other way to see Bridget's house. "Well, as you can see, I didn't break in to clean the toilets. And I'd really better get back to it so Bridget doesn't think I'm a waste of money."

Foss came closer. "You could never be a waste of money, Alaina."

Alaina swallowed. "I, uh, thank you. I really need to get back to work."

He caught her arm as she tried to turn away. "Why do you always run away from me, Alaina? I told you I'd be good to you. I'll treat you right if you let me. Nobody's gotta know but us. I know you think you like that soldier, but he's no good for you. He'll ship out and leave you behind. Then what?"

Alaina's heart fluttered like a hummingbird's wings. "He won't."

"He's not from here. He won't stay. And he won't

take you with him. Seen it before, Alaina. Trust me on this. I'm just looking out for you."

"Please let me go. I'm n-not interested in you, Deputy Foss."

"Told you yesterday to call me Patrick."

His head dipped toward her, and Alaina shrank away, tugging against his hold.

He stopped, his eyes hard. She was still clutching the toilet brush and debating the merits of swinging it up between his legs with all her might. If she did, she might manage to get away. But she'd infuriate him, and that might not turn out so well for her the next time she saw him. He hadn't pulled her over yet, but Jenna had told her she'd heard tales from the other waitresses when she was still at the diner.

If you pissed off Foss, he wouldn't treat you kindly. He'd make life hell for you.

No one would believe her if she went to the sheriff's department and said he'd been harassing her. She clutched the brush. It was only plastic, but she could do some damage. Enough to get away from him if she had to.

"Let. Me. Go," she grated.

His expression hardened even more. But then he let her go and took a step back, palms up. It was as if he could see the direction her thoughts were taking.

"You're making a mistake, Alaina. You think that soldier's going to marry you? Take care of you and that kid of yours? He's just fucking you because you're grateful, but he'll dump you when he gets tired of you. Then what?"

She was shaking with fury. And doubt, because of course she was. She'd feared the same thing herself even if Ryder told her it wasn't true.

No. Ryder was nothing like this man. He wanted to see where they could go together. She wanted it too. Anger burned through her like fire.

"And you'd be any different? You have a *key* to Bridget's house. You just let yourself in. The bed was slept in by *two* people, Deputy Foss. You and Bridget. You aren't interested in me. You just like the thrill of the chase. But you know what? You need to tell Bridget you don't really love her and have no intention of marrying her so she can move on and find someone who *will* love her the way she deserves. You need to do it before someone else does because that'll hurt her too much."

Foss moved into her space again, crowding her against the wall, his finger in her face. "You go mouthing off to Bridget, and it won't end well for you. You better think about that before you tell tales. It's you against me. Who do you think she'll believe?"

He looked mean and angry, and Alaina feared this time he might not back away. But his radio went off, squawking into the tense silence between them. He glared at her then stalked out of the bathroom, answering the radio as he went. Alaina didn't know what the codes meant that the person on the other end was giving him, but it sounded like something Foss had to respond to. His voice moved farther away as he went down the stairs. Then the door slammed and the house was quiet.

Alaina ran down to the front door and twisted the lock, then shoved a chair beneath the knob. She knew it wasn't much, but at least it was something. She was still shaking when she slid down the wall and sat on the floor in a boneless heap.

She thought maybe she should text Jenna, but what was Jenna going to do? She'd tell Ryder when he returned. And she was definitely not returning to Bridget's house again.

Chapter Nineteen

When Alaina got to the center the next day, she was determined to tell Bridget she couldn't clean her house. As much as she wanted the money, she couldn't risk another encounter with Deputy Foss. He hadn't actually hurt her, hadn't forced her to do anything she didn't want to do, but how much longer would that last?

She'd finished cleaning yesterday, but she'd rushed to get done so she could leave. She'd been worried he'd come back, but he hadn't.

If he caught her alone at Bridget's again, there was no guarantee he wouldn't take advantage of the situation. Maybe he'd be better prepared next time, off the clock, no radio to interrupt.

She didn't know what he was capable of, and she didn't want to find out. But how was she going to explain to Bridget? Her friend had been so kind to step up when Alaina said she needed the money. She *did* need the money, and she didn't want to give it up, but what choice did she have?

It wasn't so easy to tell Bridget she had to quit, though. All morning, she kept trying to find the words, but they wouldn't come. Stacie noticed something was up and asked when no one else was near.

Alaina glanced around to make sure they were truly alone. "Patrick Foss used his key to get into Bridget's house yesterday when I was there," she whispered.

Stacie's eyes widened. "Oh shit. Are you okay?"

Alaina nodded. "He didn't do anything, but he did try to talk me into starting something with him. Again."

She didn't mention that he'd tried to kiss her.

"Good God, that man. He's a sexist prick, and Bridget can't see it. He's hit on me, Lidia—probably everyone who works here at one point or another." Stacie folded her arms, looking militant. "What are you gonna do about it?"

"I can't go back there if he's going to show up. And I guarantee he will at some point because he'll know when I'm supposed to be there."

"How will you tell Bridget?"

Alaina frowned. "I don't know. I don't want to hurt her feelings or make her suspicious. I just need to find a way to tell her I can't clean for her anymore."

Stacie blew out a breath. "Damn, that sucks."

"I know. She's trying to help me and I'm about to flake out on her. I feel terrible about it, but I can't tell her the real reason."

"No, you really can't. Kim lost her cool and told Bridget to rein in her boyfriend. She'd been through a lot of shit in her life, poor thing, and she'd gotten out of a bad situation just a few months before. But telling Bridget about Patrick did not turn out so well for her. Two weeks later, she was gone. And not just from the center. Girl left town and hasn't been back. Not that I blame her. She'd been through it once before with a stalker-ex, and she wasn't hanging around when things went wrong. Besides, if she'd stayed and started work somewhere else in town, Foss would have probably made life hell pulling her over all the time and giving her tickets and shit."

A shiver rolled down Alaina's spine. "I understand why she left."

She didn't want to leave town. Leaving meant disrupting Everett's school and social life yet again. It meant removing him from the first positive male influence he'd ever had in his short life. And it meant leaving Ryder, which made her feel physically ill.

No.

She wasn't giving up her budding relationship with Ryder. Wasn't giving up his friends, who were now her friends. Wasn't giving up her life in this town. Over a cheating, lying, sleazy asshole who couldn't seem to take no for an answer? No way.

She wasn't telling Bridget that her boyfriend was a prick and she could do better. Some things you had to learn for yourself, just like she'd had to learn that Clint was a shallow douche who cared more for his own status than for her and his son.

But she could tell Bridge that she didn't want to clean for her anymore.

Stacie patted her on the shoulder. "I'm sorry, Alaina. I don't know what to tell you, but I agree you don't want to be alone with Patrick. I've heard about him forcing things along, so to speak, but I don't know if they're true. All I know is he's never tried to push me. He still flirts, and he'd take a blow job in the supply closet if I suggested it, but he's not after me hardcore. Maybe because we've known each other our whole lives, or maybe he's just not that into me. But you're still new around here, and that makes you way more interesting."

"Great," Alaina groaned.

Bridget emerged from her office and strolled down the hallway toward them. Alaina felt her cheeks heating. Fucking Patrick Foss and his fucking bullshit. She wished Ryder was home. This time she'd tell him about Foss cornering her in Bridget's house. Maybe he'd manage to intimidate Foss enough to leave her alone. Or maybe it'd make everything worse. That was another possibility, and not a good one. If Foss could harass her with tickets and crap, he could do the same to Ryder.

She didn't want to be the cause of that. But she'd promised to tell Ryder the truth. She'd have to trust he knew what he was doing. She *did* trust him. She just wished he was here now to talk to. Maybe she should have told Jenna last night, but she'd already decided to quit and she hadn't wanted to talk about it. Especially when Scarlett came over and the three of them drank wine and talked about life and kids and summer weddings. Jenna and Noah were already married, but they were having a big church wedding for family in June.

"Hey, guys," Bridget said. "What's up?"

She was smiling, so Alaina smiled too. So did Stacie.

"Nothing much," Stacie said. "Just discussing Everett spending the night with the boys again. They love having him come over to play. Keeps them occupied and gives me a much needed breather," she laughed.

"That's a good thing... Alaina, I really need to thank you for the job you did at my house. It was so nice to come home to the smell of pine and bleach. And the bathroom! You got the water spots off the shower door. I could see out of it this morning. Amazing."

Alaina tucked a lock of hair behind her ear. "It's just a little scrubbing with a solution of vinegar and dish soap. A lady I worked with back in South Carolina taught me that. Simple, but effective."

"I tried so many products. I sprayed, I left it on for the allotted time, I scrubbed. Still dull. But you've managed to clear it up. I should have hired you months ago!"

Alaina forced herself to keep smiling. "Your house is really very tidy. You don't actually need me, Bridge, but I do appreciate you giving me the opportunity."

Bridget shook her head. "Oh no, now that I know how marvelous it is to have a house cleaner, I'm not going back. It was so nice to get home and not have to clean up before dinner. Patrick and I had a lovely evening. More time for each other," she said with a wink.

Alaina nodded, her stomach tightening into a knot. "That's good. But really, if you're doing it just to help me, I want you to know you don't have to. I, um, looked at my expenses, and they aren't as much as I thought. Moving to Ryder's place has really been helpful."

"I'm serious," Bridget said. "Yes, I did want to help you out, and I've resisted getting someone for a long time, but I'm truly happy about this arrangement. One less thing for me to worry about." She looked at her smart watch. "Crap, Zoom meeting with the regional director in ten minutes. I better get ready."

When Bridget walked away, Stacie gave Alaina a look filled with sympathy. "That went well."

Alaina sighed. "Yeah. Guess I better get the flu or

something before I have to go out there again on Friday."

"Maybe you can get Jenna to go with you."

"This time, but I can't have her go with me every single time. She has her own life and responsibilities."

Stacie brightened. "Hey, I almost forgot, but I saw this lock thing online that you can put on hotel room doors to make them safer. Maybe you could get a couple of those and use them at Bridget's house. That way Patrick can't get in, even with a key. Look." She took out her phone and opened the browser. Then she opened a tab on Amazon and searched for a portable lock device. "I was going to order one. Just haven't done it yet because I'm a big-time procrastinator."

The device looked simple, the star rating was high, and it was twelve bucks for two. If it worked, it was worth the price. Even if she managed to get out of cleaning Bridget's house, it'd be good to have at other clients' places. "Can you order two packs for me? I don't have a credit card, but I can give you cash."

"Can do." Stacie clicked a couple of buttons. "There. I should have done this before but, like I said, procrastinator. Two packs for you, one for me. It'll be here next week. And now I better get back to work." She started to walk away, then stopped. "Oh, and if you want to let Everett spend the night with Carter on Friday, I can pick him up from school when I get my monsters."

"He'd love that. Thank you."

Everett was loving the air tent at Jenna's. He'd slept in it every night, though he'd finally allowed Alaina to sleep in a bed when she'd told him that grownup backs needed more padding.

But he would love a sleepover with Carter even more. The only thing that would make it more perfect was if his other friend, Nate, got to go too. She felt badly that she didn't have a place for Carter and Nate to come stay with Everett at the moment, but it would happen.

Until then, she wasn't going to stop her kid from having fun. Sleepovers were some of the best times as kids. Her aunt and uncle had always been happy to get rid of her for a night, so they'd never said no to letting her stay with her friends. Thankfully, her friends' parents had all been decent people, and she'd never been scared of any of them. She knew that was a consideration these days, but Everett was safe with Stacie.

"Sure thing, chickie," Stacie said. "Lunch at eleven?"

"Absolutely."

Stacie squeezed her arm. "It's gonna be okay, Alaina. The locks are on the way, and you can get Jenna to go with you this one time. Bridget doesn't have to know anything, and you don't have to disappoint her. One of these days, she'll figure out what a loser Patrick is. Then she'll dump his ass. Karma, baby. Just takes time."

"Thanks. I hope you're right."

But she wasn't so sure. In her experience, some men got away with being shitty human beings. Worse, they got rewarded for it.

———

FRIDAY AFTERNOON, Alaina went to clean the downstairs of Bridget's house as planned. Jenna was supposed to go with her, but Alice spiked a fever and they had to stay home. Alaina had thought about making an excuse to Bridget, but her friend said she was planning a romantic weekend with her boyfriend and really wanted the house to sparkle.

It wasn't until Bridget let slip that Deputy Foss was engaging in a prisoner transfer today and wouldn't be home until later tonight that Alaina stopped trying to think of ways to back out.

If Foss was engaged elsewhere, there was no problem. Alaina had found Stacie and told her the good news. Stacie gave her a high five. "Woohoo! Next week, you'll have the locks. Luck is on your side today, Alaina."

She hoped so. She was still missing Ryder terribly. The team had been gone for over a week now. Every day she woke up hoping it was the day he'd come back. And every night she and Jenna sat together in the living room after the kids were in bed and had a glass of wine together.

Alaina had worried at first that she was imposing by staying with Jenna, but she no longer felt that way. Jenna was warm and open, and she genuinely seemed to enjoy having someone to talk to in the evenings. They were both missing their men, both lonely without them, and both wrangling kids and life while they waited for the news their men were coming home.

Jenna had told Alaina about her life—her parents who'd died, her Aunt Maggie, whom Alaina had met at the Early Bird that one time, and the trouble she'd gotten into in Las Vegas working for an attorney who'd been doing deals with the mob. She didn't go into a lot of detail, but she had told Alaina how she, Alice, and Aunt Maggie were taken hostage and how the guys had saved them from certain death. That and how she'd jabbed the man's eye out with her keys because Noah had taught her to defend herself.

Alaina always shuddered when she thought about it, but it also made her believe she could do the same if she had to.

Not only was Jenna comforting to be around, the other women were as well. They'd gotten together for dinner last night, and Alaina had learned even more about them. How they'd met their fiancés or husbands, the trouble they'd each been in, and how finding love with a man who protected people for a living meant they'd also found a family in each other.

And she was one of them. She held that feeling close to her heart. Though nothing was settled with her and Ryder, she knew she loved him. Everett loved him too. She thought even if he didn't love them yet, he would. He was a good man. He wouldn't play with her heart.

Alaina spent a couple of hours at Bridget's house. It was quiet, though Bridget told her to turn on the Bose speaker and sync her phone to it if she wanted to play something. Alaina hadn't done it, and she hadn't put headphones in either. She *wanted* to hear what was happening outside. Wanted to hear a car pull up or a door open. She believed that Foss was gone all day because Bridget said he was, but that didn't mean there wasn't a chance he'd return early.

When Alaina was finishing up, her phone rang. It was Stacie.

"Hey," she said. "Everything okay?"

"Fine! I picked up the little monsters, and we're getting McDonald's for dinner. But Everett wanted to know if you could bring his Mandalorian jammies over later. He really, really, REALLY wants to wear them tonight," she finished with a laugh.

Alaina laughed too. "He's been wearing Thor and Spiderman this week. Now he wants the Mandalorian? Good grief."

"Yup. Oh, and he wants some movie from your

DVD stash too. Some Star Wars thing. I have no idea, but it's not one we have. Clone Wars?"

"Lord," Alaina said, putting her hand to her forehead. "Yeah, it's out at Ryder's place." She glanced at her watch. Plenty of daylight left. "I can swing by there. I need to grab some more clothes for us anyway."

"Great! I plan to feed these guys and turn them loose in the yard for a while. Then it's movie night. Star Wars and Clone Wars and who knows what else? A big glass of wine for me, of course."

"Of course. Thank you so much, Stacie. I really appreciate you having Everett over. He loves hanging out with Carter and his brothers. Mostly Carter."

"Carter is the cool kid," Stacie said. "The other two are fun as well, but at three and five, they are nowhere near as cool as a six-year-old. At least in the six-year-old's eyes."

Alaina snorted. "Gotcha. Okay, finishing up at Bridget's. I'll swing by and grab those things, then text you when I'm on the way."

"Ten-four, little mama," Stacie said. "See you later."

The call ended, and Alaina finished wiping down the kitchen cabinets and then gathered her cleaning supplies. When she heard a key in the lock, her belly clenched. But it was Bridget who walked in, not Deputy Foss. Alaina smiled her relief.

"Hey, I was just leaving."

"Are you sure? I didn't mean to interrupt, but I needed to come home and grab some files."

Poor Bridget. Always working herself to the bone. "You have to go back to work?"

"For a little bit," Bridget said, dropping her keys in a bowl by the door. "Then it's freedom for the weekend."

"That's great. You work so hard. You deserve some time off."

"Thank you," Bridget said. "I do work hard, but it's good work. Sometimes I just want to scream in a soundproof room, you know?"

Alaina did know. "Do you think maybe I could help out with the hotline again? I feel like I'm ready."

Bridget studied her. Then she nodded. "Maybe you are. You seem to have taken everything in stride."

"What other choice is there?"

Bridget arched a brow. "Melt down? Curl into a ball and refuse to come back to the center? Leave town?"

Alaina blinked. Her friend seemed almost irritated. Must just be that she was tired. "Well, I mean, yeah. I guess those are options. But not for me. I can't give up."

Bridget smiled. "I get it. I can't give up either." She picked up a glass vase and studied it. "Where are you off to, Alaina?"

"I have to swing by Ryder's place and grab some more clothes. Plus Everett wants a movie. I have to drop those at Stacie's, then it's back to Jenna's place."

Bridget knew they were staying with Jenna and Alice in town. Everyone at the center did.

She set the vase down and sighed. "If you want to take a shift tonight, you can. Come back to the center at eight?"

Alaina was tired from a full day already, but she wasn't going to say no. She loved helping people in crisis. It made her feel as if she was doing something far more important than cleaning. Maybe she'd make a difference in someone's life. Someone like her mother.

"I'll be there."

"Excellent," Bridget said. "I'll tell Lidia to expect you."

Chapter Twenty

Ry boarded an Air Force C-5 Galaxy with his team and climbed into the troop compartment in the upper deck. The mission had been brutal, but they'd survived and they'd rescued five paleontologists who'd been working on some kind of dinosaur dig in the desert. The scientists had been taken when a group of terrorists saw an opportunity to make a quick buck by ransoming them.

Hadn't worked out that way, though. Strike Team 2 had watched and planned before they'd stormed into the high rise building where the terrorists had taken the Americans, shot every last tango in the place, and extracted five men and women who were dehydrated and hungry but otherwise okay. Those people were currently on the way to Landstuhl, Germany, to the medical center there where they would be thoroughly examined and monitored before being sent back to the States.

More than anything, he wanted to call Alaina. But the team didn't have their personal cell phones on them because it wasn't safe on a mission. The pilots and crew always let them use theirs to get messages to their families though. After takeoff, Saint went up front so he could send a text to Brooke. She would let everyone else know.

Ry couldn't wait to return home to Alaina and Everett. He'd missed Alaina's warm body next to him in bed, missed being buried inside her, but he'd also missed sitting at the table in the mornings and having coffee with her, or chatting in the evenings when she got home from work.

He'd missed Everett jumping up with glee because he'd just walked in the door, and he missed the kid's questions and the way he'd light up when Ry gave him attention. Everett had started to mimic him in some things, like the way he slouched on the couch and the way he folded his pizza in half and ate it like a sandwich. Ry was touched by how much the kid seemed to admire him.

He didn't want to do anything to ruin that admiration, either. He wanted to be there for the boy, wanted to see him grown into a man. Crazy as it was, as over his head as he was, yeah, that's what he wanted.

Ry lay back on the seat and closed his eyes. It'd be

a long ride home, but at the end of it, Alaina and Everett would be there. He was going to tell Alaina he loved her. Didn't matter they hadn't been together long. She and Everett were his family, and he couldn't wait to take them to meet his grandparents in Florida when school was out. He didn't want to hide his relationship with her from anyone, and he didn't want her to feel as if she was temporary or that disaster loomed around the corner.

He understood that feeling. He'd lived with it for years after he'd found his sister's body, but life was for the living, and it was time they both got on with it.

"Muffin."

He opened his eyes to find Saint frowning down at him. The expression on his team leader's face had him rocking the seat forward as every nerve ending in his body flared to life.

That uneasy feeling he'd had before the team left the States was back. It was a stone in his gut. A wrongness. A trickle of apprehension that was fast becoming a river.

"What happened?"

"Got a message from Brooke. She says Alaina didn't come home last night."

Fear arrowed into his soul. "Everett?"

"He's with Stacie. Went to spend the night. Alaina was supposed to go over to your place to get some things to take to Stacie's, and then she was supposed to work a volunteer shift at the center. She never turned up."

———

ALAINA WOKE WITH A THROBBING HEADACHE. Her mouth was dry and her throat ached. For a second she thought she was in bed, waking from a nightmare, but the fog lifted and she knew it was no dream.

Her shoulder ached. She went to push herself up, but her hands were bound behind her back. She lay in a dark room that smelled dank. A basement? But no, that was dirt beneath her cheek. She levered herself up to a sitting position and the room spun.

She'd gone out to Ryder's to get Everett's movie and jammies as well as some more clothing. She'd texted Jenna to tell her where she was going. The other woman replied and said to text again when she was leaving.

She'd never sent that second text.

There'd been no one at the house. She'd pulled into the driveway and looked around before getting out of the car. She'd gone over to the cottage and let herself in because that's where Everett's movie was. She remembered retrieving the movie from the stack, then heading into the bedroom to get more clothing.

There'd been a noise, a shape in the doorway—

and then nothing. Something had smelled familiar, though. A sweet scent.

A chill rolled over her as she identified the smell. It was Bridget's hand lotion. She rubbed the stuff on all the time. After washing her hands, sitting at her desk, in the break room. She hated her hands feeling dry.

But that didn't mean Bridget had been inside the cottage. Alaina had been in Bridget's house earlier. The smell could have been from something she'd picked up or brushed up against while there. Maybe she just hadn't noticed it until that moment, or maybe she was reaching back and latching onto something familiar because she was somewhere completely unfamiliar.

Alaina pushed to her feet. She wobbled but managed to stay upright. What kind of building had a dirt floor and was dark inside? There were no windows, but the building was old enough that light came between the slats and around the door frame. Not underground then. Not a basement.

She shuffled to the door and tried to grasp the knob, but it wasn't easy with her hands behind her back. Once she managed to get hold of it, she twisted —but nothing happened. The knob didn't turn. She turned around to kick the door instead.

The wood was harder than it appeared. Her foot connected and she cried out in pain. The door didn't give at all. She braced herself and tried again, but again nothing. Didn't help that she was wearing a pair of flimsy canvas shoes she'd picked up at a discount store.

Alaina kicked once more, then lost her footing and fell hard on her ass in the dirt. That's when the tears came. She was cold, hungry, and scared. She had no idea how long she'd been in this place, who'd put her here, or why. What had she done to make someone so angry they wanted to kill her? Or was she just that unlucky to be chosen at random twice?

She didn't know. Worse, she didn't know if someone was coming back to finish what they'd started.

Or if they'd just leave her until she either froze during the cold nights or starved to death. For the first time in a long time, hopelessness overwhelmed her. Ryder was out of the country. His team was with him.

There would be no rescue. No reunion with Ryder or Everett.

No one was coming for her because there was no one *to* come. The only person who could help her was herself. She had to stay awake, alert, and she had to be ready if her attacker returned. She didn't know what she could possibly do to survive, but she wasn't quitting.

She had too much to live for.

———

RY WAS FRANTIC. There'd been no sign of Alaina since late Friday afternoon, and it was nearing sunset on Sunday. The team had rolled into town late last night and they hadn't gotten much sleep since. They converged on Ryder's place and set up their HQ there because it was the last place she'd been.

Jenna had called the police. Deputies Foss and Turner had been out to Ryder's house on Saturday where they'd found Alaina's car and cell phone. They'd done a search of the woods and come up with nothing.

The police were dragging the lake now. Ry didn't like looking at that operation, but he had to face facts. If the first attack hadn't been random, if someone had targeted Alaina specifically—and it now seemed as if they had—then they might have succeeded this time.

The longer there was no sign of a body, the better though. Still didn't make any of this easy. Ry wanted to dive in and help, but he had to stay where he was and work with his team to find Alaina and bring her back safely.

Because he needed to believe they *would* bring her back.

Hacker had gotten into the sheriff's department records. Deputy Foss had been at the jail the first time Alaina was attacked, and he'd been out of town on Friday when she went missing. The man was still a motherfucker, but he wasn't guilty of attacking Alaina.

Mr. Herbert had indeed claimed Keith was with him the day of the first attack. Keith's phone placed him there, though his grandfather could also be covering for him. Hacker was working on getting access to more recent phone records, but no one had seen Keith since he'd left work Friday. Not even his grandfather. Keith had told him he had a girlfriend, so his grandfather thought he was with her.

Ry turned from watching the dive boats out on the water and shot Hacker a look. "Anything new?"

Hacker's eyes were bloodshot. He yawned. "Not yet. Waiting for more phone records."

Ry growled and turned away. Fucking hell, he was going to go crazy if they didn't get a break soon. He'd promised he'd keep her safe, and he was failing. Just like he'd failed to save Sheri. He hadn't known what Sheri intended, but maybe he should have. That was the thing that'd bothered him all these years. What if he'd noticed something was wrong sooner? Told his parents? Talked to Sheri and said he loved her rather than fighting over who got the last soda in the fridge on that fateful day?

There was a knock on the door and he stalked over to answer it. Stacie stood on the other side, looking wide-eyed and worried.

"I wanted to see if I could help," she blurted. "Jenna told me you were back."

Ryder had an urge to drag the woman into his arms and hug her just for being Alaina's friend. He thought that might scare her though. He'd spoken to Alaina's other friends, Lidia and Bridget, but Stacie was the first one he'd actually seen since his return.

He raked a hand through his hair and shook his head. "You've done a lot by taking care of Everett."

"He's no bother. He wants his mother, though. He's been happy all weekend, but he misses her by now and wants to go home." She turned and looked back at her car. He saw the four children seated inside. One in particular stood out.

"Jesus," Ry said, his eyes filling at the same time his heart did. He jogged over to the car and pulled open the back door. "Hey, little dude."

Everett barreled out of his seat and into Ryder's arms. "Mr. Ryder," he cried. "You're back! Where's Mommy?"

Ry dropped to his knees and hugged the kid tight, his eyes stinging. He could lie, probably should lie, but he wasn't going to do it. He pushed back until he could look into Everett's eyes.

"I don't know, Everett. Mommy isn't home, but I'm working on finding her, okay?"

Everett nodded in that exaggerated way little kids had. He knew she wasn't there but he wasn't old enough to think all the dire thoughts Ryder and his crew were thinking. Thank God.

"It's my job to find people. And I'm gonna find

her."

Everett rubbed an eye. "I want to stay here with you."

"I want that too, little dude," Ry said. "But I need you to go and keep Miss Stacie company for another night. You and Carter can go to school together in the morning."

"I don't want to!" Everett started to cry as he clung to Ry again. Ry felt like absolute shit as he picked the kid up and wrapped his arms around Everett's little body. Truth was, he didn't want to let Everett go anywhere without him right now. He wanted to keep the child close, but he also needed the freedom to take off and follow a lead if necessary.

A Jeep turned into the driveway then. Jenna was driving, bringing Easy back after he'd gone home to shower and change. Ry made eye contact with them both as they parked. He mouthed one word. "Help."

Easy got Alice out of the back while Jenna walked over. "Hey, Everett," she said, rubbing her hand on his back. "How you doing, honey?"

"Miss my mommy," he wailed, really getting into it now. Ry held on and started to bounce him like he'd seen Jenna do with Alice.

"I know, honey," Jenna said.

"Want to stay with Mr. Ryder."

Jenna met his gaze. Ry shrugged. He had no idea what to do now, and his heart was about as shattered as the kid's. Not only that, but he didn't want Everett to go because then he'd worry that someone would come after the boy, too. He didn't know why anyone would, but rationality was impossible at the moment. Someone had taken Alaina from him, and he wasn't going to let them take Everett too. It would break him worse than he already was.

"Okay," Jenna said. "How about you and me and Alice go inside and find something to do while Mr. Ryder does his job and searches for your mommy? He'll be here with us, and if he has to leave, we'll be waiting when he comes back. That work for you?"

Everett sniffled. "Yes."

"Okay, good. Want to come inside now?"

Everett held onto Ry and shook his head. Ry didn't want to let him go, either. "It's okay," he said roughly. "We'll go inside together."

He thanked Stacie for bringing Everett and asked if she wanted to stay with them. She was hesitant at first because she had her three boys in the car and they needed to be fed, but she finally agreed to stay and bring the boys inside when Ry told her two of his teammates were picking up food and it was easy to add to the order. Sure, it meant chaos in his house, but he welcomed the distraction. And it made Everett stop crying.

Once inside, the kids began to play in the living room while Easy called Zany and Gem to tell them to pick up more burgers and fries and to grab more snacks at the grocery store. Hacker was still tapping away on the computer. Wolf, Mal, and Harley were out searching for signs of Keith. Saint was at home with Brooke but would be back soon.

Ryder looked at them all working hard for Alaina and felt overwhelmed with grief and love. The past couple of days had been some of the worst of his life, but it also showed him how much he had in these people. The best of friends, his brothers in arms. Their women were his sisters. He missed Sheri like hell, but he had these people. He still had his grandparents and parents, though he was much closer to Gram and Papa.

He had a good life, but it wasn't the best it could be. He needed Alaina for that. She'd gotten under his skin, her and her son, and he didn't want to imagine his life without them. He wanted to come home after a long day at work or a hard mission and find them waiting for him. He wanted to make love to his wife and play with his son. Yeah, *his* son. He wanted that right, and he wanted to ask Alaina if she would allow it.

"Fucking hell," he muttered as he headed toward the bedroom to take a moment and relocate his balls before he sobbed like a drunk at a wedding.

"Hey," Easy said. "Who's that?"

Ry turned to follow Easy's gaze. A man walked toward them from the direction of the woods. A skinny, surly man that Ry recognized instantly.

Keith Herbert.

Chapter Twenty-One

ALAINA WOKE TO THE SOUND OF A KEY SCRAPING IN the lock. The door squealed open on creaky hinges, and her heart lodged in her throat. A flashlight swept over her, shining into her eyes before she turned her head. Fresh pain stabbed at her temples. The headache was still there. Worse, her mouth was drier than before. She didn't know how long it'd been since she'd been taken, but she'd had no food and no water in all that time.

Someone stepped into the building. The door stayed open behind the vague shape making its way toward her. Hope flared as Alaina thought maybe she could distract them and make a run for it.

But her body wouldn't obey her command to move, which meant it wasn't going to happen. She was too weak and clumsy to escape. Whatever this person intended, she couldn't stop them. Not as she was.

"Water," she croaked, hoping for at least that much.

"Sorry, but no."

Alaina gasped, her lips cracking as her throat closed. "Bridget?" she forced out.

A foot kicked her in the thigh and she cried out in pain.

"You shouldn't have tried to steal him, Alaina. I liked you. *Helped you.* But you had to go and turn his head, didn't you? Wanted to clean my house so you could meet him there. Thought nobody would know, didn't you? But I knew. I watched and waited, and sure enough he showed up."

Alaina's mind reeled. Bridget?

Bridget, her friend. Her boss. The woman who *counseled* abused and suicidal women because she had a freaking degree in psychology and counseling. Bridget had attacked her and brought her here because she thought Alaina was trying to steal Deputy Foss? Had she been the one to attack her the first time, too?

It was too much to process. Too much to understand.

"No, Bridge, I—"

"Shut up," Bridget screamed. "I know better! Kim tried to steal him, too, then she told me *he* came on to *her.* As if he ever would. As if my Patrick would *ever* want anyone else. I tried to warn you, Alaina. I tried to tell you to be careful, but you wouldn't listen."

Alaina couldn't see Bridget's face, but she could hear the touch of hysteria in her voice. Bridget was hardcore delusional if she thought Alaina wanted her boyfriend. Alaina recalled the conversation she'd overhead between Bridget and Foss that day. How she'd said she got jealous at his flirting and he'd told her not to worry about it, it was nothing, that he was just making people comfortable. The hell he was. And some part of Bridget must have known it.

"I'm in love with Ryder," Alaina said with a throat made of sandpaper. Tears welled in her eyes, surprising her. She wouldn't have thought she had any moisture left for tears. Her heart was beating faster than usual because she was dehydrated, and her head pounded, but she still managed tears for what might have been.

Ryder and her and Everett. A family. Maybe he would have wanted that. *She* wanted it, but she knew better than anyone that she never got what she wanted. She wished she could see Ryder and her son again before she died. Wished she could tell them she loved them both and they'd made her life better just by being in it.

Ryder had made her feel like she had a home and a family with his team. He'd made her and Everett a part of his life, and she regretted she hadn't gotten to tell him how much it had meant to her. She should have said so when he'd called her the day he left the country.

"Liar," Bridget growled. "You want Patrick. I've seen how you look at him. But it's not going to work. I know what you are, Alaina, what kind of cheap trash you are. And I'm not letting you steal what I've worked so hard for. Patrick and I are getting married, and we're having kids, and you can't stop that. Not you, not that stupid Kim, not anyone!"

Alaina swallowed even though there was no spit in her mouth to make it easier. "W-what are you going to do?"

Bridget kicked her again. Pain exploded as Bridget's foot connected with Alaina's stomach. She couldn't breathe, couldn't suck in enough air. She rolled to her back and lay there, gasping. She wanted it over. Silence, darkness, peace. If she had to die, then she wanted it done with.

Part of her, a deep, deep part inside, raged against the violence and the unfairness. That part wanted to fight. That part wanted to hook a leg around Bridget's and bring her down hard. But she didn't have the strength. All she could do was wait.

Bridget squatted beside her, her eyes gleaming in the light from her phone as she set it down on the floor. "I'm going to take out the trash, Alaina. They never found Kim, and they won't find you." She laughed, and the sound sent a chill scurrying across Alaina's skin. "I'm smart, and I watch true crime shows. I know how to get rid of a body. Did it once before, and I can do it again."

Alaina heard a rustling sound, and then the light flashed off a needle as Bridget took off the cap and dropped it. "A little something to make you sleep. You won't feel a thing. It's more than you deserve but easier for me."

That part of Alaina that wanted to fight flared bright as Bridget bent over her to look for a vein. Alaina pictured everything in her head, and then she summoned every last bit of meager strength she had to lever herself up and knock her head against Bridget's nose as hard as she could.

She knew she'd succeeded when the other woman screamed. Something hot and warm hit Alaina's face. Blood. Bridget fell backward, dropping the syringe as she did so. Alaina didn't see where it went and didn't care. She couldn't use it anyway with her hands behind her back.

Get up! Run!

Alaina struggled to obey the voice in her head. Everett needed her. Ryder needed her. She had to fight for *them*. Had to get away for *them*.

Bridget was still crying, but she was starting to move. Alaina found some reserve of strength she didn't know she had and somehow stumbled to her feet. Then she started for the door.

But an arm hooked around her legs and dragged her down again. "You aren't going anywhere, bitch!"

Alaina landed hard, but she didn't let the pain stop her. She screamed her rage as she flipped herself over and kicked Bridget in the head. She kicked again and again, until Bridget let go. Then she pushed and twisted until she got herself upright once more.

Somehow she was out the door, stumbling through the fresh air.

She would escape. She *would*. Her breath heaved in her chest, and she had to bite down on the urge to vomit. She knew she wasn't moving fast enough. She was too dehydrated, her heart pumping too quick and hard, and she wasn't going to get far before she collapsed again. The only advantage she might have was that it was dark. If all Bridget had was her cell phone light, that might not be enough if Alaina could get far enough away before Bridget caught up. Maybe she'd find a road, or maybe she'd hide in the trees until daylight.

"You won't get away, Alaina!" Bridget screamed behind her. *Too close* behind her.

Alaina pushed herself to go faster, but there was nothing in the tank. Her foot hit something—a tree root, a stone. Didn't matter, though, because she lost her balance and went down. The ground beneath her was damp and cool, and she wished she could burrow beneath it and hide.

Footsteps crunched in the leaves. A pinpoint of light got bigger. Alaina tried to get up again, but she couldn't. She'd used every last bit of energy she had to escape the first time.

This was how she died, then. In the dirt. Cold, hungry, thirsty, and utterly defeated.

But you tried. You didn't give up.

No, she hadn't given up. She'd tried to escape, and she'd nearly succeeded.

"Fucking bitch, you broke my nose." Bridget sounded angry and stuffy. "Think I'll leave you alive? This time, I'm making sure you're dead. You should have *never* survived the first time. Not in that freezing water with nothing to keep you warm. You wouldn't have if that idiot soldier hadn't seen you. I should have taken you farther up the lake, but I was in too big a rush to get it done. Not this time. I've planned carefully, and I've waited. I've even pretended to be upset that you're missing. Nobody will ever suspect me. And they'll never miss *you!*"

Alaina couldn't even cry now. She was no longer shocked. She was sad and angry and too helpless to do anything. She wanted to tear Bridget's eyes out. But she didn't have the ability.

"Fuck. You," she whispered hoarsely at the woman standing over her. She might have no strength left but she still had words, though her voice was almost too weak to say them.

Bridget grabbed one of her arms and tried to pull her upright. Alaina lay still and didn't move. She was too spent. Besides, Bridget wanted her to cooperate, and she wasn't going to do it.

"Get up, you fucking whore," Bridget grated.

"Fuck. You."

God that felt good to say.

"Okay, if that's the way you want it," Bridget spat.

Then she wrapped her hands around Alaina's neck and squeezed.

———

"GOT BRIDGET'S SIGNAL," Hacker said. "She's on her own property, but not inside the house."

Ry put his truck in reverse, whipped it around, and sped down the driveway. Hacker, Saint, Mal, and Zany were with him. Easy, Gem, Wolf, and Harley were in Gem's Jeep. Hacker had managed to get access to real-time data on Bridget's cell phone location after Keith told them what he'd seen on Friday. Saint had called Ghost and it was a done deal within minutes.

Thank fuck.

Keith Herbert, bless his stalker-ish soul, had been following Alaina around town when he wasn't at work. He was lovesick for her, and he'd been working up the courage to tell her. He was the one who'd been walking around the cottage that day when Everett had seen him, and though he was probably the person who'd shined the light in the woods, he wasn't admitting it. But when Alaina drove to Ry's place on Friday, Keith had been planning to finally talk to her. He'd driven past the house, but then turned and headed back, working on his courage.

That was when he saw a car pull off the road and a woman get out and walk toward the house. He'd recognized Bridget's car, and he'd driven farther down and parked where he could cut through the woods. His plan was to wait until Bridget left, then go talk to Alaina.

What he saw instead, when he reached the edge of the woods, was Bridget driving up to the cottage. Then she carried Alaina's limp body outside and put it in the back seat.

Ry had nearly lost his shit then. That was Friday afternoon and now it was Sunday evening. It might already be too late to save Alaina. Too much time had passed, and Keith fucking Herbert hadn't thought it important to tell anyone until now.

"They work together, man," Keith had said. "I thought maybe she was sick and Bridget was trying to help her. Take her to the doctor."

Ry didn't stick around to find out why Keith had finally decided to tell someone or why he'd gone to the lake instead of the sheriff's department to report what he'd seen. Wasn't fucking important anyway. All that was important was finding Alaina.

He told himself she was alive. If she'd been dead, he'd have felt it. The unease in his gut was the same, not worse, so he told himself that was a good sign. He still had a chance to save her.

The team parked the vehicles in a field adjoining Bridget's property and hiked toward the signal. They didn't have NVGs because their equipment was at HOT HQ, but they didn't need it to scout the terrain and find two women.

Yes, *two* women. Ry repeated it to himself over and over. Two women. Alive.

Hacker stayed in Ry's truck, directing them through the comm link. It didn't take a whole team of special operators to do the job, but nobody else on the team wanted to stay behind while Ry and one or two others went after Alaina.

"Alaina is family," Easy had said. "We're going."

That had settled that. Now they were ghosting through the woods toward the location of Bridget's cell phone. She wasn't in her house. A satellite photo of the property on Google Earth showed tree cover over most of her five acres. It had once been the site of an older home that'd burned down years ago, but the original smokehouse, barn, and well were still there.

"You won't get away, Alaina!"

The scream carried across the night air. Ry felt two things at once. Relief because his woman was still alive, and desperation because Bridget was clearly in pursuit.

Ry broke into a run, sprinting toward the sound.

His team was with him, running for all they were worth, trying to reach Alaina and her attacker before it was too late. He couldn't process everything yet, couldn't understand *why* Bridget had done any of this. All he could do was run as fast as he could to make it to his woman's side and save her.

Because he didn't want to live without her. Couldn't imagine trying.

A fresh burst of speed propelled him forward. He couldn't hear any voices, but he kept running toward where the sound had come from.

Hacker was in his ear. "Left three degrees. Straight, straight, straight… Almost there."

"Okay, if that's the way you want it." It was Bridget's voice coming from a few feet away. Ry sent a hand signal to the men nearest him, knowing they would pass it down. They fanned out, stalking quickly toward the target. But Bridget was his.

Ry slammed into her with the force of a freight train. Bridget didn't make a sound because he barreled into her so hard she didn't get a chance. She simply went flying off Alaina. When she didn't move, he turned to drop beside Alaina. Someone else would take care of Bridget now.

"Alaina," he choked. "Baby. You with me?"

There was blood on her face, but he determined it wasn't coming from her. He patted her cheek softly. Her eyes fluttered open. A moment later, she smiled.

"Heaven," she whispered. "I'm in heaven."

His throat tightened. "You aren't in heaven, baby. You're right here on earth with me."

She lifted a hand, curled weak fingers around his wrist. "It's real? You're here?"

"Yes. Need to examine you, honey. Can you tell me if you're hurt anywhere?"

"Hurt. Everywhere."

Ry continued his examination while someone held a light so he could see. He didn't look up, didn't know who it was. He simply worked his way over Alaina's form. She'd been hit in the ribs and stomach judging by the red marks. Her pulse thrummed far too fast, and a quick test of her skin showed she was dehydrated. Best thing for that was IV fluids but they didn't have any.

"We have to get her to a hospital. Gonna pick you up now, Alaina. It'll hurt. I'm sorry."

"S'okay."

He slid his arms beneath her shoulders and knees, then cradled her against him and stood. She moaned, and his heart cracked. Ry strode back to his truck with Alaina in his arms, her soft crying breaking his heart anew with every sound. Zany opened the door for him and he climbed inside with her in his arms, settling her on his lap while Mal got behind the wheel.

"Bridget," Alaina said, her voice so weak he had to drop his head to hear her.

"We got her. She's alive, which is more than she deserves."

"She… killed… Kim."

"Kim?" Ry met Zany's gaze. Zany shook his head. "Ask. Stacie."

"Okay, baby. I will. I love you, Alaina. Don't you leave me. Everett and I need you."

"'Kay…"

Her eyes dropped closed and her body went limp. Ry checked her pulse. Still beating, but thready. He pressed his lips to her temple and whispered to her to fight. Then he held her close all the way to the hospital.

Chapter Twenty-Two

THE NEXT TIME ALAINA WOKE UP, SHE WAS IN A hospital bed with beeping machines disturbing her rest. There were tubes in her arms, a tube under her nose, and the smell of antiseptic everywhere. She tentatively moved her head—and it did as she commanded. She remembered having a headache, but that was gone now.

She looked around the darkened room, searching for Ryder. He'd been there the last time she woke in a hospital bed. She'd assumed he'd be there this time, too. She thought she remembered him telling her that he loved her, but she wasn't sure she hadn't been hallucinating.

Clearly, he *had* found her and brought her here. Just like last time. But maybe her memory of what he said wasn't quite clear. She was still so tired. She might have dreamed the words.

A shadow crossed the threshold, and she turned toward it. Ryder was at her side in an instant, bent over the bed, his fingers on her cheek.

"You're awake."

"Yes," she rasped. Her throat was dry, but she didn't feel dizzy with thirst anymore.

"Here." He picked up the giant cup with the lid and straw and helped her take a drink. Just like last time. "You're gonna be okay, Alaina. You're safe now. Everett's at Easy and Jenna's, sleeping in his air tent, and he's coming to see you tomorrow. Unless you don't want him here."

Her heart throbbed. She didn't want to expose Everett to the ugly side of life, but she couldn't shelter him forever. People had accidents. People died. He would encounter it sooner or later. And she wanted to see him. Desperately. She'd thought she never would again when Bridget had been choking the life from her.

"It's okay. Want to see him."

Ryder gripped her fingers in his and pressed them to his mouth. "I thought we'd lost you, Alaina. I never want to go through anything like that again."

"Me neither," she joked, though inside she trembled with how close she'd come to dying. Again.

"Bridget," she said, tears pressing against her eyelids. "I had no idea."

Ryder's eyes were bloodshot. She realized for the first time that he had a pretty good beard going. It was sexy on him, but she knew he'd end up shaving it again. Jenna said the guys often came home unshaven and with longer hair, but they got back to regs soon enough.

Either way, Alaina thought Ryder was the sexiest, handsomest man she'd ever seen. And he was hers. She knew it in her bones. Even if she wasn't sure he'd actually said the words.

"I don't think anyone did, honey. Something's broken inside her. She kept it hidden for a long time. No more. She's gonna pay for what she did to Kim Lucas, and for what she did to you."

Alaina blinked and a tear fell down her cheek. Bridge and Lidia and Stacie and her. Friends, or so she'd thought. How many times had Bridget given her extra hours, or arranged the schedule so she could be off when Everett had a day off school? How many times had Bridget bought lunch, or given everyone a pep talk. How many times had she helped women who truly needed it?

It was all so unreal and sad.

Ryder caught the tear on her cheek. "I know she was your friend. But she really wasn't, Alaina. It's not your fault. It's hers, and maybe even a little bit Patrick Foss's for not being fucking decent enough to be loyal to her... Fuck, what am I saying? It's not his fault. He could have been one-hundred percent into her, and she'd have still reacted the way she did if she thought another woman was trying to steal him. She was always a block of explosive waiting for the detonator. Kim was one. You were another."

"I didn't do anything. I never told her about Foss harassing me. Never."

"I know, Alaina. I think she knew what he was up to. She must have seen him with you. Or maybe someone told her they saw you together. He stopped you in places other than the center, right?"

"Yes," she whispered, anger and frustration swirling inside. She closed her eyes and saw Bridget's angry face looming over her. How long would it take to stop seeing that? She opened bleary eyes to look at Ryder again. She was still so tired, but she was also afraid to sleep. Afraid to see Bridget again.

No matter how she tried, her eyelids drooped until it was harder than ever to keep them open. She gripped Ryder's hand. "Please don't leave me. I don't want to be alone."

He kissed her fingers again and rubbed his cheek against her palm. "Not going anywhere, Alaina. I'll be here when you wake up. I'll always be here for you. Shoulda said it before I left town, but I love you."

She smiled sleepily. "Me too."

———

RY TOOK Alaina home two days later. She was bruised and tired, but he wanted her there as much as she wanted to be there. Everett was in school, but he'd be there later when Stacie dropped him off.

Ry settled Alaina on the couch with a blanket, but when he went to turn on the television, she stopped him.

"I want to look at the lake. Will you sit with me?"

He dropped beside her and put his arm around her. She snuggled into him and wrapped one arm around his waist. He closed his eyes and pressed a kiss to the top of her head.

Since he'd found his voice and told her he loved her, he didn't seem able to stop saying it. The beauty of it was that she said it back to him. With a soft smile and shining eyes that told him she not only believed him when he said it, she felt exactly the same as he did.

He worried about her, though. She'd been quiet all morning. He hadn't wanted to push her to talk about it since she'd been through so much, but he knew she was thinking about Bridget and what she'd tried to do.

"I still don't know what happened the first time she attacked me," she finally said. "I'm not sure I'm ever going to remember it."

Ry wanted to growl in helpless frustration. He couldn't fix it for her, and he wanted to. "Trauma does that sometimes. You can remember everything right up to the minute you're in an accident and then nothing about the aftermath. Your brain's protecting you."

"My nails were torn, so I must have fought back at least."

"She tried to smother you, probably with your coat. When you struggled, she hit you over the head to make you stop. The blow is why you don't remember."

"Then she kicked and punched me and dumped me five miles away in the lake. But the second time she took me to that old smokehouse on her property and left me there for two days before she came back to kill me."

Bridget hadn't said much in custody, so he didn't have an answer for her. Nobody knew why she'd done the things she had other than she wasn't sane. A fact she'd hidden very well from everyone. Including her boyfriend, who'd seemed visibly shaken when he'd been one of the responders to the scene. That didn't make Ry like him any better though. The man was still a bullying asshole, and Ry was still going to take him down if he ever bothered Alaina again.

Ry ran his fingers up and down Alaina's arm, soothing her.

"I think I know why she came after me the first time," Alaina said. "A couple of days before it happened, Deputy Foss was at the center. The day we reported the belligerent man outside. He was flirting hardcore that day, leaning in, touching my hair. She must have seen him do it. Maybe she thought I was into it since I didn't push him away. I was still trying to be nice then. I didn't actually tell him to leave me alone until after I went back to work. I should have."

That fucking made him mad. "No. There's no blame, Alaina. Fucking men like that use their power to make women uncomfortable because they can get away with it. Even if you'd kneed him in the balls, it wouldn't have mattered to her. Kim told her to make him stop and she still saw the woman as a threat. Bottom line, no matter how inappropriate Foss behaved, Bridget's response was completely divorced from reality."

"He acted that way with more than just me. That's what I don't understand."

"I know, honey. I don't either. Maybe it's because you weren't from around here. Kim wasn't either, and Bridget got away with making her disappear. She probably thought nobody would care if you died either."

She shivered. "I guess what really gets me most is how normal she seemed. She *killed* someone. And she tried to kill me. Twice. Because she couldn't bear the thought of her boyfriend leaving her. It's fucked up."

He heard the undercurrent of anger in her voice. He understood it. A lot of things didn't make sense to him in his line of work, but he mostly got on with it. You could spend far too much time being angry over things you couldn't change. He'd learned that one firsthand when Sheri died. Something he still needed to tell Alaina about when the time was right. He didn't want her upset for him when she had crap of her own to work through.

"It is fucked up. She won't get another chance to hurt anyone else, though. She'll end up in prison or at a psych facility."

"And her boyfriend will still be annoying women with his bullshit."

Not if Ry could help it. He and Deputy Foss had a reckoning coming, but it'd have to wait until another day.

They sat that way a while longer, Alaina talking, Ry listening. There was still a lot to say between them, but for now he just held her and let her work things out. The plumber came by to work on the busted pipe, and the security cameras arrived. Ry was still putting them up, even if the immediate threat to Alaina was over, because security for his family was important to him.

"I don't want to move back to the cottage," Alaina said over lunch. "I want to stay here, and I want to tell Everett we're a couple."

Ry's heart swelled. He hadn't intended to push her on those things, though for him it was a done deal. They loved each other. But they also loved Everett, which meant if they needed to move a little more slowly for him, then they would.

"I'm not saying no to that."

She grinned. First smile he'd seen today. "He's under the impression that we should sleep together anyway. Nate told him adults who like each other sleep in the same bed. Plus he wants his own room."

Ry laughed. "Honey, his wish is my command."

She reached for his hand across the table. "You don't think this is too fast for you? You just bought this house, and now we're moving in before you've even finished painting your kitchen cabinets or doing all the other projects you wanted to do."

"Alaina," he said, "this is *our* home. Yours, mine, and Everett's. It's not too fast. I've been waiting for you both for a lifetime. I just didn't know it."

She came to him and sat on his lap, wrapping her arms around his neck and kissing him sweetly. "I love you. And I want you, but I don't think I'm ready for that quite yet. Which is *very* frustrating, believe me."

He held her lightly. "I love you, too. We've got nothing but time, honey. I can wait."

His cock was swelling from her proximity, but he'd live with the deprivation until she was better.

Her eyes turned glassy. "I never thought I'd find someone like you. I thought it'd just be me and Everett until he was old enough to move out, and then maybe I'd find a nice guy to date."

"Not to quibble or anything, but I found you first."

She laughed. He'd hoped she would.

"You definitely did."

———

EVERETT TOOK the news of them staying with Ryder and of her moving into Ryder's room with sheer glee. He didn't understand anything about adults in the same bed, but he did understand he was getting his own room. His. The first one he'd ever had, which made Alaina's eyes tear up. Ryder rubbed her back in support, and she managed not to cry.

"Can I have Mandalorian stuff in my room? Please?"

"We'll have a look around and see what we can find," Alaina said. She still had to worry about money, though maybe not quite as much as before. Ryder said it was their house, but she wanted to pay her share. She didn't even know if she still had a job though. No matter. She'd find another one if she had to.

"Is Mr. Ryder gonna be my daddy now?"

Alaina's heart stuttered. She hadn't expected that so soon, but she should have known. Everett wasn't a dumb kid.

"Well," Alaina began.

Ryder took her hand in his and held firm. "I'd like that, little man. But your mom and I have to talk about it first, okay? It's a very important job, and she needs to be sure I can do it right."

"I think you can," Everett said. "Nate has a daddy, and all he does is cook on the grill and take Nate to soccer practice. His mommy does everything else."

Alaina bit the inside of her lip and tried not to laugh.

"Is that all there is to it?" Ryder said very seriously. "I guess you're right that it doesn't sound too hard."

"But you have to get married first," Everett said. "Nate's mommy and daddy are married."

This kid.

Alaina's cheeks heated. She should have known that was coming. Everett didn't miss much, and she wasn't about to give him the speech about how people didn't have to be married, blah, blah, blah. Time enough for that another day.

"How about you do your homework now?" she said brightly. "We'll get the rest of your things and make your room nice and neat after. How's that?"

"Cool!"

Alaina watched him get his backpack and start taking things out of it. The kid was easily distracted, thankfully. Ryder was still beside her, still holding her hand. He chuckled under his breath. She did too. Then he led her to the kitchen and backed her against the counter just out of sight.

His kiss was just what she needed. It made her ache with desire—as well as frustration that she wasn't well enough for sex yet.

He broke the kiss and kept her caged between his arms. His green eyes were bright, his handsome jaw clean shaven again. She wanted to trail kisses along it.

"About that marrying thing," he said.

"I'm sorry about that. Everett gets ideas about things and—"

He put a finger over her lips. "I want to. Maybe this isn't the way you wanted a proposal, but I want to marry you. I can do the proposal thing later if you want a romantic one with flowers. But right now, I need you to know it's what I want."

Her eyes were filling with tears again. "Dammit, you're making me cry. Yes, I want to marry you, and no, I don't need a fancy proposal."

He grinned. "Then I guess I can be Everett's daddy, huh?"

She wrapped her arms around his neck. "Yes, you can be Everett's daddy."

And then she kissed him.

Chapter Twenty-Three

Two months later...

"DADDY! I GOT A BIG ONE!"

Ry got out of his chair and went over to Everett's side of the dock. His pole was bent over, his cheeks puffed out with exertion.

"Careful, kid. Don't reel too hard. Bring him in slow and steady."

Everett did as he was told, reeling a little slower but still going too fast. He did it every time, so Ry got the net ready. Better to scoop the fish when it appeared than have the line break and watch the disappointment on Everett's face.

Everett bounced on the dock. "Can I hold him? Please?"

"Yep. Give me a minute here." Ry pulled the fish

from the net. It wasn't real big, but it would've felt like a whale on Everett's lightweight rod and reel. Ry unhooked the fish and reminded Everett how to hold it as he handed it over. The boy studied the fish with pride.

"Mommy!" he yelled as Ry took a video. Alaina had walked outside, no doubt when she saw the commotion on the dock. "Look what I got!"

Alaina came sashaying down the dock in a long sundress and sandals, and Ry thought he'd never seen a more beautiful sight in his life. His wife. Because, yes, they'd gotten married at the courthouse a month ago. He hadn't wanted to wait, and she didn't seem to care about having a big wedding. They'd had a reception instead, right here at their house. They'd invited all their friends and partied in the backyard and on the dock for hours. Their first dance as a married couple had been right over there beneath the big oak tree with fairy lights dangling from its branches.

His grandparents had come and stayed in the cottage, but his parents sent their regrets because they were on assignment. Of course. He would have expected nothing less. He'd told Alaina about finding his sister in the pool and how his parents had grown distant afterward. How they'd stayed distant over the years. When they didn't come to the wedding, at least she wasn't surprised. Though she was angry for him. He'd told her it didn't matter.

And it didn't. He had her and Everett. He had his

Gram and Papa. His parents were still hurting, still blaming themselves probably, and seeing him only reminded them of what they'd lost. Hell, maybe they blamed him, too. He didn't know and it wasn't important anymore. None of them knew why Sheri had done what she did and they never would. He'd made his peace with it the best he could. He hadn't been able to save her, but he'd saved many, many other people over the course of his career.

Including the woman he loved with all his heart.

"Oh my goodness," Alaina exclaimed when she reached them. "What a gorgeous fish, baby."

Everett beamed. "We gotta let him go now. Daddy says we have to let the fish grow bigger before we can eat them."

"That's very wise," Alaina said, winking at Ry as Everett turned and knelt on the dock to put the fish back in the water. "Think you can go inside and get cleaned up for dinner now?"

"I want to fish some more," Everett said with the hint of a whine.

"And I want to eat," Alaina said. "Mommy's hungry."

"Come to think of it, I am too," Ry said, rubbing his belly. "Gotta keep up the strength to fish another day."

Everett pouted. "Can I watch the Mandalorian after dinner?"

"Haven't you seen all the episodes?" Alaina asked.

"Yes. But I like them all."

She ruffled his hair. "Okay, sure, you can watch again."

Everett grinned. "Yay!"

Then he picked up his pole and trotted up to the house, propping it on the back porch before going inside to wash up.

"Stacie called," Alaina said as Ry put an arm around her and started for the house. "Patrick Foss has been relieved of duty."

"Couldn't happen to a nicer guy."

"My thoughts exactly."

Ry had enjoyed the delightful opportunity to punch Foss's lights out for him not long after Bridget had been taken into custody. Foss had come out to talk to Alaina when Ry was running errands. Alaina told him about it the instant he got home. She'd been angry because Foss had gotten into her personal space and wouldn't back off when she'd told him to. He hadn't touched her, but he'd made her uncomfortable.

That was enough for Ry. He'd gone looking for Foss and found him at the Early Bird. He told the man if he ever upset Alaina again, he'd knock the shit out of him. Foss got angry and said a few things. Ry walked away, but Foss tried to jump him from behind. That was all Ry needed to put the man on his ass.

Everyone present swore that Foss had been the one to attack first. Soon after that, the first accusation of sexual harassment rolled into the station. Several more followed until Foss was put on administrative leave. Looked like the sheriff had made a final determination about the complaints after all.

"What did you fix for dinner?" he asked, moving the conversation to something besides Patrick Foss.

When he'd offered to help her cook earlier, she'd refused, telling him to fish and let her handle it. So he had. He'd taught her a few things about cooking, but then she'd started watching YouTube videos. She was a very fast learner. She had more time these days because she no longer cleaned houses or the center. She'd gotten a part-time administrative job, and she still volunteered too, but she'd wanted to focus on making their house a home.

Ry was fine with that. In fact, he was looking forward to the day they added another baby to their family. When the time was right, of course.

"Shrimp fettuccine with Cajun Alfredo sauce and a tomato salad. You're going to love it."

His stomach growled. "I don't doubt it."

They went inside to the gorgeous kitchen he'd painted the way she wanted. White uppers, pale blue lowers, gold handles and pulls. He'd gotten a butcher block island for her and a farm sink too. She hadn't mastered cookies yet, or his Gram's famous muffin recipe, but she said it wasn't necessary when she had him for the baking. He could bake and she'd cook. The perfect partnership.

He was teaching Everett the recipes, though. Ry

had learned how to bake when he wasn't much older than Everett. They'd started by working together, Ry measuring everything and telling Everett how to add and mix. The kid made a hell of a mess, but when the muffins came out of the oven, he proudly served one to his mom, who pronounced it the best ever because it was made with love.

Fuck yeah, it was made with love. Everything Ry did these days for his wife and kid was done with love. He was a lucky, lucky man.

"Oh, we're talking about having a HOT potluck this weekend," Alaina said, cutting into his sappy thought train. "At Scarlett and Mal's. Mal wants you to bake that chocolate layer cake he loves so much."

"Of course he does. Damn thing takes hours."

"It's his birthday, Ry."

"Yeah, yeah, okay." An idea unfurled in his brain. "Oooh, what if I get some of those fake cockroaches and put them inside the cake?"

"Eww."

"I owe him after what he did."

Alaina laughed. "You mean the throw blanket he had made for me? The one that has your sweet little boy picture and the word Muffin emblazoned across it?"

Ry grumbled. "I wish you'd throw that thing away."

"No way. It's cute. But I promise not to bring it out when anyone's here but us."

"You need to burn it."

Alaina sighed and lifted up on tiptoe to kiss him when they reached the back door. "I'm not burning it. But go ahead and get the roaches. Fake, of course. And make a second cake for the rest of us. I am not cutting into a slice of cake and encountering a roach, fake or not."

"I wonder if I can find them made out of spun sugar? Then they'll crunch like they're real."

Alaina put a hand over his mouth. "Enough, babe. No more discussion of bugs and food."

"Party pooper," he said when she let him go.

"I'm just looking out for the rest of us." She frowned. "You better make sure that Cade distracts Brooke when Mal dives into that cake."

"Good point."

Brooke was in the second trimester and puking at the oddest things. He'd make sure to warn Saint ahead of time. Saint wouldn't let Mal in on the gag because he loved it when Mal got pranked. *Especially* when Mal got pranked since he was the main prankster on the team.

Ry held the door for Alaina, his eyes dropping to her ass as she walked into the house. He was so getting his hands on that curvy behind later. She went into the kitchen to get the food. The salad was already on the table, which she'd set with a white tablecloth, white cotton napkins, and flatware. There was a ceramic pitcher of water on the table and glasses at each setting. She'd also placed a vase with cut hydrangeas in the center of the table.

Ry stood and took it all in. His house, the beautiful, peaceful retreat he'd found for himself, was a home. A welcoming, cozy home with the kind of feminine touches he'd have never chosen but couldn't imagine living without now that he had them.

"Ry, can you grab the parmesan and the bread for me?" Alaina asked as she carried a big bowl of pasta over and set it down.

He dragged in a breath, happiness like a sunburst inside him. Damn, this was everything. The life he'd wanted. The life he hadn't known would be as fucking amazing as it was.

"Yeah, babe, I got it."

———

LAS VEGAS, *Nevada*

ZANE SCOTT WOKE SLOWLY, trying to remember exactly where he was. He could hear water running. He had an impression of a crowded bar, laughter, and voices.

His little sister's twenty-first birthday.

She'd wanted to celebrate in Vegas, and he'd flown out to meet her and her friends because she'd asked him to. His parents were there too, but they'd bowed out long before the evening ended. He remembered drinking tequila shots, thinking there was no way Mia was old enough to drink, and scowling at the random dudes who came by to chat with Mia and her friends.

Her friends were all around the same age, and they flirted outrageously with him. He didn't mind. He knew better than to bang any of them, no matter how drunk he got.

He had a sudden impression of skin on skin, hot sex, and the satisfaction of at least two orgasms. He'd definitely banged someone last night. But had it been one of Mia's college friends? A shudder rippled through him.

God, he hoped not. They were pretty enough, but they were kids. He was thirty-one, a full ten years older than his baby sister. No way would he have let down his guard enough to fuck one of her friends. Would he?

The water stopped running. He pushed upright slowly, his head aching. He didn't usually drink so much, but it'd been a long few months and he'd welcomed the break from work. All his teammates were married or getting married. Some of the wives were pregnant, or soon would be. It was downright domestic at HOT HQ these days. He was the only one still up for spontaneous bar hopping or for darts and wings at Buddy's Bar & Grill.

The guys still went to Buddy's, but they tapped

out early, saying they had to get home to their women. Zane sighed. It was a lonely business being the last unattached operator on the team.

He told himself to snap out of it. He *liked* being single. Banging a different woman every night if he wanted. Not being tied to a schedule for going out or coming home. He reached for a bottle of water on the bedside table and drank it down. He set it back on the table when something glinted on his left hand.

He blinked. Stared. Spread his hand to stare some more.

There was a ring on his left hand. He lifted it to stare at it a bit closer. Gold, smooth, encircling his ring finger. As if he'd gotten married.

The chill that shuddered through him earlier became an ice storm.

Married. Oh, shit.

He'd gotten married. It'd happened. He remembered standing in front of Elvis, saying vows to a woman with red hair and luscious lips that he'd wanted wrapped around his cock.

"Oh Jesus," he groaned. Of all the stupid fucking things.

He'd married a woman he didn't know last night. For some hot sex and a blow job.

Fucking hell…

Who's HOT?

Strike Team 1

Matt "Richie Rich" Girard (Book 0 & 1)
Sam "Knight Rider" McKnight (Book 2)
Kev "Big Mac" MacDonald (Book 3)
Billy "the Kid" Blake (Book 4)
Jack "Hawk" Hunter (Book 5)
Nick "Brandy" Brandon (Book 6)
Garrett "Iceman" Spencer (Book 7)
Ryan "Flash" Gordon (Book 8)
Chase "Fiddler" Daniels (Book 9)
Dex "Double Dee" Davidson (Book 10)

Commander
John "Viper" Mendez (Book 11 & 12)

Deputy Commander

Alex "Ghost" Bishop

Strike Team 2

Cade "Saint" Rodgers (Book 1)
Sky "Hacker" Kelley (Book 2)
Dean "Wolf" Garner (Book 3)
Malcom "Mal" McCoy (Book 4)
Noah "Easy" Cross (Book 5)
Jax "Gem" Stone (Book 6)
Ryder "Muffin" Hanson (Book 7)
Zane "Zany" Scott (Book 8)
Jake "Harley" Ryan (HOT WITNESS)

SEAL Team 1

Dane "Viking" Erikson (Book 1)
Remy "Cage" Marchand (Book 2)
Cody "Cowboy" McCormick (Book 3)
Cash "Money" McQuaid (Book 4)
Alexei "Camel" Kamarov (Book 5)
Adam "Blade" Garrison (Book 6)
Ryan "Dirty Harry" Callahan (Book 7)
Zach "Neo" Anderson (Book 8)
Corey "Shade" Vance

Black's Bandits

Jace Kaiser (Book 1)

Brett Wheeler (Book 2)
Colton Duchaine (Book 3)
Jared Fraser (Book 4)
Ian Black (Book 5)
Tyler Scott (Book 6)
Dax Freed (Book 7)
Thomas "Rascal" Bradley
Jamie Hayes
Finn McDermot
Roman Rostov
Mandy Parker (Airborne Ops)
Melanie (Reception)
? Unnamed Team Members

Freelance Contractors

Lucinda "Lucky" San Ramos, now MacDonald (Book 3)
Victoria "Vee" Royal, now Brandon (Book 6)
Emily Royal, now Gordon (Book 8)
Miranda Lockwood, now McCormick (SEAL Team Book 3)
Bliss Bennett, (Strike Team 2, Book 2)
Angelica "Angie" Turner (Black's Bandits, Book 3)

Book 1: HOT PURSUIT - Matt & Evie

Book 2: HOT MESS - Sam & Georgie

Book 3: DANGEROUSLY HOT - Kev & Lucky

Book 4: HOT PACKAGE - Billy & Olivia

Book 5: HOT SHOT - Jack & Gina

Book 6: HOT REBEL - Nick & Victoria

Book 7: HOT ICE - Garrett & Grace

Book 8: HOT & BOTHERED - Ryan & Emily

Book 9: HOT PROTECTOR - Chase & Sophie

Book 10: HOT ADDICTION - Dex & Annabelle

Book 11: HOT VALOR - Mendez & Kat

Book 12: A HOT CHRISTMAS MIRACLE - Mendez & Kat

———

The HOT SEAL Team Books

Book 1: HOT SEAL - Dane & Ivy

Book 2: HOT SEAL Lover - Remy & Christina

Book 3: HOT SEAL Rescue - Cody & Miranda

Book 4: HOT SEAL BRIDE - Cash & Ella

Book 5: HOT SEAL REDEMPTION - Alex & Bailey

Book 6: HOT SEAL TARGET - Blade & Quinn

Book 7: HOT SEAL HERO - Ryan & Chloe

Book 8: HOT SEAL DEVOTION - Zach & Kayla

HOT Heroes for Hire: Mercenaries
Black's Bandits

Book 1: BLACK LIST - Jace & Maddy

Book 2: BLACK TIE - Brett & Tallie

Book 3: BLACK OUT - Colt & Angie

Book 4: BLACK KNIGHT - Jared & Libby

Book 5: BLACK HEART - Ian & Natasha

Book 6: BLACK MAIL - Tyler & Cassie

Book 7: BLACK VELVET - Dax & Roberta

———

The HOT Novella in Liliana Hart's MacKenzie Family Series

HOT WITNESS - Jake & Eva

———

About the Author

Lynn Raye Harris is a Southern girl, military wife, wannabe cat lady, and horse lover. She's also the New York Times and USA Today bestselling author of the HOSTILE OPERATIONS TEAM ® SERIES of military romances, and 20 books about sexy billionaires for Harlequin.

A former finalist for the Romance Writers of America's Golden Heart Award and the National Readers Choice Award, Lynn lives in Alabama with her handsome former-military husband, one fluffy princess of a cat, and a very spoiled American Saddlebred horse who enjoys bucking at random in order to keep Lynn on her toes.

Lynn's books have been called "exceptional and emotional," "intense," and "sizzling" -- and have sold in excess of 4.5 million copies worldwide.

To connect with Lynn online:
www.LynnRayeHarris.com
Lynn@LynnRayeHarris.com

Made in United States
North Haven, CT
20 May 2023

36758751R00195